VICTIM OF
THE AURORA

Books by Thomas Keneally

THE PLACE AT WHITTON

THE FEAR

BRING LARKS AND HEROES

THREE CHEERS FOR THE PARACLETE

THE SURVIVOR

A DUTIFUL DAUGHTER

THE CHANT OF JIMMY BLACKSMITH

BLOOD RED, SISTER ROSE

CONFEDERATES

NED KELLY & THE CITY OF THE BEES

PASSENGER

GOSSIP FROM THE FOREST

VICTIM OF THE AURORA

SCHINDLER'S LIST

TO ASMARA: A NOVEL OF AFRICA

FLYING HERO CLASS

SEASON IN PURGATORY

BULLIE'S HOUSE

THE PLAYMAKER

A FAMILY MADNESS

THOMAS KENEALLY

VICTIM OF
THE AURORA

A HARVEST BOOK
HARCOURT BRACE & COMPANY
SAN DIEGO NEW YORK LONDON

Requests for permission to make copies of any part of the
work should be mailed to: Permissions Department,
Harcourt Brace & Company, 6277 Sea Harbor Drive,
Orlando, Florida 32887-6777.

Library of Congress Cataloging-in-Publication Data
Keneally, Thomas.
Victim of the aurora.
I. Title.
PZ4.K336Vi   1977   [PR9619.3.K46]   823   77-84391
ISBN 0-15-693534-1 (Harvest: pbk.)

Printed in the United States of America

First Harvest edition 1985

C D E F G H I J

FOR BOB HAWKE

↓ MEMBERS OF THE STEWART EXPEDITION ↓

Captain Sir Eugene Stewart R.N.   Leader

Dr. Alec Dryden   In charge scientific staff, chief zoologist

Harry Kittery   Physicist

Paul Gabriel   Zoologist

Rev. Brian Quincy   Chaplain and parasitologist

Dr. Waldo Warwick   Meteorologist

Barry Fields   Geologist

Isaac Goodman   Asst. Geologist

Anthony Piers   The narrator, expeditionary artist

Victor Henneker   Representing the press; the victim

Peter Sullivan   Photographer-Cinematographer

Byram Hoosick   Biologist

Lt. John Troy R.N.   In charge of stores

Lt. Par-axel Beck, Royal Swedish Army   Ski instructor

Capt. Warren Mead, Highland Light Infantry   Ponies

Harry Webb   Dogs

Norman Coote   Tractors

SAILORS

Walter O'Rielly   Cook, R.N.

Nikolai   Dog handler

Petty Officer Percy Mulroy   Sledger

Alexandrei   Pony handler

PO Ernest Henson   Stores

PO Bertram Wallace   Sledger

PO Richard Jones   Sledger

AB Bernard Mulroy   Stores

AB Russel Stigworth   Steward

VICTIM OF
THE AURORA

ONE

Once, sometime in the 1930s, when journalists pressed me about the Henneker rumors, I cried out, "We were the great New British South Polar Expedition." We were the apogee, I was implying, of old-fashioned Britannic endeavor. If we lied, then all institutions were liars.

Perhaps it was some kind of Antarctic susquatch or wild man who got him? the journalists pursued. I made a face as if they didn't deserve an answer. We were the great New British South Polar Expedition ...

Journalists don't press any more. Could you imagine young Woodsteins flying out to the West Coast to grill me concerning Henneker's south-polar fate?

Other conditions have changed as well. I suffer long patches of what could be called coma. I am sitting in the sun on a Tuesday morning, say. From the terrace of the rest home south of Los Angeles I survey the golf course of the township called Sageworld, where sixteen thousand aged people live in apartments and manors. When they lose the capacity to drive, chip, and putt they will join me in the rest home, unless of course a massive stroke or heart attack graduates them directly to Forest Lawn.

I squint at the sun, chewing over Sageworld's geriatric ironies. I blink and it's all at once Wednesday afternoon, and I am no longer on the terrace. I am watching the rain from the reading room. I have a different shirt on. Who put it on me? Where did yesterday go? I know by questioning the nurses that I went on sitting. I ate. I watched the 7 P.M. news and drifted off to sleep during an episode of "Maude." I rose in the morning, dressed myself and ate—that's what they tell me. I remember it no more than a vegetable remembers the spring.

Sir Anthony Piers, ninety-two-year-old designer and one-time official artist to the New British South Polar Expedition is frightened not so much of conventional death, but of the way death comes ravening up to him while he's still at his ease under the sun, and bites chunks out of his days.

He...I...doesn't...don't know why I should want at this late hour to write a little record of the expedition. Why I should write down the things Eugene Stewart asked me never to utter. It isn't simply that Stewart and the sainted Dryden and Hoosick and Sullivan and Beck and Kittery and all the rest are dead now. It isn't simply that at this distance, Henneker's assassin—for he had an assassin and it was not some form of polar ape-man—is himself a victim. I think it's because I believe what I told the journalists. To me, the world was simple and the lying hadn't begun when I joined the expedition. The world grew complicated and the lying set in with Henneker's death, and ever since the world has been fueled and governed with lies. *That* is my concise history of the twentieth century. *That* is why I wish to define what was for me the century's first lie.

There's one good thing. Decay takes away my consciousness one day and doesn't give it back till the next. But the same process also sharpens my sense of our hut on Cape Frye in that Antarctic winter, in the innocent years before the First World War. I can for example smell the cocoa and the acetylene lamps, the drying thermal underwear before the stove and the acid smell of Siberian pony dung when the door to the stables is opened. I can see them now in their young bodies, my colleagues, a supposed polar elite, selected from thousands by Captain Sir Eugene Stewart. They sit at the large table in the middle, writing reports. Or they move to the laboratory, to the dark room or the naturalist's alcove, or out-of-doors to read temperatures or visit the magnetic hole, an ice cave three hundred yards to the north of the hut. Or they dress to go trolling for biology specimens through holes in the ice of McMurdo Sound or even to ski across to the Barne Glacier to help Harry Kittery with his measurements of ice movement.

As well as the Cape Frye hut, I remember to the last nuance of language the manner of my recruitment to the expedition.

In 1909 when I was twenty-four years old I had my first exhibition in a Bond Street gallery called Brenton's. It may amaze the film buffs, who know me as a movie designer of the thirties, forties, and fifties; it might amaze equally the corporations, airlines, armies, and fashion experts who employed me as a design consultant, to find out that I was once a bona fide artist, a landscapist no less. I did not in fact design my first stage set until 1925, when I was nearly forty.

At the time of my first exhibition then, I considered I was an artist, would always be an artist. And if the craft of designing movies had been available to me I would have despised it as a bastard activity for any true talent.

It was a golden frivolous year, the year I was twenty-four. The summers seemed longer then and the women seemed allied to the summer and dressed in the colors of the sweet pea—mauve, pale rose, and lavender. Even their makeup seemed an extension of the sunniness of the age. It was the great decade of peaches and cream, except in the slums of East London and in the cities of the north where, in any case (so we all believed), tuberculosis and squalor would eventually yield to progress and good will.

In 1908, I had earned £200 from sales of paintings and lecture fees, and that was enough to allow me to move amongst the happier complexions. You didn't need much money. We lived under a king who would make love to any of his subjects as long as she was pretty. Farmers' wives and boilermakers' daughters could dazzle him, make him get down out of his carriage and speak softly to them. He was a fat satyr, and appalling as any fat satyr. Yet I knew a pretty cook called Rosa Lewis for whom he bought a hotel, the Cavendish in Jermyn Street, which she went on managing in remembrance of her king well into the 1950s.

She had beauty. And I suppose in a way I must have had it then. I was tall and dark-haired and blue-eyed. I looked as spiritual as an artist ought. You should see what's happened to it all now, the tallness, the dark hair, the blue eyes—above all, the spirituality.

So I had been able to attract and to be attracted by a woman six years older than me, sixty times more wealthy, and unhappily married to one of London's most celebrated trial lawyers. We'll call her in this record Lady Anthea Hurley, and she was supposed to be there, at Brenton's of Bond Street, pretending to be an acquaintance of mine and adding for me an edge of beauty and secret sexual triumph to the hoped-for artistic triumph of the evening.

Though she'd warned me the affair was ended, I didn't believe she would fail to come that evening. But by nine I began to believe. Not even strangers turned up at nine. I stood smiling but lost among my oils and water colors.

The paintings were mainly of Tyrolean glacier scenes, for I was much taken with the way light came off or through great gnarled bodies of ice. I suppose Turner was my favorite painter, and he had painted scenes as if light and its reflections were the main realities and the solid objects were nothing. There is his famous painting of a train on an embankment, and the train is nothing and the light is everything. And that is the nature of light when it strikes and permeates stretches of ice.

Brenton, the gallery owner, was a fashionable Londoner. He owned, as well as the gallery, a restaurant called the Xanadu Gardens to which, sooner or later, came anyone of importance in business, politics, the arts, and even the sciences. He would then invite these people to his next opening. The gallery, as it were, fed off the restaurant. That was how I first met Sir Eugene Stewart. He and his wife had been taken to the Xanadu Gardens for their fourth wedding anniversary, and there Brenton had mentioned me and my ice paintings and suggested they would be of interest to a polar explorer who must have a more intimate acquaintance with ice than most people have, hah hah!

Brenton inserted his two guests through a gap in the scrimmage line made up by my parents and brothers, and critics from the *Times,* the *Telegraph,* the *Sketch,* the *Evening Standard,* and other journals, among all of whom I stood bilious from the non-arrival of Anthea Hurley.

"Sir Eugene and Lady Stewart," said Brenton, "this is our artist, Anthony Piers."

Sir Eugene said before I could what an honor it was. He was a husky man, dressed unfashionably in an old lounge suit.

"Tell me," he said, pointing to one of the glacier paintings, "the light . . . the ice . . . the exact glacier tones . . ."

When you met a great man then, it was an entirely different matter from meeting a great man these days. We have been trained to mistrust greatness, to look for the manic flecks in the pupils of the eyes, to look for the pathological twist in the way the great man walks or speaks to his wife. We have been taught that at the basis of greatness lies a great disease. It wasn't like that then. I believed while the dew still stood on the century that at the basis of greatness stood a great sanity. I looked at Sir Eugene now in those terms.

His head was held sideways, his brows lowered. A questioner, a listener, a man who believes he has much to learn. He kept that posture till the end of his life. I saw him approach other men the same way, even out on the Ross Ice Shelf with the wind cutting at his face. Stewart listening to Troy recount details of supplies cached at Ross Lip Depot, at Sitka Cache, at the White Mountain Fodder Depot. Listening to Harry Webb the dog man or Mead the pony expert. It endeared him, of course, to the lot of us.

"Tell me," he said again. I was excited by the respect he had for me, the care he took framing the question. But before he could put his question together, Lady Stewart torpedoed him.

"I think the watercolors," she said, "are even more superlative than the oils. Splendid, Mr. Piers. Splendid."

She wore no hat. That was a sign of extreme individuality in that age. Like many other women she had given up wearing the savage corsets that forced the female body into an S shape. She wore a dress of gray and apricot under wide, glittering brown eyes that distracted me from my loss. She also had the sort of nose Greeks and Edwardians both were crazy about.

I mention all this not because Lady Stewart had a large part in the incidents of the expedition, but simply to show how the husband and wife physically differed. Lady Stewart dressed, spoke, walked with a passion, and that, even the passion of her loyalty to his Antarctic ambitions, rather frightened Sir Eugene.

She didn't buy one of my paintings. All the Stewarts' money had gone to pay for her husband's 1905 expedition, and now he was—in the quaint phrase of those days—"putting together" another.

At last Sir Eugene had his question ready. "Have you ever painted an auroral display, Mr. Piers?"

"No sir. I've never had the good fortune to spend the winter in the Arctic."

"Ah. The aurora is brilliant not only in the Arctic, Mr. Piers. In my experience the aurora australis of the Antarctic night is even more startling."

I told him I had heard that and believed it.

"You painted these pictures in situ, Mr. Piers?" he asked. "I mean, actually perched on ice falls above the body of the glacier? Or sitting on the lip of a crevasse?"

"It's the only way to do these things, Sir Eugene."

He took a cardcase from his old-fashioned jacket and passed a card to me. "Please, could you manage to call at the expeditionary office. I am there next Monday to Thursday in the afternoons. Would, say three o'clock Monday be satisfactory?"

There was some reason why it was not, and we settled for Tuesday at the same time. Before she left, Lady Stewart took my hand in both of hers—an act that wasn't common in public in those days—and squeezed it, telling me in a low voice how talented I was.

It's said that Zimmerman, the American millionaire, paid out $150,000 on the weekend Edward VII spent with him in Surrey. That was the sort of vapid event for which money could be found, but wealthy Edwardians weren't nearly as ready to put money to more sober causes.

So the expeditionary office turned out to be two small rooms above a café in Holborn. In the outer office was a man about my age and one overworked typist. The young man was the expedition's secretary, McGuire, and he took me into the inner office where Eugene Stewart and the chairman of the expeditionary committee, Sir Dexter Milburn (there *were* such names in those days) sat at a desk signing correspondence.

"Ah, Mr. Piers," Stewart called out, and went on signing and glancing at me between signatures. It was Milburn who put his pen down and began talking, saying who he was and what his powers were. "You come to me with high recommendations," he said sourly.

"I don't come to you with any recommendations, Sir Dexter," I told him. "I called in to see Sir Eugene. I haven't come for a job."

I felt red in the cheeks. Didn't this old man know I'd been treated kindly by critics, sold out my exhibition, and become a public figure?

Stewart put his pen down. "Forgive us, Mr. Piers. We're

overworked and we come to the point at a great pace, don't we Sir Dexter?"

In fact I didn't know till the expedition was finished and became history how hard the two men were working when I first met them—writing begging letters to manufacturers of biscuits, chocolate, dehydrated and canned meats, canvas and windproofs, tractors and woolens, hydrometers, anemometers, aneroid barometers, signal equipment, and so on and so on; inviting companies to enhance Britannia's name by giving their goods and/or a cash donation to the New British South Polar Expedition. Not only that, but processing the thousands of applications for membership in the expedition, and traveling the country by second-class rail, speaking anywhere a crowd could be expected, speaking also at schools, many of which gave an Arctic stove here and a tent there or a down sleeping bag or even, where the masters were enthusiastic, the cash for a dog or a pony. Both Stewart and Sir Dexter had been working a ninety-hour week for four months. They could be pardoned for forgetting that I was one of London's young lions.

"Can you ski?" Stewart asked. Exactly the way he'd asked me if I could paint auroras.

"A little."

"A little," sniffed Sir Dexter, as if I'd avoided the ski slopes just to annoy him.

"I spent a fortnight at Zermatt."

"Well, you can manage to ski cross-country," Sir Eugene said as a fact. "You start off ahead of most of the members of the expedition."

I blinked, because he had so randomly opened up an Antarctic vista for me.

He continued. "No matter how well an expedition is planned, there is always a debt at the end. Sir Dexter and I have cast about for means of alleviating the debt. I mean, people aren't interested in making donations to an expedition that's over, are they?"

"I don't suppose so."

"Now this is confidential, Mr. Piers. We've approached a renowned popular journalist to come with us and document our efforts. He was virtually the first staff member to be approached and accepted. We have already sold his articles under contract—before they're even written—to newspapers and magazines the world over: England, Germany, Sweden, the United States. Of course, we won't get the bulk of the fee until the articles are delivered, which will be, for the most part, when the expedition is over."

He paused for me to comment. I couldn't speak. Was he in fact inviting me into the expedition? I didn't think that for an irreplaceable eighteen months of my young life I would be without women and theater and good food and modest adulation. All I thought was that soon I'd be on the ultimate ice, watching the world's farthest sunlight burst and dazzle on and through it. As for the golden haze of London summers, the sweet-pea colors, the dalliance and the sparkle, it would all be there when I returned. Perhaps by then the world would be entirely rid of the S-form corset.

"The journalist's name—*entre nous*—is Victor Henneker," Sir Eugene told me. "Do you know him?"

"The poor man's George Bernard Shaw," I said.

That was what people called him. Henneker was, in fact, a cross between Shaw and say Lowell Thomas. His fame was dazzling in those days, and his death became a journalistic issue. But if you read him now (as I have, perhaps the last reader he'll ever have), you see he was just a glib hack. He had been on the expedition to Tibet in 1905. Afterward he wrote a famous article about the ridiculous nature of the exploring urge and said he'd never do anything so fatuous again.

It seemed he'd changed his mind. Normally he interviewed politicians and generals, and reviewed theater, art, and even motion pictures with a stylish barbarity.

"Similarly," Stewart went on, "we've employed Peter Sullivan the cinematographer to make a moving picture that will be exhibited all over the world when our efforts in Antarctica have come to a conclusion. As for you, Mr. Piers, we were wondering if—under similar terms—you would like to be the expeditionary artist."

I couldn't answer straightaway. I was a little dazzled by Sir Eugene's intention to exploit the media. It was a new idea then. When I did speak I found myself saying, "You mention terms?"

Sir Dexter took over. "Your wages as an officer of the expedition will be five pounds per month. When the pictures you paint are exhibited you will receive forty percent of the net profit. The net profit will be calculated on the price the picture sells for minus only the normal advertising and framing charges and the gallery's commission, if any."

"My wife," Stewart explained, "has connections with gallery owners who will very likely give us free hanging space. You have to remember, the interest in such an exhibition would be intense and therefore the prices paid would be high. Clubs, universities, museums, and private patrons can be depended on to compete for the paintings. Our profit depends on your output, Mr. Piers. Therefore we'll leave you as much free time as we can. Just the same, I would expect you to do some sledging and depot-laying and help out as energetically as any other member of the party at busy times. I should tell you that now."

It wasn't sledging and depot-laying that worried me. "Sir, I think I ought to take fifty percent. I'm sure you agree." It felt blasphemous to argue with a great Englishman; yet I had a sort of market place stubbornness from being a farmer's son.

"Oh look," Sir Dexter growled, "the world's full of artists."

"I'm sure most of them would take fifty percent. I'm sure Mr. Henneker is taking fifty percent."

Sir Eugene laughed. "You shouldn't use that name against me. I mentioned the names of Mr. Henneker and Mr. Sullivan to show you we were employing the top talent."

"I have to say, Sir Eugene, I would have asked for fifty percent anyhow."

"Sir Dexter," said Stewart, "would you consider fifty percent if Mr. Piers forgoes his wages?"

At last Sir Dexter grunted. An affirmative grunt. Stewart turned to me.

"Mr. Piers? All found. Free food. Free shelter. I want paintings that will stand prominently on the stairwells of this nation; I want the essence of Antarctica set down. We won't expect you to work yourself into the ground."

I was actually tearful, in front of Stewart and the harsh old man. "I'm grateful to accept. I'm honored . . ."

"I think you'll do a lot of water colors," said the polar knight. "You'll find oils sluggish in those temperatures."

That was how I was recruited. I suppose it was the same for most of us, captivated by Lady Stewart, cajoled by Sir Eugene Stewart, bullied by Sir Dexter. Not that we all needed cajoling. Three thousand members of the Edwardian middle classes lined up to apply for positions on Sir Eugene's staff.

Like most of the expedition's younger men I presumed that Sir Eugene's suavity derived from his genius and Sir Dexter's snarling arose from mediocrity. Henneker eroded some of this innocence.

It was the morning we left the Thames. The expeditionary ship, a third-hand Norwegian whaler renamed *McMurdo* for the sake of the journey, was moored in the river at Rotherhithe, and the Bishop of Southwark came off from the shore in a barge to bless it. After the blessing there was, strangely enough, a champagne breakfast on board. All the executives and officers of the expedition brought their mothers, wives, and girls. Byram Hoosick the American, for example, had brought his mother. The press said of Mrs. Hoosick that she was a notorious chaser of royalty and had once thrown herself at King Edward's feet as he walked down a hotel corridor in Biarritz. I had always imagined her as a massive New World woman, entirely jamming the king's corridor with an ample body, while half a dozen royal equerries struggled at her various extremities to clear her away. I saw now that she was a frail, short, sick-looking woman, speaking quietly at Byram's elbow. My mother, down from the country in a lacy summer dress, would make far more noise at the champagne breakfast than Mrs. Hoosick.

We were all crowded on the small quarter-deck. The main deck, below us, was piled with a lumpy cargo of oil and paraffin drums, coal sacks, lumber, and scientific gear. The cartwheel hat had come back into fashion that year, even Lady Stewart was wearing one this morning, and I remember that quarterdeck as a delightful clutter of hat brims and flowers and osprey feathers and oriflammes.

Although the ponies and dogs would not be loaded until New Zealand, I was amazed how low the *McMurdo* sat in the water.

"I don't like this ship, Anthony," my mother told me. "It's nearly awash now."

"Some ships look like that," I told her. "Look, don't be superstitious."

On the way to Westminster from Kensington that morning we'd passed a great number of houses that had straw laid down in the street in front of them to quiet the wheels of passing traffic. In those days, straw in the road meant someone indoors was sick. My mother had seen all this morning's straw as an omen.

Now, on the quarterdeck, we found ourselves in a group hard up against the railings. Here Henneker, Sir Dexter and a man called Lord Stonehurst were the luminaries. Stonehurst was Commodore of the Royal Yacht Squadron, and for some reason I couldn't then understand, the *McMurdo* had been registered with the squadron as, of all things, a yacht.

"It lies low in the water," my mother said in a gap in the talk.

"I beg your pardon, Madam," said Sir Dexter.

"This ship," said my mother, "it lies down in the water a lot."

"My dear lady." Henneker leaned over her. He was tall and dark and worldly in his light flannel suit, whereas Sir Dexter and Stonehurst were dressed too heavily for the morning in dark, thick official-looking clothing. "The *McMurdo* wouldn't be permitted to sit half so low if his lordship here had not so kindly permitted us to load it to the gunn'ls."

"I don't believe you, Mr. Henneker," said my mother. "You make it sound like a plot—"

Henneker gestured with his hands to silence her. She was fascinated—they were more or less the same age. "You see, if this ship were registered in the normal way, with anyone but the Royal Yacht Squadron, it would have to have a Plimsoll line. And if it had a Plimsoll line, we wouldn't be allowed to load aboard half the things we need in the Antarctic."

By the railings Lord Stonehurst was coughing and seemed angry. He half turned to walk away from us, but clearly decided he had to stay.

Mrs. Dryden, a small, pretty woman and the wife of the chief scientist, muttered at Henneker, "Why do you have to raise issues like this, Mr. Henneker?"

"Professional bias, Ma'am," Henneker told her mysteriously and with a bow.

Lord Stonehurst growled. "The Royal Yacht Squadron

agreed to register the *McMurdo* purely so that we could be associated with a great British enterprise."

But my mother wasn't stopped. "If they load it below where the Plimsoll ought to be," she observed, "they won't get to Antarctica at all."

Henneker said, "There are some who claim that polar heroes should enjoy all the safeguards that ordinary seamen sail under. Others, however, think the sea will overlook our little omissions on account of our holy cause."

"Infamous, infamous!" Lord Stonehurst was growling.

I got my mother away from Henneker and spent an hour reassuring her. I wished I had a girl there to say a painful good-bye to, someone to part from sharply, deeply, less stupidly.

As it turned out the *McMurdo* did nearly founder—twice: Once off Spain and once in the Antarctic Ocean. In the Antarctic Ocean, for example, the pumps clogged with balls of coal dust and oil and I served with the bucket brigade that emptied the engine room, one end of the line working naked and waist-deep in warm water, the other on deck and freezing in polar clothing. I remember thinking, dazed and amazed, that the exalted kinship of *McMurdo* and the Royal Yacht Squadron was merely a ruse to avoid certain Admiralty regulations.

TWO

If your quaint fancy is to read the classic books of Antarctic exploration, you would notice how the authors—usually the expeditionary leaders—go to so much trouble to praise their staff. There has never been, they seem to say, a happier band of brothers landed on the ice.

On Midwinter's Day, the year I remember so keenly, at the deepest point of the Antarctic darkness, Stewart made a speech that was typical of this genre.

"First we faced storm," he said, "the fiercest the Southern Ocean could provide. The pumps were manned without cease until they clogged. Then we passed buckets of bilge hand-to-hand, sleeping where we stood. As the storm eased we found ourselves confronted with the worst pack ice in human record and battered at it until we found a clear passage. It was during those days I saw the kind of colleagues I had.

"When we came into McMurdo Sound and put out our ice anchors, we made up for the lateness of the season by unloading our stores and fabricating our hut all within a fortnight. Then, despite the lateness of the season, we laid depots to a distance of two hundred miles across the ice shelf. So that, as we celebrate here, the supplies that will be the basis of our success next summer, the pemmican, biscuits, oil, and tea, are waiting cached in the ice within sight of the great glaciers we must climb to approach the Pole. No other group of men I could possibly have chosen in England or any other nation on earth could have done more, performed so superlatively. I salute you . . ."

The plum pudding had been eaten when this was said. The boxes of cigars had been broken out and port and Benedictine were being passed about as we all listened to the visionary, the polar knight, and believed him. As Par-axel Beck would often say, "We work bloody bloody hard, Tony."

In fact we were frankly proud of ourselves. You don't have to be told that in those days people weren't always examining their motives for volunteering in such projects as the Stewart expedition. If we were asked why we had offered ourselves for at least a year and a half of isolation far more intense than the isolation of astronauts in command modules, we would have said we were doing it because we loved adventure or because it was a manly thing to do. They would have been the orthodox replies for that age. We didn't question whether our withdrawal to Antarctica meant we were insecure in the real world, or were frightened of women, or were latent homosexuals. So we believed in duty and believed as well that what we were doing was sane and not suspect. The fact was that we were tough and efficient—most of us—and deserved some praise from Sir Eugene Stewart. Yet elites are very hard to achieve, since those who seek them have one way or another suspended their belief in original sin.

It had been a good party. After the entrées of fried seal liver and galantine of penguin, we ate roast beef and dumplings and there was much wine. The hut was hung with sledging flags and naval pennants, and beneath them the speeches and the arguments took place. The arguments were diverse—on politics and rock formations, initiated by my friend Barry Fields, a red-haired Australian; on the superlative qualities of Scandinavian girls, sentimentally initiated by Par-axel Beck; on the relative value of ponies and dogs in polar conditions, initiated and carried on by Captain Mead, the pony man, and Harry Webb, the dog expert from northern Quebec. Isaac Goodman, Waldo Warwick, and Harry Kittery argued about the geological history of the continent—Goodman was already thinking in terms of continental drift. Eugene Stewart and John Troy debated Germany's naval intentions; Paul Gabriel and I questioned the impact of photography on painting; Dryden and Hoosick were probably talking about fish, art, or Italy; the Reverend Brian Quincy and Norman Coote listened to Henneker tell scandalous stories about peers, actresses, industrialists, and courtesans. And, at a point near the door to the sailors' quarters (the expedition was run on a naval basis, and the petty officers and ABs had separate living space), Peter Sullivan, the maker of early movies, held a carbide flash above a tripod-mounted camera and called on us to hold our positions.

After the speeches—I've already referred to Stewart's—everyone brought out his special luxury, the item he had brought with him in his pack to celebrate this deepest point of the polar year. Beck had a bottle of schnapps. As he poured the first glass he said, "My friends, I am certain of it that if I offered you all a glass it would do no one much good and that I would only be a hypocrite, which Christianity forbids me to be. Therefore, I will drink this personally myself and toast the each of you one at a time." Which he then went on to do. Red-headed Barry Fields had a half-dozen bottles of his native Australia's heavy beer. He brought a dozen to Antarctica with him, concealed in the ponies' fodder, but half a dozen of them exploded when the contents froze. He once confessed to me that he knew little of cold climates and had never seen snow until he came to England a year before the expedition left the Thames. Now he offered Stewart one of the bottles, but Stewart declined. Henneker had Highland malt whisky and the Reverend Quincy three Philippine cigars. Hoosick, who did not drink, produced peanut brittle, and Kittery put some liqueur-filled chocolates on the table. And so it went.

Then "the men"—as Stewart called his sailors—came through the door into our quarters. Everyone toasted the cook, Walter O'Reilly, who was awarded a chair by the stove and sat in it smiling, a pint of bitters in his hand. The dog handler, Nikolai, performed a dance and sang some wistful Siberian sledging songs. Petty Officers Henson, Wallace, and Jones staged a comic performance during which they impersonated everyone: Stewart, Dryden, Beck, Hoosick, Henneker, Quincy—the lot of us. Wallace and Jones were lost in their roles, but I remember that Henson was brilliant, that I went red in the cheeks when he did his characterization of me.

Next, a sailors' choir sang a sentimental song about the king:

> *There'll be no wo'ar*
> *As long as there's a king like good King Edward,*
> *There'll be no wo'ar*
> *For 'e 'ates that sort of thing.*
> *Mothers need not worry,*
> *As long as we've a king like good King Edward,*
> *Peace with 'onor*
> *Is his motter,*
> *So God save the king.*

We didn't know the king and the age had died in our absence just the month before, the king fading into a coma from bronchitis caught when the proprietor of the Porte-Saint-Martin theater in Paris turned the heating up too high.

Lieutenant John Troy stood up on his chair. His blockhouse shape wavered there; he had a parrot-like grin beneath his long nose. "No better time, gentlemen," he said, "to introduce to you the definitive version of the John Troy nose protector. You might remember," he continued when his colleagues began catcalling him, "that you all carry about with you an extremity called the nose, that you have all been ice-bitten on that extremity, and that I then had to suffer the indelicate sight of grown men staggering about the hut with their noses half sloughed off. You might remember that conventional nose protectors didn't work because your breath froze them and so things were as bad as ever. My nosepiece, however, combines a sensible conical profile with a triangular shape."

Then he put on his windproof jacket and buttoned the nosepiece to it. It looked ridiculous, and everyone began to laugh at his bemused eyes, one either side of the apex of the windproof nose cloth.

You could see his hurt. "All right," he said. "I was going to run up three dozen of these. But . . ."

Some of us stopped laughing, but others went on as if punishing him in a small way for mentioning the cutting winds while we were feeling so well fed, brotherly, and immortal in the hut's warm core.

I noticed now that Par-axel Beck was asleep in his place at the table. None of us had drunk liquor in any quantity since the ship landed us, so that now there was a sharp, vinous gleam in the eyes around the table.

Men drifted from the table to argue at closer range. I saw Henneker sitting on my bunk with Paul Gabriel. Paul had his glasses in his hands and wore the blind, bemused look of all very shortsighted people when their spectacles are off. Henneker was reading him a letter or something similar, some piece of documentation from one of the scandalous stories he'd been telling that night. They were both dark men, Henneker tall and piratic, Paul wedgelike and, liquored, reminding one of some dark young Irishman or a Welsh miner. Henneker spoke quickly, quietly, smiling crookedly, and Paul seemed to be in that unpleasant state when you're trying to make up your mind either to be sick or to fall asleep.

The arguments grew louder. Barry Fields burned his hand on the stove while playing indoor soccer with the American, Hoosick. Through it all, Stewart sat smoking and with his head inclined as if he could learn something from all of this too. He watched Coote, the tractor man, and Isaac Goodman tote Beck to his bunk and pull his inner shoes from his feet.

Alec Dryden, a married man, thirty-eight years old, had offered to be watchman that night and make notes of the aurora in the appropriate auroral record book. Only he was left at the table at eleven o'clock that night when Petty Officer Percy Mulroy went to the acetylene hut at the rear of the men's quarters and cut off the gas supply to the lamps. The last drunks collided, laughed, and rebounded to their bunks. I asked Paul Gabriel, prone in the upper bunk, if he needed any help. He said no, he was just tired.

Alec Dryden cranked the gramophone and pointed its red enamel trumpet across the littered dinner table. His favorite record "Night Hymn at Sea," sung by Clara Butt and Kennerly Rumford, wheezed out across the hut.

I heard Victor Henneker, in the bunk beside mine, mutter, "Clara Butt is a dismal old tart," and begin to sing softly a song of Gaby Deslys's.

> Sur la plage, sur la plage
> Men are full of persiflage.
> When I take my bain de mer
> All the boys just come and stare ...

Lost in images of Gaby Deslys's rich little body, I closed my eyes.

Then Dryden had the night to himself. On the hour, he left the hut by the laboratory door to view the great prismatic veils of green and gold and blue that hung vertically from the stars. There were means of making observations from Waldo Warwick's meteorology room if the weather was too bitter, but that night of Henneker's penultimate sleep was clear and still, and the temperature a mere −38° F.

I didn't sleep well. Not by Antarctic standards anyhow, for sleep there—when it comes—is deep and long. I was awake at 7 A.M. I could hear faint sounds of the cook, Walter O'Reilly, clanging his pans next door. I was awake when AB Russell Stigworth came in quiet as a church warden at 7:30, broom in hand. He swept the floor four times a day and washed the mess traps and tidied—a thin-faced little man who prided himself on his work and grew radiant when Stewart and Dryden or any of us praised him for it.

He spent so much time on these duties I wondered if he had seen or absorbed the auroras or been awed by the ice shelf or the mountains across the sound with the moonlight on them. What would he tell his grandchildren of his Antarctic experience? I suppose he could always tell them Sir Eugene Stewart had called him a fine hand with a broom. I studied Stigworth out of one eye as he shunted his broom through the debris of the midwinter feast and extracted Beck's schnapps bottle from the floor and put it in his Hessian bag of rubbish.

At eight I heard the men next door rousing and, soon after, a faint whinny from the stables as Alexandrei arrived to feed the ponies their morning hay. They slept standing all night, those ponies. The floor of the stable was too cold for them to lie on, but Warren Mead said they were comfortable and had a locking joint in their knees that took the weight off their hoofs. It was the way they slept in Siberia, said Mead, since the time they were foals.

A little later I heard the dogs greet Nikolai. They occupied a slight incline to the north of the hut, most of them leashed to two thin cables. They too were from Siberia and were all post dogs used to deliver mail, or else the offspring of post dogs. When blizzards came they sat and let the dry snow cover them and, so insulated, slept the time away. When Nikolai came to them each morning with their frozen seal meat they applauded him madly. Some of their howling was like that of ordinary dogs, but they could also sing better than a coyote, and keen better than a wolf.

Next I heard the thud of the men lifting slabs of snow, cut with coal shovels out of the ice embankment behind the hut, into the snow-burner.

Every morning "the strongmen"—the haulers and sledgers like POs Mulroy, Wallace, and Jones, had to melt down a day's supply in a blubber-fed burner near the acetylene tanks. The water dripped slowly from the burner into a (somehow never full) tank in the galley area, and from it Bernard Mulroy, Percy's brother, issued us our daily ration.

At 8:30 I saw Eugene Stewart emerge from his curtained compartment and cross to the stove rubbing his hands gently, like some old monk to whom even the cold is a gift. Stigworth, the sweeper, brought in two bowls of snow and put them on a table near the darkroom. Alec Dryden and Troy stood up naked and rubbed the snow all over their bodies. Their pale hind quarters glistened and quivered.

This was a workday. I was in no mood for it. But I got up anyway. Everyone else in the line of five bunks on our side of the hut seemed stertorously asleep. They had only another few minutes to sleep off their drunks.

I confess with embarrassment to what worried me. You have to understand that in those days the attitude to homosexuality was one of breathless abomination. "Sodomy was accursed," says a historian of the era, and the law and public opinion destroyed the sodomite. No homosexual should be let anywhere near children or public office. In 1908, the German emperor had dismissed his oldest and closest friend, Philip von Eulenberg, because of a homosexual scandal.

I was a child of my age and suffered from all its frantic prejudices.

I was now afraid, that morning of June 23rd in Antarctica, that Henneker might be trying to seduce Paul Gabriel. I am embarrassed to have to relate the diffuse and ridiculous origins of this suspicion. But I must.

The last port of call all those classic Antarctic expeditions made before they vanished into the ice was the port of Lyttelton in the South Island of New Zealand. It was a beautiful little haven with high ridges above its bowl of harbor, and over the ridge and in the plain was the city of Christchurch.

When we docked in Lyttelton all the best families of Christchurch vied to have us in their homes. Some of us wanted to be free agents and raise whatever hell those southern cities offered. But Stewart insisted we take the invitations, and John Troy was delighted, because it meant a saving of stores.

Paul Gabriel and I found ourselves guests in the home of a Christchurch wool merchant. He and his wife drank nothing at dinner, and their three teenage daughters were not permitted to add anything to the conversation except requests for salt or Worcestershire sauce. The wool merchant spoke of "home"— that is, England—so fervently that you wondered why he lived so far from it.

His father had been a factory hand in Nottingham, and he delighted in passing on to us horror stories of the Nottingham slums.

"So in a way," said Paul, "Britain so deprived your forebears of a decent income that your father was forced to come as far as the South Pacific to find one?"

"I wouldn't put it like that," said the merchant. He had once entertained a cousin of the Prince of Wales, he told us, and our names went on some honor roll of distinguished visitors from "home" he kept in his billiard room. Even Paul Gabriel, who was a pleasant boy and could suffer anyone gladly, thought the man was a bore.

Late on our second afternoon there, Barry Fields arrived by cab, asked to see us, and was shown into a front parlor. Then we were fetched by a maid, who took us in to Barry and withdrew.

"Hell," Barry said. "What is this? A bloody doll's house?"

"It's worse," I told him. "It's a morgue."

"Bloody colonials," he said.

"You're one yourself," said Paul.

"No, I'm not. I'm a socialist and have no country."

He always said that when he was cornered. In fact, he went into conservative politics in Australia before he was thirty-five years old.

"The place I'm staying," he told us, "is very humane—a pretty wife, pretty daughters, their old man very liberal with the good things that come from bottles. And the son is a secret heller and had the good taste to give me the address of a first-rate seraglio. He says the governor-general of New Zealand even uses it when he's in town. I thought it would be only civilized to invite you two to visit the place with me."

At the end of this speech he flourished an imaginary rapier in the air, touched its tip to the tip of his boot, and bowed. It was a habitual gesture of his, as habitual as saying he was a socialist.

I said, "I think we could look the place over."

I didn't want to shock Paul Gabriel, who still had the look of a senior prefect. But the sight of the pretty women of Christchurch had aroused me. It was useless trying to seduce any of the girls we met socially. There wasn't time, for seduction was a long business in those days. In any case, Stewart had asked us to behave. And why should a nice Christchurch girl give in to us anyhow, when we were about to go into the void?

I was pleased to see Paul understood that in a funny way Fields's offer was a gesture of friendship. "Yes," he said. "Yes."

"I mean," said Barry, "if we don't like it, we can have a drink and leave."

We made some excuse to the wool merchant's wife about having to attend a dinner and met Barry in the lounge of the Imperial Hotel. After one Scotch each we caught a cab. It was a beautiful September evening, the beginning of the southern spring, and the parklands in the center of the city, each tree and every leaf, seemed delineated by the prismatic light, sometimes blue, sometimes a golden brown as sharp as the points of lances.

We passed the cathedral where the parklands ended. Nowadays, in the square by the cathedral stands a statue of Sir Eugene Stewart in polar gear. It was not, of course, there then, and we rolled through the square feeling kingly and tremulous. In a quiet street full of good houses, the cab horse halted, as if he knew the particular gate. The cabman certainly did. When Barry paid him he winked and wished us a happy evening of it.

A maid answered the door and showed us into a parlor. There were antimacassars and a picture of a stag, as well as portraits of Victoria and Albert and an engraving of Sandringham Castle.

"Are you sure it's the right place," Paul Gabriel asked Barry.

"No risk," said Barry. "This is window dressing."

At last the Madam, Mrs. Bryant, came in. She was a small, pretty woman of about forty-five years. Barry said Mr. Stevens had recommended us and had telephoned her to that effect.

"Oh yes," she said, "you're the brave gentlemen who are going to Antarctica."

"That's right."

"My house is yours. Please follow me."

She led us upstairs. The furnishings up there were somber too. She opened a door on a small room where there was an ottoman and two easy chairs and a coffee table. As she told us to be seated, a maid came in with a silver tray on which stood Scotch and soda and three glasses.

"Gentlemen," said Mrs. Bryant, "some of my dear friends will join you soon. Drink what you wish, but remember there is only one rule in my household: I never admit drunks and I will not tolerate any drunken assault on my friends. I ask you to be responsible with the Scotch."

"Of course," I said, piqued a little, and she left.

Barry poured three Scotches and passed them around. There were two doors into this waiting room. One of them opened, and through it came three pretty girls dressed in summer frocks as modestly as girls at tea parties. One had reddish hair, and Barry Fields held his hand out to her, saying, "Hello, my name's Barry and I'm a Viking too." That also was one of his continuing statements: Redheads were Vikings.

A small dark girl sat beside me. "I'm Betty," she said. "You're going to the South Pole, you poor fellow."

I had noticed that the people of Christchurch, like the people of London, used Antarctica and the South Pole as interchangeable terms. But I wasn't going to argue with anyone so intensely pretty. I took a second to glance at the girl who had landed at Paul Gabriel's side. She was large. I smiled at the idea of his taking her in through his minus-vision lenses.

Betty said, "Let me in on the joke."

"There's no joke," I said. "I'm delighted to meet you, Betty."

We sat together for a while, nudging. I smelt her cologne and felt the pressure of her breasts on my upper arm. At some stage Barry Fields growled like a triumphant bear and took his fellow Viking out through the door. Betty asked me to come with her and we walked out. In a sober bedroom she forced me back on her bed.

At some delicious point of my arousal I heard a yowl from somewhere in the corridor of bedrooms. I tried to ignore it and the sound of footsteps in the corridor, but Betty would not. She got up from the bed and went to inquire.

Mrs. Bryant was in the corridor. She said to me, "How dare you bring an inebriated friend into my house." Barry emerged from another door and she said the same to him. Paul Gabriel had been sick over the body of his large girl, and Mrs. Bryant said she would call the police, who were, of course and quite credibly, friends of hers.

We dressed and went into the large girl's room and dressed Paul. His eyes were distant amongst the stink of bile. As we helped him downstairs, Barry said, "did you—"

"No. Did you?"

"Oh hell!"

A cab was passing the corner, and seeing us, its driver turned into the street to collect us. Paul Gabriel was still gasping and dry-retching and once in the cab, he turned toward a corner, brought his knees up like a man with stomach cramps, and became comatose.

"I hope he's all right," I said.

"You mean, as regards health? Of course he's all bloody right. He just caught it from Henneker."

"Caught what?"

"They used to tell me when I was a kid. Half you bloody English are that way."

"What way do you mean?

"Henneker's a closet queen. Haven't you seen him going after young Bernard Mulroy?"

"No."

"No, that's the trouble. You're all so bloody busy separating the 'gentlemen' from the 'sailors'!"

"A second ago, half of us had strange tendencies. Are all Australians as prejudiced as you?"

"I'm a socialist. I have no bloody nationality. And I'm not so much a 'gentleman' that the sailors don't talk to me. Before we were over the equator, PO Mulroy came to me and asked what he thought he ought to do about Henneker and his brother." He had grown less rabid now, recovering from the unconsummated relationship with his hired Viking. He said, "Of course, this is between us."

"Of course."

Barry's information at once reminded me of a friend of mine who, when I told him Henneker was an expedition member, said, "You'll want to guard your flanks. They say Henneker's a regular at the Icarus Club." The Icarus Club was a notorious homosexual brothel in Piccadilly.

I asked Barry, "Do you really mean Henneker and Bernard Mulroy were—?"

"That's dead-on what I mean, mate."

"In any case, it's got nothing to do with Paul here."

Barry's frustrated lust was abating, as was mine. He patted Paul on the back of the neck. "I suppose not. Poor old Paul." He leaned close to him and murmured, "What did you have for dinner, mate—escargots?"

When I got Paul back to the wool merchant's they were waiting up for us. Paul was still dazed and in misery and I had to help him in. Our host's suspicions coincided with Mrs. Bryant's. "What have you done to the poor fellow?" the wool merchant demanded. It shows that both the righteous and the reprobate share the same moral prejudices.

I helped Paul to bed. As I was leaving him he grabbed me by the arm and said, as if it explained everything, "My mother told me I was a child of love." I knew his mother by her reputation. She was Thea Gabriel, a renowned *danceuse* and forerunner of the Isadora Duncan breed. Like Isadora she hadn't put much store on paternity and had given Paul her own name. I had never asked him if his father was, as London gossip said he was, Howard Middleton, a chocolate magnate, himself a sufferer from shortsightedness, who had built a mansion in Berkshire for Thea. (She had occupied it for two months.)

I didn't know what Paul meant by a "child of love" or how it would help me when I went downstairs to face our hosts.

But what I had heard of Henneker that night began to disturb me when, in the winter at Cape Frye, I saw him questioning Paul, or Paul laughing at his stories. It seemed that the evenings often ended with those two in conclave, and Henneker listened as vidly to Paul's stories of Harrow or Magdalene as Paul listened to Henneker's tales of the beau monde.

The trouble was, Paul was innocent. His scandalous and ethereally worldly mother had worked as strenuously as any churchgoing mama to keep her boy uninformed about evil.

When the "gentlemen's" rising hour of 9 A.M. came that morning of June 23rd nearly sixty-five years ago, Lieutenant John Troy had to go amongst the bunks bullying my colleagues to rise. On our side of the hut, Kittery and I were up, but all the other occupants of those five double bunks, named the Cloisters by Henneker in honor of the Reverend Quincy, had to be shaken by the shoulders and bullied upright. I heard Beck moaning and someone farted thunderously, probably the Reverend Brian Quincy, who was afflicted with hyper-active bowels, a crucifixion for a man of such painful sensibilities. He sometimes shamefacedly blamed the condition of his bowels on the foul food he'd been served in his first curacy in rural Yorkshire.

In the upper bunk Paul sat up suddenly, too suddenly for a man with a hangover. He looked wanly at me.

"Are you all right?" I asked him.

"Today," he said, looking at his hands, "I'm going to begin the stuffing and mounting of a skua gull. It is the first flying bird I've attempted."

"Good luck with it," I told him.

"Thank you."

I saw Henneker pulling on a woolen cap for his visit to the latrines. It could be cold out there in the morning. As he passed Paul's upper bunk he stopped a moment and looked up tentatively toward the boy. (I automatically call Paul the "boy," though he was only two years younger than myself.) Paul was still contemplating without joy the task with the skua or something more secret. It was Henneker's eyes and mine that met.

"Spry after the Saturnalia?" he asked me.

"Yes. You, Victor?"

"I feel as if a division of the Sudan Camel Corps have camped in my mouth. But I can perform a mime of health and industry, I think."

I can remember still his tall movements as he made for the stable door, the polar crapper, walking like a man on his way to his tailors. Insofar as he represented the shallowness of his age, he was totally unsuitable for an expedition. But he represented its toughness as well. He was a hauler, a skier, a marcher. We liked his stories even though they sometimes turned vicious. Dryden and Hoosick shyly pretended he didn't exist, but he was popular with some of the more unlikely and innocent men, the Reverend Brian Quincy and Paul Gabriel.

Within ten minutes we were all at the table, eating one of Walter O'Reilly's fortifying breakfasts. Beck, after one mouthful, cried, "Oh God, why do you torment your good friend Par-axel this way?"

Just to make talk, someone asked Alec Dryden what the aurora had been like last night. "Poor," he said. "Rather bleached. A weird green arch whose highest point didn't coincide with the meridian, about two hundred and eighty-five degrees south-southwest. Some green wreaths above the mountains, but so thin they were practically streamers." You never asked Alec Dryden a question without getting a highly explicit answer.

Kittery, who was a puckish little man with glasses, told us, "You'll be happy to hear the weather's deteriorating. No afternoon pony walks."

Unless there was a blizzard on, each of us had a pony to exercise after lunch. All the hungover at the table wanted to know more about the barometric pressure and the low-pressure system that was swirling down from the Pole. They didn't care to take some bouncy pony out onto the ice at the end of a jarring rope.

"Waldo," they all began calling, seeking the expert word. We all noticed then that Waldo Warwick wasn't at the table. John Troy stood on a chair so that he could tell whether Waldo was still in the upper bunk where he slept.

"He's there, Harry," he told Kittery.

Kittery flinched. In the midst of his great task, which was to document the formation and behavior of ice in glaciers, on the ice shelf, and on the waters of the sound, he kept forgetting prosaic details, such as fully rousing his bunk mate or reporting him ill. His work and even the jokes he made at table were directed at showing Eugene Stewart that he could be trusted, that he really was a polar praetorian. For some reason Stewart persisted in giving the young physicist something less than an open-handed greeting. In his journal at this stage the leader praised Dryden and Troy and Mead, and even Waldo Warwick and myself, without making any wavers. But of Kittery he was writing, "I do not know if he is yet aware of the size of the task that faces him. There is no doubt he is very talented, but if he is not successful in his work it will be because he is confused about his objectives and does not understand that he was employed to study all the superficial ice of our part of shelves and glaciers. He can be forgetful."

Yet it turned out that Kittery was one of the successes of the expedition. He sledged for two summers. He managed dogs well and could out-stubborn most ponies, and when the dogs or ponies perished he put on the harness himself. Above all, he gathered the largest body of ice data ever put together up to that time, and his work, *On the Glaciology of West Antarctica,* is the founding classic of ice physics. He had forgotten however to rouse Waldo.

"Waldo?" Henneker called from his place at table. "Waldo! Is it one of your little fits of catatonia, old chap?"

"I hope not," John Troy muttered. He had to take the weather room if Waldo was sick.

Harry Kittery went to look. He stopped some feet from the bunk, calling, "Waldo?" Then he moved closer and stood on his own bunk, below Waldo's, so that he was now head and shoulders level with the meteorologist. He saw Waldo lying rigid, eyes open, stark, unblinking. On the handsome, lightly bearded face there was an expression of mild distaste. Harry asked Waldo three questions: "Are you well? Can you hear me? Do you want to see Alec?" (Alec Dryden was a physician, along with his other talents.) It was clear Waldo could not hear or (at some guerrilla headquarters deep in the unconscious few of us had heard of then) *would* not hear.

"Alec?" Harry Kittery called. "I think you ought to look at him."

At the head of the table Sir Eugene Stewart seemed impassive and even reached for more of Walter O'Reilly's fresh-baked bread. He accepted these spasms of Waldo's, because he liked him, because the fits never lasted more than a day or so, and, some of us had noticed, never occurred at times of crisis, when Waldo—as the people of my adoptive homeland would put it—was working his ass off. Stewart never mentioned the fits in his journal. If he forgave you anything, it was as if the fault or crime had never existed, and he forgave Waldo his catatonia.

Alec Dryden went and took Waldo's pulse, felt the temples, pinched the cheek. He mixed up a bromide and asked Kittery to hold the patient's head so that the draught could be poured down the throat. Everyone at the table paused in his meal at the sound of Waldo's gullet reluctantly taking down the sedative.

Bromides worked well on Waldo's state. After a while he would relax and fall asleep and wake at the end of the day, sheepish and full of energy.

When Alec returned to the table, Sir Eugene said, "Did Waldo drink much last night?"

Alec smiled. "I think he had less than anyone. It has nothing to do with drink."

Harry Kittery had taken his place again and grabbed his tea mug frowning. Across the table, Henneker raised his own mug as if in a toast. "Our little ice martyr," said Henneker, as he often did. Kittery didn't answer. He was very angry, hating to be called that, hating Henneker for defining the trouble between Stewart and himself.

Kittery, like most of the staff members, came from a particular background—middle class, private schools (they call them *public* schools in England), the services, the Oxford-Cambridge axis. It was a background even Paul Gabriel's hectic mother had imposed on him, by main force. The three I mentioned, Barry, Henneker, and I, were all farmers' sons. Henneker had a cruel rural wit, the kind of blood-raising tongue some of his brothers had. He made his fortune by refining it and using it on public figures. My colleagues did not understand this. They were well-mannered and clubbish Englishmen and they did not often have replies for him.

John Troy sighed from his place at the table. He had had

plans of his own for the day, working on the sledging rations for the summer and keeping his catalog of supplies up-to-date. Now he had to spend his time in the meteorology room, making entries for Waldo in the various journals, taking hourly readings from aneroid barometers, wind and precipitation gauges, magnetometers, and an ion-bombardment gauge that Waldo and an older scientist had, between them, invented.

Victor Henneker and I also stirred in our chairs.

"Tony," Troy asked me, "would you do the ten o'clock readings at the outside screens? And, Victor, would you do the two o'clock readings?"

At five minutes to ten I put on an extra sweater, my windproofs, and a pair of snow boots, found a lantern, pencil, and paper, and went into the naturalist's room. From there a door could be opened that gave onto outer Antarctica.

Paul Gabriel stood at his workbench in the naturalist's room. Before him lay a frozen skua that had been killed the previous autumn and stored in the ice cave behind the hut. Paul merely contemplated the iron-hard gull. He seemed glad that it defied his taxidermist's skills and required him to wait on its slow thawing.

He looked up at me. "If you like, I'll take the notes for you."

"Gladly, Paul," I said.

He stared at me with his hungover eyes, magnified by glasses. "I need the air," he said.

Our hut was a fragment of heat on the flanks of the great ice organism, amoeba-shaped and larger than the United States and Mexico together. There was no moisture or mercy in the flesh of the organism. Even the sun did nothing more than color it. And now there was no sun. To conserve our tight little bubble of heat, our doors were double, even the door from the naturalist's room to the outside. You opened the inner door and were in a little porch. Before you opened the outer door you made sure you shut the inner. Doing so, Paul Gabriel and I found our way out into the dark but spectacular winter's morning. The moon was a sliver away to the north. We looked across the sound and could see the ice solid and gleaming by the light of the stars and the radiance of the aurora. We saw too, in the strange, luminous dark, the mountains beyond the sound, the great mountains that Scott, with more gratitude than gift for imagery, had disappointingly named the Royal Society Mountains. The aurora had become more intense than Alec Dryden had reported it. The arch of light to the southwest had vanished, but straight across the sound and above the mountains hung great translucent curtains of green and gold and blue. They seemed to be suspended from the highest point of night, to cover an area of sky vast as a continent. Giant ripples of light—white, blue, yellow—ran through them so that it looked as if a furious astral wind were blowing. The base of the aurora blurred and faded at a point that still seemed miles above the mountains.

It was Waldo Warwick's task to study this phenomenon. Measuring the great atmospheric draperies, he was as uncrowded by rival experts as Adam was in Eden. He concluded that the auroras were the fruit of some sort of electrical discharge from the earth's magnetic field (for the earth *was* a magnet, I had discovered, and we were, of course, near its south pole). Waldo, inconvenienced only a little by his fits, wanted to show that the intensity of the phenomenon was connected to the magnetic storms that his gauges could, in a rudimentary way, detect. Scientists have since told me Waldo's theory is either wrong or unpopular—with scientific hypotheses it can amount to the same thing.

The aurora did not yield to the arts, either. Peter Sullivan, using the finest Lumière color plates, had found it impossible to photograph. I was finding it hard to paint in its exact effect of solidity and wispiness. Peter thought he was helping me by telling me he would have called his abortive photographs *The Stage Curtains of the Gods,* but coy figures of speech were of no use to me. In the end you have to paint things for what they are, not for the images they evoke. That's what I thought anyhow.

Paul and I stood on the rise behind the hut. The view of the sound was never the same; there were always variations of light in the darkness, always new dimensions and grandeurs and omens.

"We're the only human beings out-of-doors," I said. "In the whole of this, we're the only ones."

"Except Forbes-Chalmers," he said.

"Except him." Forbes-Chalmers was the name of a certain illusion, a trick of light that had caused members of the expedition (Kittery was the first) to report having sighted a man high up on glaciers or far out on the ice of the sound. Forbes and Chalmers were two members of Holbrooke's expedition of 1908 who never returned from a journey across the sound to study the Taylor Glacier. Stewart now gave their names to a phantasm created by light refraction.

It was the only memorial they had.

"Some things are too much for a person to take in," Paul told me suddenly. He still sounded as numb as he had on waking.

"Are you all right?"

"As a matter of fact I don't feel well." Then he laughed. "But Waldo's preempted the sickbay for the moment."

I told him he should go to his bunk for the day if he needed to.

"Please," he said. "If Beck can walk this morning, I can."

The little weather screens were the visible signs of our expeditionary seriousness. They stood like tabernacles atop poles that last autumn we had sunk into the permafrost. While we visited the screens and read their instruments, keeping records that no one else of earth was keeping, we remained a worthy priesthood.

The first screen stood on a small hill no more than a hundred yards to the north of the hut. Above the box spun the small cups of an anemometer. They turned lazily that morning, for there was hardly any wind. I put the lantern between my feet in the drift snow and opened the doors on the screen. Inside were five weather gauges. One was the anemometer gauge. When I lifted the lantern I was able to read that the wind on the hill had a velocity of a mere three knots, and blew from the south-southwest. I told Paul this. He took a glove off and wrote it down on the pad of paper. We were in a warm snap, and because there was little wind, his hand retained its sense of touch, but on the colder days you saw men who had been to the screens, seated groaning by the stove, waiting for the blood to return painfully into the meat of their hands.

I read him the overnight maximum and minimum from the appropriate thermometers. I read the present temperature, $-31°$, and the present barometric pressure. I forget what that was, but it was dropping. The temperature always rose and the barometer always fell when a blizzard was coming. I reset the maximum and minimum thermometers by pulling a cord, and then closed the screen up.

As we walked around the hut to read the screen Waldo had planted on a little elevation to the south, the dogs away to our right began baying all together. All at once the cold (even today's moderate cold) and the loneliness touched me in a way that wasn't physical. The snug life of the hut in winter had softened me. I began to doubt if I could travel far in this night.

The trouble was, I had offered to. On a sunny day in the previous summer, I had nominated myself for a seventy-mile journey to Cape Crozier to find an emperor penguin egg. The eggs are laid in midwinter. If someone thought that such a journey sounded like the apogee of Edwardian craziness, I would forgive him. The truth was, however, that no one had ever been able to retrieve an emperor penguin embryo, and Dryden and Paul Gabriel would achieve a zoological triumph if they managed it.

The dogs were really keening now, like Irish widows.

I said, "The egg trip—"

"Oh yes," said Paul. "We must have a conference. You and Alec and I?"

"The end of June? You still plan it for the end of June?"

"Yes," he said with no enthusiasm, "a week from today."

"God," I said. I hadn't realized. "A week." I couldn't help asking, "You're still keen, are you?" Because he had sounded so flat.

"Oh yes," he told me, lifelessly.

It was Paul's vision of the emperor embryo that had enchanted me in the first place. Between bouts of racking seasickness he would come into the wardroom of the *McMurdo* and tell me about the emperor. How it was a survival from that strange evolutionary moment (lasting, of course, millions of years) when certain serpents developed flippers and beaks and grew feathers. The debate between Paul and Alec Dryden was whether they had ever flown or not. If we could get an egg, it was likely we could see the history of this development in the embryo, see in the embryo's rudimentary quill pores, in its physical arrangement, the shape and biological history of its ancestors.

Oh he had been fervent about the task; he was rabid very nearly. Between vomiting he drew me diagrams. "There are other reasons for studying the emperor embryo," he told me. "The emperors mate in the autumn on the ice at Cape Crozier.

At the beginning of winter the female lays an egg and leaves the male for half the winter to tend it. He sits on the ice with his back to the Pole, and the egg lies on his feet and is covered with a flap of belly blubber. Imagine. He stands there through blizzards of force ten. He stands there when it's minus eighty degrees. He eats nothing. How can he do it? How is it biologically possible? He is blood like us. He is flesh. The answer is in his body and his blood. But more basically still, it is in the embryo."

I went to Alec Dryden and suggested I go to Cape Crozier with Paul and himself. "You understand," Alec said, "it has to be a midwinter journey. By the time the sun comes back they've hatched the eggs. If we want an egg at an early embryonic stage, it *has* to be midwinter."

I told him I understood that. Raising the Azores, with the sun on our deck, it was easy for me to say I understood.

But now the journey was a week away, and Paul didn't seem to have any appetite for it, and I had tasted the night.

After we had recorded the scarcely different results from the screen to the south, we stood again for a while. The dogs had stopped their noise, and we took in the quiet and the overbearing scene. I could tell Paul wanted to utter something, so I waited. In that place it was easy to spend three or four minutes without speaking. A sort of mystical humility came down on you and speech seemed futile.

At last he said, "They never forgive a fellow for having a *danceuse* for a mother."

"What?"

"Their fathers all saw mother dance. They were all enraptured. Yet they don't forgive you for being her son."

During the year I'd known him, he'd never said that sort of thing before. I asked him who the unforgiving *they* were, and what signs he had had of their unforgiveness.

"It's obvious you don't know. Sir Eugene went to eight men yesterday. He told them they would be the final two sledge teams. From them would come the four men for the Pole."

"I take it you weren't one of the eight."

"No. No. Alec Dryden. John Troy. Petty Officer Mulroy. Victor Henneker to record everything. Brian Quincy—"

"To hold the services?" I asked, agnostically, a little bitter for Paul's sake.

"Because he's strong." He paused but lost control. "Because he's legitimate and his mother wasn't a dancer and his name will look good in the papers."

I thought, Henneker might be the first sodomite at the Pole.

"Then there's Mead," Paul went on, "and Par-axel Beck and Harry Webb."

"He left out Isaac Goodman," I pointed out. "He left out Barry Fields. Despite the fact their mothers aren't dancers."

Paul stared at me. For a moment there was great anger.

I said, "What I'm trying to say is that Stewart doesn't give a damn what your mother was. There are other factors—"

"My shortsightedness, I suppose."

"Yes."

"I'm rather sick of hearing that reason."

"Oh look, I have to say it. You were accepted for the expedition later than anyone else. Why? Stewart was warned about your eyes. That's the only reason. Your breath rises to your glasses and freezes round the inside of the lenses. There are some days when you couldn't see an open crevasse at a yard's distance. Listen, the night journey—shortsightedness won't matter there. We'll all be equally hindered. Forgive me for being frank. We'll all be equally hindered. And it will give us glory enough."

"You don't understand, Tony. I'm not looking for glory. That's a luxury for those who already have a name. What I'm looking for is a name of my own."

"Your name's Paul Gabriel," I told him, "and that's enough for me."

But he still looked leaden, sauntering back to the hut. He had never raved like this before about legitimacy and his mother's reputation. Some deep balance in him had been marred.

I remembered the time Thea Gabriel got back from the United States, bringing with her a superb black bodyguard whom she called her Nubian. Around the Nubian's neck hung a placard:

"I BELONG TO THEA. PLEASE RETURN ME TO HER."

And I imagined Paul as a schoolboy, facing the elegant jocks who ran sporting affairs in the great schools, being told that he could not wicket-keep or stroke or play stand-off half because his eyes weren't fit. And wondering, without knowing he wondered, if in fact he was suffering for his mother's exotic dancing and her strange black bodyguards who, if separated from her, had to be returned by finder.

As I took off my windproofs, I saw Henneker lying on his bunk, reading *To the Polar Plateau,* an account of Holbrooke's expedition. I often saw men reading Holbrooke. Because five of his men had died and all had shown signs of scurvy and malnutrition, the book had become a sort of negative textbook for all of us.

I congratulated Victor.

He said, "Thank you, dear boy," and went on reading.

"You sound as if it was a foregone matter," I said, "your getting chosen, I mean."

"Oh well, it was. I mean, that was the stipulation the newspapers made to Sir Eugene. I was to go to the Pole. I mean, that's fair enough. They paid us quite a price, dear boy, and contracted to pay more—I would say, the largest amount in the history of the newspaper business."

I felt immediate disappointment in Sir Eugene. He had let Paul Gabriel work so long without telling him that not only was one place reserved on the polar team, Sir Eugene's own place, but Henneker's was reserved as well. I felt disappointed not only for Paul but for all the others who could have been chosen: for Barry Fields and Beck, for Mead and Webb, for Coote and Goodman, for Petty Officers Wallace and Jones. In protecting them from the truth about Henneker, he was debasing them, pretending to believe that if they knew, their work would not have been so willing.

I went to the door of the laboratory, looking for Quincy. I saw Kittery first, but I knew he had no grievance. He had to stay around McMurdo all summer, studying the Barne Glacier and the glaciers across the sound. Goodman was in the corner, grinding geological specimens on a stone table. His fingers were slick like a potter's with the clays of the rock he was working on. I didn't speak to him in case he too felt hurt, in case he painfully suspected that anti-Semitism was in operation, even in this far place.

I went through into the weather room, where John Troy was writing up records, and then into the biology lab. Quincy and Byram Hoosick, the American, were identifying a parasite they had taken from the gut of an Antarctic cod. Hoosick, the extent of whose decadence the night before had been lemonade and peanut brittle, looked up at me grinning like a farm boy in love. Quietly, in their little compartment, they had found a previously unknown parasite. It was something they managed to do about once a week.

I went to lunch depressed. I had been working badly for the last two hours on water color sketches for a large painting of the aurora. It seemed everyone else at the table was a little jaded and subdued, and I speculated on the reason. Maybe it was still last night's boozing, maybe it was the news that the final elite had been chosen, the ones to stand at the Pole, and that therefore, in a way, that most spectacular area of the expedition was closed off now from the rest of us.

John Troy stood up after soup. There was no catcalling as when he'd announced his new conical nose protector.

"Gentlemen, because of the imminence of the blizzard, the ponies will not be exercised this afternoon."

There was no cheering. Perhaps by then we all wanted a pony walk as therapy for our sense of midwinter anticlimax.

People drifted from table early. By two o'clock only Hoosick and Quincy were still there, holding some biological conference.

". . . blood sample from the fish . . ." said Quincy.

". . . saline composition , . ." said Hoosick.

Ridiculously I wanted to sleep—sleep was a suitable refuge from my bad art. My easel was only a yard from my bunk. I sat heavily on the stool and stared at the last sketch. The real aurora pulsated continuously. How to get the pulsations in. As I considered the question I saw Henneker hauling on his windproofs and lighting a lantern for the two o'clock reading. He passed me, opened the door to the naturalist's room. That was the last I remember seeing of him.

All at once the afternoon changed for me.

I had gotten my formal art training as a scholarship student at an academy in Paris called the Evraire. My landscape instructor had told me, "Monsieur Piers, you are a barbarian. Train yourself with water colors to be less of a barbarian. If you make love the way you fling paint, no woman would want you."

I had tried for so long and so well to restrain my tendency to large, barbarous gestures that now I had managed to paint the aurora as a mere color profile. I had not conveyed its movement, its arrogance or barbarity.

I began to paint again, as wildly as I could with water colors, the throbbing undulations, the vast electric shards of color. Only once or twice did I listen for a second to the blizzard wail or hear men carrying the news around the hut that the wind had grown to force eight.

The Reverend Brian Quincy put his hand on my shoulder a little after 4:30. "Could you join us, Tony?" he asked.

I turned and saw everyone, including the sailors, gathered around the table in the middle of the hut, all except Waldo, who was still sleeping off his catatonia. They all looked dismal, like members of a kangaroo court. I was alarmed that they had convened under cover of my artistic absorption.

I followed Quincy. Stewart was the only one seated. Flanked by large men all of whose names I knew, yet who suddenly seemed to be strangers, he looked up at me. "Have you seen Victor? Victor Henneker?"

My life was about to be subsumed by a murderous event, but I didn't understand that when I answered.

"No. I saw him go out at two."

John Troy seemed petulant. "You must have seen him since two!" he insisted.

I shrugged and gestured toward the easel. "Sorry to disappoint you, John," I said.

Stewart said, "I want you all to put on finnesköe and windproofs. The wind has leveled at force six, very fierce. I want no one, *no one*, to suffer frostbite. Dr. Dryden will direct the search from this hut. You are to report to him at this table within sixty seconds."

For a minute the hut was full of the strange sounds of flexing windproofs, as everyone dressed, whispering like monks when they spoke at all. As Paul was about to cover his head up, I saw his hands arrested on either side of the fur-lined hood. His eyes glazed.

"If he's been gone since two o'clock ..." He had a concealed dread of what the cold could do. Once, in May, he had been lost on the sea ice during a sudden blizzard. He'd had no compass and had trudged ten degrees off course, reaching a little ice-bound islet called Middleton Island and mistaking it for the coastline near our hut. Struck by the sudden suspicion that he might have a compass after all in a pocket inside his windproofs, he took his glove off to search for it. He found nothing, but his hand was frostbitten and useless now, so that he could not get the frozen mitten back on it. He pulled snow about him and slept for a while and opened his eyes once, having already lost interest in consciousness and life, to see a gap in the blizzard. And in the gap a flare rose into the sky. Therefore he had come home. But the hand was frozen and covered with elephantine blisters in which the fluid had frozen. It hung by his side heavy with the ice of his own subcutaneous liquids. Sullivan took a photograph of that hand, and I believe it is still used as a cautionary picture on scientists and sailors being briefed for Antarctica. Somehow, with salves and dressings, Alec Dryden quickly mended the hand, but the memory stayed with Paul that ice can render a body monstrous in the same manner as fire.

"Two and a half hours," he said, thinking of Henneker.

At the next bunk, which he and Henneker shared, Brian Quincy overheard. "But he hasn't been gone for two and a half hours." Squinting up at us, Quincy buckled up his finnesköe, the furred polar boots from Finland. "I saw him an hour ago."

We asked for no explanations of the chronology. There wasn't time. But the idea that Victor had left the hut an hour before we went to look for him became the reasonable doctrine among us.

AB Stigworth had placed two dozen storm lanterns on the table and was lighting them. It was strange to see him in his blizzard gear, the thin sober head rising from the furry hood.

Dryden had made a diagram for the search and written names down in various sectors. He told us how the flares would be fired and the hour by which we were all to return in any case. I think it was 5:40, but am not sure. He told us to take our personal compasses. I remember some of the unexpected groupings of men. Alexandrei and Henson were to search together, and Kittery and Stewart, Stigworth (the sweeper) and Nikolai, Beck and Mead. Paul and I were to work to the south of the hut.

We all took our lanterns and left, the northward searchers by way of the naturalist's room, the southward through the porch near Peter Sullivan's darkroom.

We milled in the porch awhile covering our noses and mouths, all but our eyes. We southward searchers had to walk into the blizzard. Though my mouth was now muffled by a swath of windproof cloth, I mumbled toward Paul, suggesting we might tell Dryden we wanted to search to the north. Paul understood that his glasses would ice within seconds and be speckled with drift snow.

"It doesn't matter," he said. "You'll be as blind as me in this weather."

"I didn't mean to imply you were blind," I told him, tired of his readiness to be insulted.

But I could see by his eyes he was grinning. "We'll be just as good south as north. We can lean into the wind."

Barry Fields opened the outer door. Stepping out into the blizzard, he yelled some warning or expletive, which was carried away north. He vanished as absolutely as a parachutist disappears from the door of a plane.

Paul and I stepped out crouching, in case the wind blew us on our backs or tore the lanterns from our fists. The blizzard, being a medium unto itself, forced on us the gait of sumo wrestlers. I had again the usual blizzard feeling—that my senses had battened down in a little haven under my ribs, that I was remote from my hand that numbly held the lantern. Snow spun quickly in the small patches of night we lit. First our shoulders were against the back outside walls of Mead's stables, made of bales of hay set between bracing uprights of timber and cara-paced iron-hard with ice provided by the climate.

There was no comfort to us in that wall. So, bent, we turned south and stood for a while wondering if we could successfully take a further step. My locked knee joints jiggled under the wind's attack, and I could feel the small vacuum at my back that my body and the wind made between them.

While we walked, I thought of nothing—not of art nor of women, nor of the wonder that all the snow butting me and biting my eyes was not freshly fallen but snow from another place, perhaps from a ridge farther inland than any of us had been or a glacier where Harry Kittery had never set a bamboo flag. There was numbness and no wonders for me in that wind, that whirl.

In ten minutes we reached the weather scene, turned our backs to the south wind, and got down on our haunches. It was, of course, like walking beneath a waterfall or across a canyon.

"If he's in the snow asleep," I roared at Paul, "we won't find him by going in a straight line."

"No," Paul agreed at full throat.

"I suggest we go back on our tracks but sideways." I made zigzag motions of my gloved hand to indicate a lateral search of the area we had been given. "I mean, against this wind, he wouldn't have gone on past the weather screen here."

Paul yelled in reply, "I think a little farther—say, four hun-dred yards—and then back and forth, back and forth."

"I don't know," I said.

But he insisted.

We continued, some seven yards apart and, as agreed, look-ing at each other and at the snow between us and on both sides.

My brain became a small, numb cube, all protein but no spark.

It jumped and reared, however, when Paul's light vanished. I looked to the rear. Paul was hunched a yard behind me. I let the wind blow me toward him and to my knees as well. It was pleasant to give in to it even in small ways.

He had found boot tracks, in spite of his iced spectacles. We knelt together, viewing them. They crossed our own. Flakes settled on them but were blown away. That was the way of wind, snow, ice in that place. A bootprint or a ski track compacted the surface snow so that later snowdrift found it too slippery to settle there. I remember that later during the expedition Peter Sullivan took a photograph of months-old bootprints standing up six inches above a wind-eroded ice surface, like little buttes. Originally they would have been sharp and indented like the boot tracks we were watching by the light of two storm lanterns.

We followed them and found Henneker, though not easily, because snow had fallen at his back and mounded him over. He lay facing the Pole. We had to walk around him and squat with our backsides to the south. His open eyes were very bulbous in the light of the lanterns. His tongue stuck out. It was black, a frightful excrescence, hopelessly frostbitten. The panels of the face—cheeks, forehead, jaws—were bloated and already blackening.

Paul ripped the covering from his mouth and vomited in the snow. I had felt nothing yet; my senses were still all in hiding, and I saw the corpse and the problem distantly.

"We have to carry him," I called.

I saw Paul button up his mouth covering and shake his head. I felt anger. It spiked my throat.

"Paul, damn it!" I screamed. "Take his legs!"

He obeyed me. It was obvious the body had already stiffened in the cold. Somehow, as we were blown north carrying Victor, we retained our lanterns. Possibly we were too numb to understand they were still in our hands. I was shocked and useless and dropped the shoulders twice. Paul seemed patient with me.

Some yards back, we stumbled on Stigworth, the sweeper, and Nikolai, the dog handler. Under Stigworth's eyes were frozen tears.

"The bastard won't move, sir," he yelled at me. "He's hexed."

Nikolai sat in a snowdrift, shivering, his eyes closed.

"It's all right. We've found Mr. Henneker."

I must admit that the class consciousness of the day required me to call our weird load "Mr. Henneker."

"Oh good, sir." Stigworth screamed. "This bloody Roosian, he hates the dark, sir. He just sits there. You'd think, sir, in bloody Roosia, they'd be used to the dark."

He kicked Nikolai, who opened his eyes, saw us and the corpse we carried, and began screaming.

That was the way we took Henneker back to the hut—Paul, Stigworth, and I hauling him and a demented Russian wailing in our wake.

THREE

Sir Eugene Stewart had an alcove of his own. It was formed on three sides by a tall bookshelf, a plywood partition against which his bed stood, and the wall of the hut. The fourth side was made by a curtain hung from a rod. The curtain was rarely closed, but even when it was pulled back you could still only see in there from the corner where Dryden and Troy slept.

In this way Sir Eugene expressed both his accessibility and his desire for privacy.

On the night of Henneker's death the curtain was pulled firmly across, making a private room out of the alcove. Stewart had Alec Dryden in there, conferring with him. The rest of us were also finding it hard to digest Victor's death. We sat at the table, reading or writing, or else working numbly in our appropriate places. Paul, for example, had gone back to work on the skua, Hoosick was writing up the day's discovery in the biology room, Peter Sullivan was developing copies of last night's photograph in the darkroom. Quincy sat in a hard chair by his bunk, the bunk he had shared with Henneker. We presumed he was praying or mourning meditatively, in the manner of a clergyman, but he was the sort of man who would have thought it in bad taste to do it on his knees around people who were working.

I was still too bemused to be any use with a brush. When Waldo woke at eight, I took him to the table and fed him tea and the last of Walter O'Reilly's bread for that day. I was in a state of mind that made me wonder if there would be bread tomorrow. It was clear to me that Victor Henneker had been treated violently and not survived the treatment. Therefore, all the bonds and shared duties that made our life possible were under question, if not ruptured. It mightn't be long before everyone in the hut understood that—before things fell apart, the stove went out, the blankets iced, the drinking water froze over.

"Waldo," I said, "something happened while you were asleep."

"A blizzard came up," he said. He was embarrassed about that—that the weather should change radically while he was unconscious. "Poor John Troy. All that extra work."

"It wasn't just the blizzard. This afternoon Victor Henneker went out without telling anyone. We can't ask him why. But he fell and hit his head, and I'm afraid he died of exposure before he could be found."

Waldo looked at his hands, clenching the fingers as if he could read in the arrangement of the knuckles a clearer account of the death. He said at last, "You say, *of exposure?*"

"Or of a head injury, or of both." I knew it, and his incredulity annoyed me. "Does it matter, Waldo?"

Waldo did not say. He still wore the contrite look that he always had after one of his fits.

"He . . . he wasn't reading the weather screens?"

"No. No, he did the two o'clock reading but came back safe from it. John Troy and PO Mulroy are doing the eight o'clock now. But it was late this afternoon Victor went out again, nothing to do with readings, nothing to do with anything. As I say, we can't ask him."

After a while, Waldo said, "Death by a freak. Poor Victor. You'd think, in a great . . . *enterprise* like this, you wouldn't die in that way. A bump on the head. Thanks for telling me, Tony." He stood up, wavering a little. "I think I'd better go and see what's happened in my office today while I was . . . while I was sick."

He was usually a wry young man who made jokes quietly,

out of the corner of his mouth. But guilt over his fits left him wooden.

At the end of the table the two geologists, Fields and Goodman, had been playing a dispirited game of chess. Usually they contested noisily, making speeches about their strategies, calling in other men to watch them make crucial moves. "See what I'm doing to this colonial gentile," Goodman would say in invitation. "Look at this, I've got his bishop and check," Fields would announce. "Sheep farmer," Goodman would say. "Gefilte merchant," Fields would respond. They were the only two who mentioned Goodman's Jewishness openly. They did it without any awkwardness. Tonight, though, there were no rantings or exclamations over the chessboard. Goodman beat Fields easily but seemed to get little joy from the triumph. Barry murmured his congratulations and drifted down the table to the place where Waldo had left me.

"You're shocked," he suggested gently. "I can tell."

"I suppose so."

"Do you mind talking? About finding him and so on?"

"Well . . . " Alec Dryden had asked me not to—to pretend shock and reluctance even if I didn't feel them. Of course I felt them.

Barry blinked, staring directly at my eyes. I wanted to laugh. He had the oversolemnity and overfrankness of a child. "I mean, you found him. Did you really think he'd hit his head? Just that? Sorry if this is painful. But what did he look like?"

I couldn't frame words. "Yes. I don't know. Blisters. His face was blistered. I don't know." I wanted my ignorance to sound like the last word.

"You and Paul and the sweeper brought him back. Did Alec look closely at him? Listen, you've got to bloody forgive me. I've got reasons for asking."

"We put him on a bench in the naturalist's room . . . —"

And as soon as we had done it Paul went and leaned his

brow against the wall. Stigworth sat moaning with a frostbitten hand and rubbed it furiously against his chest far inside his polar clothing.

Alexandrei was keening by the door. Only I—and I don't know why—watched Alec work with Victor. First he felt Victor's temples, then he wrestled with the frozen gauntlets, seeking a wrist pulse. His attempt to close the eyelids failed because they were frozen to the eyeballs.

He touched Victor's bloated and frozen tongue and realized that even if it were thawed, it would not fit properly back in the mouth again. Then, unbuttoning the iced windproofs from around the neck, he put his fingers toward Victor's carotid and saw, before he touched the cold flesh, what I also could see— the various purple bruises of strangulation on the throat. Alec stared at me a second, pulled the windproof collar back into place so that the marks were not so visible and asked me alone to help him carry Victor through our quarters, maneuvering his stiffness around the end of the table, then into the sailors' quarters, and so through into the workshop. I held Victor upright while Alec cleared a bench of hammers and chisels. When that was done, we placed the corpse on the bench.

"There's no one else to ask," he said, "so would you mind getting some blubber and lighting the stove here?"

The temperature in the workshop was probably close to freezing, but the room had an unused blubber stove, which, if lit, would be likely to give out enough heat for the thawing of Victor's body.

I went out of the workshop to the space beside the men's latrines where frozen blubber was heaped. Men like Mulroy and Wallace flensed it away from the meat of any seal they caught, cut it in blocks, and stacked it here where, of course, it froze. Every day sailors took a supply through to the stables for Mead to use in the stove there to keep the ponies warm.

I loaded myself with four blocks—enough, I thought, to

warm Victor's corpse—and brought them into the workshop. Alec had already covered the body with a blanket. "It's from his own bunk," he said. I could dimly hear the explosion of a flare in the blizzard outside. Stigworth or Paul must be doing that duty, pointing the flare pistol southward over the hut, so that the flare exploded in the blizzard above our heads.

I put the blocks of blubber in the perforated bin at the top of the stove. As they melted they would give off an unpleasant fatty smell inappropriate to respect for the dead, so I covered the bin with its steel lid. Next I opened the slide beneath the bin and lit the small oil burner inside the stove. I closed the slide. What would happen now was that the burner would melt a little of the blubber, the blubber oil would drip through the bin perforations and feed the flames, which would melt more blubber still. And so a heavy, sooty warmth would grow in the workshop.

"Thank you," said Alec. He took a chair and began filling his pipe.

"Aren't you shocked?" I asked him. I thought the pipe was indecent.

He put it on the floor, near his foot, and put both hands on his knees. "You'll have to forgive me, Tony."

"It's all right," I said. A sweet, narcotic fog of blubber heat was already rising in the room. "Go ahead," I said, pointing to the pipe at his feet.

"No," he said. "No. What if you get us both a nip of brandy?"

"Very well."

"But first, Anthony, could I ask you not to speculate? About Victor, I mean."

"Do I look like a gossip?"

"Of course not."

I went into our quarters and poured us a half tumbler each from the brandy bottle. In the doorway near the darkroom and the porch beyond the naturalist's room, returning searchers were arriving and questioning and talking of the blizzard. Paul was sitting silent but thoughtful at the table, which Stigworth was serenely preparing for supper.

When I took the brandy back to the workshop, Alec raised his glass toward me. "To reticence," he said solemnly.

At the dinner table later, Stewart had announced Victor's death and had even proposed aloud that it may have followed a heart attack. Yet the obvious signs, he had said, were of head injury and exposure. "God rest his soul," said Sir Eugene in conclusion.

With such guidance, I could now only be what Alec had suggested—reticent. I felt I risked bringing on a final chaos if I said, "The leader—the chief—Sir Eugene—is lying into his soup."

So when Barry pestered, I gave my colorless answers.

At last he kept silent, knowing he'd pressed me too much.

"You said you had a reason to ask," I suggested.

"Yes."

"Well?"

"It's that Henneker was a thorough man. In his field he was a damn sight more thorough than I am in mine. I can't—in fact, I don't—believe he'd let himself die that silly way."

I thought that was a stupid reason, but didn't say so. I said what Alec had already said: "That sort of speculation is very dangerous."

"Did Alec take Victor's personal belongings? Papers and so on?"

"I don't know. I imagine so."

He patted my wrist. "You ought to have a hot drink and fall asleep early," he said. "And I'm sorry. For nagging you, I mean."

He went and found a novel and sat by the stove reading it. I sat alone, and the longer I sat the better I came to like Barry's thesis. There is a Graham Greene short story about a man who is killed by a pig that falls from a balcony in Naples. Why? Because he is the kind of man of whom falling pigs take advantage. The story is actually about the son of the man, who is exactly the sort of person to be ridiculously orphaned. But Victor *wasn't* the sort of man on whom pigs fall. I knew that. Victor's death had the stature of an assassination.

I raised my head. Alec stood beside me. His pipe was unashamedly fuming between his lips. "Have you got a moment for the leader, Tony?"

I stood up and followed him. We went into Sir Eugene's little alcove, and Alec rearranged the curtain so that we were unseen from outside. Sir Eugene sat with his side to his table. He wore his stained white sweater and was frowning at some papers. When he saw me he put his head to one side as if I could immediately give him crucial information.

"Sit on the bed," he told me. I did so, arranging my legs on either side of the scarred leather suitcase that protruded from under the bed frame. Peter Sullivan at one time or another took a photograph of Sir Eugene working as he was now, frowning over papers against the background of books, bed, and tattered luggage. Lady Stewart loved the photograph so much that this one—not the heroic open-air shots of Eugene be-furred, beskied, visionary in the polar glare—was the one she hung in her living room from 1913 till her death in 1952.

"I'm not going," Sir Eugene announced, "to make you take an oath or anything ridiculous. But we are concerned about rumors being started . . ."

I said I understood.

"I've asked AB Stigworth not to gossip," Alec told me dolefully, as if he'd been forced to suspend all civil liberties.

"He had a frostbitten hand," I said. "*That* seemed to pre-occupy him."

"Quite. And Paul was in a condition of shock."

"And as for Nikolai," concluded Sir Eugene, seemingly reading from some notes in front of him, "he appears to have been hysterical. Nor is his English adequate for spreading rumors."

With a little shudder he turned the note paper over.

"Cause of death!" My aggression took even me by surprise. "What was the cause of death?"

Sir Eugene made a little affirmative grunt and inclined his head farther.

Alec said, "First he was hit. There's a lineal fracture here." He patted the back of his own head delicately. "Then he was strangled. You saw the bruising around the trachea and carotid. In addition, there was the blistering of the face and the freezing of the limbs."

"We can't tell these things to everyone," Sir Eugene said. "It would throw everything into doubt—trust, the manners of men, the expeditionary purpose." He began dismantling and inspecting the bore of his pipe. I have noticed the annoying obsession with pipe cleanliness in other men at times of bereavement and crisis.

"The temptation," he went on, "is to pretend, not just to others but to ourselves, that it was an accident of climate. Only ourselves and the person responsible would know we were lying. But *that's* a mental trick I can't quite manage."

I was thinking of Barry and his questions and the absurdity of Barry breaking a brother's skull and choking him with big, bruising thumbs, putting an onus of investigation and punishment not on some impassive outside authority but on the people of the hut. I thought of Waldo and Kittery and Paul and Quincy. It was all ridiculous.

Sir Eugene picked up more note paper and read the timetable of Victor's afternoon. Victor had done the two o'clock reading and left the results in the meteorology hut. Then he spent a short time watching Paul embalm the skua. (So Paul had mentioned aloud at the dinner table that night.) Perhaps he'd rested and read more Holbrooke then. Then, toward 3:30, the Reverend Brian Quincy went looking for him and found him in the latrines. The Reverend Quincy and his friend Hoosick had made a new parasite discovery, and Brian considered it of sufficient news value to inform Victor about it. Victor promised to come and see Quincy and Hoosick as soon as he was finished in the latrines, but he did not keep the promise. Instead, dressing fully, he'd gone out for a walk in the blizzard, and had met somebody. "With what results we now know," Sir Eugene concluded.

We sat silent a while. The blizzard wail had such intimidating resonances.

Sir Eugene murmured, "Alec has a suggestion that may save the sanity of all of us."

"Yes," Alec began instantly. "Last autumn three men reported seeing a human figure in McMurdo Sound. Harry Kittery was first. He said he was working on the Barne Glacier, sinking a core for an ice sample. He looked up and saw a man standing on a moraine ridge two hundred yards away. He called to PO Henson to look, but when PO Henson did the man was gone. Next Barry Fields claimed to have seen a man at Hut Point. The distance involved was half a mile, which is no great distance in this atmosphere. Barry said the man seemed to be clubbing a seal at the edge of the tide crack."

"I hastened," Sir Eugene confessed, "to label it an illusion: The Forbes-Chalmers effect. It seemed to me no human could occupy Antarctica long on a solitary basis. I didn't believe it to be biologically possible, and I certainly considered it wasn't— what will I say?—emotionally possible. Now that this has happened I am tempted—merely tempted—to revise my ideas."

Alec continued, as if on a cue, to whip up an outline, an acceptable silhouette.

"Even after the leader had given the phenomenon that name, PO Percy Mulroy claimed to have seen a man walking across the lower slopes of Erebus. It was from a distance of at least a mile and the weather was deteriorating, but Percy certainly believed—and believes still—in the man's reality."

Alec began hammering the palm of his hand gently with his own pipe bowl. For a second, he bit his lower lip. "I saw the man too. It was just like the time Harry Kittery saw him. We were at the Adélie penguin rookery half a mile down the coast. I had Paul Gabriel with me and PO Bertram Wallace. Bertram was catching the birds—he has a gift for it; his father was a falconer, you know, not that falcons and penguins have much in common. Wallace would hold the Adélies while Paul put a numbered tag on their ankles and I took note of the number on a sheet of paper. We wanted to see if the numbered penguins would come back to the same rookery next spring for their mating. Anyhow, I looked up while Bertram was chasing some penguin chick and the man was only a hundred yards away on a rise. I couldn't see him in detail because the light was behind him. I could tell he'd run if I shouted, so I hissed at the other two, but by the time they looked he was gone. I . . . I didn't make much of it because it's not one of the purposes of the expedition to find Antarctic Crusoes, and in any case the light in this country does perform tricks, not subtle ones either. But that's four of us who thought we saw a man. I think now we must have."

"I pray," said Sir Eugene, priming him, "that you must have."

"Of the men counted as dead on Holbrooke's expedition, only the bodies of Forbes and Chalmers weren't found. As you may know, Forbes and Chalmers started on a journey from Holbrooke's hut further down this coast for the Taylor Glacier. It's a contracting glacier on the other side of McMurdo Sound and the valley it leaves as it contracts is dry—it doesn't fill with snow, no one knows why. It is one of those Antarctic puzzles. Anyhow, Forbes and Chalmers began the journey in autumn. It happened that the autumn that year was one of ceaseless blizzards and Forbes and Chalmers neither returned nor were they found. Later Holbrooke was pilloried for negligence and delay, for not supplying them adequately. But they could have disappeared no matter how well they were equipped, given the weather. If, however, there is a man—other than ourselves—in McMurdo Sound, it must be Forbes or Chalmers."

Sir Eugene murmured, "The Forbes-Chalmers effect is therefore well named."

I had noticed before that the relationship between Sir Eugene and Alec was a perfect king-chancellor one. Sir Eugene made the pronouncements and Alec did all the annotating—as he immediately began to do again.

"Last February some of us visited Holbrooke's hut. I noticed two things that surprised me. For example, Holbrooke says in his journal that when the relief ship turned up in February of 1909 the expedition was down to one crate of cocoa, a hundred and twenty pounds of biscuit, ten pounds of butter, twenty-five pounds of rice, eighty pounds of pemmican. Enough to keep twenty-five men alive for ten days. He says that the members of the expedition were so delighted to see the ship that they left all the food behind as a sort of tithe to the fates that had saved them. I was surprised to find no supplies in the hut. But I found something written on the wall. It said, "John Forbes, dead in Christ, 1908." Large lettering. Done in charcoal. It . . . well, it didn't look like the sort of thing Holbrooke would have wanted on his walls."

"Too accusatory," said Sir Eugene, "for Holbrooke's taste.

He didn't want to be reminded of his dead. He still resents it if he's questioned . . ."

I could see that Alec believed heartily in this surviving man who wrote on walls and took and ate the tithe Holbrooke had left for the gods. But at the same time I sensed Sir Eugene encouraged this belief only as a mental therapy for Alec and me, to keep us sane. The way an atheist father wants his daughters to believe in God on the grounds that the belief will make them behave more chastely.

Alec, however, was now deep in his thesis.

"My theory, therefore, is that Victor—who was a newspaperman of the modern style—somehow made contact with Forbes-Chalmers and was to meet him again today at a certain time; that Victor, in spite of blizzard, skied out this afternoon in case Forbes-Chalmers (we don't know which one of them it is, though the inscription at Holbrooke's hut indicates Chalmers), in case he kept the appointment. After all a powerful journalistic motive would have been at work in Victor. An appointment of that nature would be the only sane reason for going out this afternoon. Discovering Forbes or Chalmers would have been a journalistic tour de force he may not have wished to share with the expedition. My theory, then, is that Forbes-Chalmers must have repented, for some mad reason, of meeting Victor and killed him to protect a manner of life that must be barbarous and painful yet, in Forbes-Chalmers's mind, superior to meeting us or returning to the world."

We all three sat silent for a while, relishing for a second Alec's hypothesis that we were whole again, the Cape Frye community—that the cancer wasn't interior. But I think Sir Eugene, like myself, wondered why anyone would set and, more still, keep an appointment in the midst of a Beaufort scale eight blizzard.

Sir Eugene studied my face awhile. "You understand," he said, "the necessity of the lies at the dinner table? Death from exposure, following an accidental head injury, and so on? If I tell them Victor was killed by Forbes-Chalmers, a theory I can't accept totally myself, then it will raise the parallel possibility that he was killed by one of them. Lies are a risk, but I hope I'll be forgiven. You know and Alec knows and I know that Victor was murdered. As a result, our heads are spinning; we are dazed; we don't know what to believe. If all the people knew the cause of Victor's death, the confusion—the stupefaction—would grow tenfold, possibly by the square of ten. Where would we go to hide from each other, to be safe from each other? What doors could we lock? What authorities could be called in? I won't admit to them how Victor died. It is information that would make us barbarians."

I felt a rush of panic at being elected to this inner committee of three. "Why?" I asked. "Why plague me with the truth?"

Because you already know it, they told me. I asked further, why not Paul Gabriel? Paul Gabriel's view of Victor's injuries had been confused by shock and nausea. Besides, Sir Eugene told me, Alec had spoken to him and made sure. Paul's apparent confusion was real.

Alec had spoken to him, for Sir Eugene wasn't confident of his ability to talk to men directly. He was happier making a speech, his eyes traveling from man to man, taking in the collective not the individual face.

Alec Dryden picked up a piece of paper and told him, "We find that of all the expeditionary members, only Waldo, yourself, and myself were in the living area the entire afternoon. Waldo and you and I—we didn't even visit the latrines."

"Good for you," Sir Eugene murmured with a brief private smile. He suffered from a condition called tenesmus. It was a cruel form of constipation that *Webster's* defines as "a feeling of urgent need to defecate or urinate, with a straining but unsuccessful attempt to do so."

Alec had taken up another sheet of paper. "I have a crude list of other people's movements. It's not something we can ask directly—'Where were you, so-and-so, when Victor was killed?'—but men have naturally tended to say what they were doing when Victor was dying. They're tantalized, you see, by the thought of how easily they could have dropped what they were at and gone and found him."

"I head the said crude list," Sir Eugene announced. "And, of course, if I'm the responsible party, then we're all finished."

Alec read. Sir Eugene had visited the latrines after lunch and then wrote his journal and a memorandum for Harry Kittery concerning ice formations. The leader pestered Harry with dilettante theories about the conditions that cause sea ice, the sequence of states it goes through until it is pack ice, its decay until it becomes ice cakes and brash ice. Sir Eugene's theory was that the sea began to turn to ice only when water vapor fell out of the air and made the first ice crystals on the ocean. Harry Kittery believed that the ocean froze from within. A major question, you might say. Yet Sir Eugene often wrote Harry notes about it, as if to put the boy on the right track.

After this, Sir Eugene (according to the list of movements) had gone to the sailors' quarters to help in the repair of sledges. He was fetched from there by the news that Victor could not be found anywhere.

Alec himself spent the afternoon in his corner, writing and illustrating an article on the embryology of Adélie penguins. Harry Kittery had been in the laboratory, reading the memorandums from Sir Eugene perhaps. Paul Gabriel had been embalming his skua. Brian Quincy examined and discussed with his partner, Hoosick, the function of a new parasite they had retrieved from the gut of one of their more important catches, an Antarctic cod.

In fact, for Quincy and the restrained American, the examination of this tiny bug that infested the intestinal tract of an impressive fish had produced a further and greater scientific success. As the little parasite lay under their microscope it had bled out its minute body secretions, which during the lunch hour, while Quincy and Hoosick were taking a quick meal, had turned to crystals. Hoosick, who had more chemistry than Brian Quincy, tested the crystals and discovered that they were salt. Both men instantly felt a creative excitement, a potent intuition. They knew with a certainty of the blood, rather than of the deductive mind, why Antarctic cod could live unarmored, unblubbered, and yet healthily in polar water, at depths where the temperatures were actually *below* the surface freezing point and should very quickly freeze the cod's blood. If the small sea vermin got its saltiness from the cod, then maybe the explanation for the cod's success was salt. They had already refrozen the cod's carcass. It lay in Walter O'Reilly's storeroom to the east of the hut, the room you got to through a door from the galley. They rethawed the cod by plunging it in hot water and got what smears of blood they could from it. The results of their tests were not, therefore, of the highest clinical quality. Nonetheless, they found that the blood of the Antarctic cod was a broth of salt and hemoglobin, that it would go on flowing when a salmon's blood was long frozen.

Quincy went looking for Victor when the blood was ready for testing, sure that Victor would want to be present for one of marine biology's more splendid moments. They had delayed the test ten minutes, waiting for Victor to finish in the latrines, but then they had gone ahead anyhow.

On a normal night Sir Eugene would have made a little speech honoring them and there would have been fish talk all evening till PO Mulroy cut the lights at eleven. But none of us had wanted to talk cod that night.

The list continued. Barry Fields took notes and Isaac Goodman ground the geological specimens. Peter Sullivan was in the darkroom developing a mediocre plate of the aurora and hand-tinting the results. John Troy worked partly in the meteorology room, partly on the sledge and ration packs being assembled in the sailors' quarters. Par-axel and Harry Webb helped the sailors repair sledge runners.

Warren Mead stayed in the stables. "One of the ponies," Alec explained, "Tulip I think it is, has symptoms of glanders. Alexandrei was with Warren, melting snow on the blubber stove. Tulip, of course, needs a great deal of drinking water."

"No symptoms in any of the others?" asked Sir Eugene, as if glanders were suddenly the main problem.

"Not yet. Warren is confident . . ."

In Sir Eugene's mind, ponies were the innovation that would bring him success. He was sentimental about dogs in any case and found it distasteful to budget into his plans the dog meat that would become available as the dogs failed in their traces and were shot. He was not so sentimental about Siberian ponies and intended to use them on the glaciers and polar plateaus, as long as they would last. A pony could drag eight hundred or a thousand pounds of food and gear, he'd told us—if the pony were well. Yet there were other, more obvious contrasts between dogs and ponies that Sir Eugene seemed to understand as poorly as any of us did that winter.

For instance, Harry Webb, the Canadian dog man, tethered his dogs in the open, fed them frozen seal meat, left it to them to eat enough snow for good health, and had to tend them only when males fought over leadership or bitches. Warren Mead, on the contrary, had to build stables for his ponies and spend most of every other winter day melting water (since they didn't fancy snow), making mashes, dosing and mixing dosages, working out a dietary balance for them, and watching for symptoms of glanders, a sort of horse mumps that had already killed two of his ponies. He was an all-day mother to his troop of fifteen animals. No one liked to mention to him that they would probably all have been eaten by the following autumn, for he seemed to love even the mean shaggy Siberian creature I used to exercise—a gelding called Igor. Igor could, even wearing blinkers, throw a hoof sideways and crack your shin just where the most nerves crossed the bone. When, limping, I returned Igor to the stables one afternoon, I said to Warren, "I'm glad they castrated the bastard. He deserves it." But Warren did not laugh. Pipe in mouth, chunky, his head cropped like a cavalry recruit's, he inspected Igor all over, as if I might have bitten him.

That night in Sir Eugene's alcove it was not news to me that Warren Mead spent all afternoon with the ponies. Nor that Norman Coote had worked on one of the two tractors. Norman was attentive to his machines. They sat with drained engine blocks in a garage you could get to from the laboratory. The garage was unheated and Coote always used to be testing oil blends on the moving parts, seeking a lubricant that would not freeze and choke the engine. He spent the winter taking those two machines apart, considering the moving parts, even designing new treads for their tracks and tooling them in the workshop. Later, whenever I visited a technological museum, I always thought of Norman in that distant winter, of the brave red paint, the brass polish, the fine oils he used on his two darlings, keeping them spotless as exhibits in the Smithsonian. This was the way he consoled himself for the loss of the third one, the one that lay a hundred fathoms down in McMurdo Sound, that had fallen through the ice with John Troy in its saddle. Everyone had been grateful John Troy didn't go down there amongst the salt-blooded codfish with it. But Norman had been bitter about the loss and believed Troy had lost the tractor through reckless driving or lack of the sensitivity men should have for machines.

Norman spent so many hours, dressed in a greasy greatcoat,

dealing with his tractors, because he believed they were central to the expedition, that they would take Stewart across the ice shelf all the way to the base of the Beardmore and—depending on conditions—a long way up it. He believed that the automated future had already come and that when Stewart stood at the Pole he would say, "The tractors made this possible." So Norman looked on Warren Mead and Harry Webb as keepers of quaint polar pets and on himself as the logistical center of the enterprise. As the winter went on and we all became more eccentric, he began to say as much. He spent so much time in that unheated garage; he had so little conversation other than about tractors; he had so much mechanic's arrogance that he was an outsider. It was only the following summer, when both his tractors broke down beyond repair after logging a mere hundred miles between them, that he was forced to take an interest in the rest of us and won friends and became an expert sledger.

So Norman Coote was in the garage. Walter O'Reilly was cooking in the galley, occasionally visiting his storeroom for cans of meat for pudding. The rest of the sailors worked in their quarters. They repaired sleeping bags, made sailcloth containers for supplies, sewed up dog or pony harnesses, mended ski equipment, bound or reinforced the framework of sleds. As a sort of quartermaster's mate, Henson clerked in a corner by the bunks. Last of all, the Mulroy brothers made new runners in the workshop. The woodworking lathes had whirred all afternoon.

Alec asked me did my experience contradict anything in this roster of his. But my afternoon had been experienced as blocks of color and not in terms of the movements of my colleagues. I apologized.

FOUR

A manila folder lay on Sir Eugene's table. I saw him open it. It was fat with documents.

"I went to Victor's bunk," he said, "and took his bags from beneath it and so took possession of his personal effects and documents. He's written what looks like six excellent articles on our winter work, absolutely suitable as far as I can tell for publication in quality newspapers. He has also written a half dozen more whimsical articles, rather mocking in tone. They would have been his business—he could have published them in suitable magazines. Here's one. "How to Live with Polar Explorers." It's clear he thought some of us a little ridiculous." Sir Eugene chuckled without malice. "You should both read these—there may be something in them, some indication... Here's another. "Hygiene and Male Fashions at −50°." There are also a number of letters from public figures. Poor Victor obviously took them everywhere with him. Here's a blistering one from Mr. George Bernard Shaw." He read aloud:

Dear Mr. Henneker,
I have heard you described at one of the less challenging dinner tables of this city as the poor man's Bernard Shaw. May I say that I believe that the poor suffer from sufficient economic disadvantage, are cossetted too regularly with the promise of heaven's draughty porticos and, in any case, suffer from such deplorably bad teeth that some benevolent editor might well believe they should be further discriminated against by being given a substitute Shaw to chew upon. I can only warn you that even the severest social and political discrimination has not barbarized them to the point where they can stomach you.

'And more of the same. Poor Victor. He wasn't easy to insult, was he?"

"He wasn't insensitive," said Alec bravely. "He had a very good journalistic reputation. Of course, Mr. Shaw thinks all journalists are barbarians."

Sir Eugene put the letter down delicately, like an honorable epitaph. "There are others, even a death threat from the Sinn Fein. Oh dear." He was silent a second. I thought he might even shed a tear. Victor was a terrible man, but most people found him hard to hate unless he had injured them in cold print.

Sir Eugene packed the articles and letters back into the manila folder and closed it. He stared at the knuckle of his right index finger and kneaded it with the fingers of his left hand. "It's incredible that I should ever have to speak like this. Victor has been treated by someone as an object of fear and hate. Alec has sketched a reasonable motivation for Forbes-Chalmers to treat Victor in that manner." The way Sir Eugene spoke, a stranger might have believed Forbes-Chalmers had maligned Victor at some dinner table. "We have to consider whether any of *us* had motivation to fear and hate." He coughed again and looked straight at me. "You see, we three are a kind of Committee of Public Safety. It's ridiculous, but before this affair is over we may have to be brutal with our friends."

There was silence. It grew and weighed. They wanted me to speak first. I was aware, as Stewart had said, that we would all have to speak painfully in the end, for the good reason that anarchy threatened our breath and the tenuous warmth of our blood.

"I have only the most random thoughts," I said. But they still waited for them to emerge.

"Well," I said, "it seems the news that Victor had been chosen for the Pole party . . . that it had been predetermined that he was going . . . it could have disappointed some of us."

"Not you. Surely not you."

"Some of them . . . They might think they should have been told earlier."

Sir Eugene nodded, taking the criticism in. Taut aggression and florid apology were equally foreign to him.

It was Alec who made the defense. "I was in my garden two years ago," he said, "down near Exmouth. My wife and children were blackberrying at the end of the garden and I was simply reading. I saw a taxi—a rare sight on those country roads—let off a lady and a gentleman at the bottom of our lane. As they got closer I saw it was Sir Eugene and Lady Stewart. Before I had time to warn my wife and children, Sir Eugene called to me. He said, 'Alec, I'm going back, all the way to the Pole this time. I would very much like to stand at the Pole with you.' My point is that it's always been agreed that I would go to the Pole, yet none of the expedition was ever told in so many words."

I remember I shrugged. He didn't need to argue the matter with me.

"The eight men," he pursued, "who were approached yesterday and notified of their selection . . . they were told to keep it secret. But one of them was so pleased or so well-liquored he passed the list on . . ."

Sir Eugene understood me exactly. "Anthony has touched on an incentive for violence that is credible however incredible. I could see such motivation operating in the case of Paul Gabriel, who believes that only his shortsightedness stands between himself and the reaching of the Pole."

I flinched at the specific name. Sir Eugene had begun to take more notes. When he had finished he looked at the curtains beyond me. "Now," he said, "do you have any more to tell us?"

My throat became instantly dry. I must restate that the values of the day made "homosexual" the worst label you could put on a man. Pimps and confidence men and sellers of stocks in Peruvian or Australian gold mines were considered moderate enemies of society. But when you said "homosexual" you were speaking of an outlaw, a man who couldn't be redeemed. It was like saying "Communist" in the Hollywood of the 1950s. You didn't willingly apply the word even to the dead.

I began to mutter something about Petty Officer Mulroy's distress—about Victor's attentions to young Able-bodied Seaman Mulroy.

Even before I began speaking I was obliquely aware of a new wailing—separate from, sharper than, the monotone wail of the blizzard. I thought it might have been the big kettle boiling madly in the men's quarters. Because, as I said, "This is third-hand information . . . ," the shrilling got louder, as if the door between our quarters and the sailors' had been opened.

As I mentioned Victor's proclivities, someone began hammering on the outside of Sir Eugene's bookcase. The volume and heftiness of the knocking indicated urgency, and that the curtain was not instantly pulled aside suggested that it was a sailor pounding the bookcase; yet, politely, not announcing disaster until requested to, Sir Eugene nodded to Alec, who rose and pulled the curtain back. By now I could tell that the distant noise was a human lamentation, in there, in the sailors' quarters.

Petty Officer Percy Mulroy stood by the bookcase.

"Sir," he said, "one of the Russians has gone crazy."

Sir Eugene instantly got up from the table. I had the impression for a second that he was as pleased to have the distraction of a plaintive Russian as I was.

At the open door into the sailors' quarters, Barry Fields, Isaac Goodman, and the Reverend Quincy stood. Barry held out a hand to delay Sir Eugene. "Watch out, leader," he said, "the lunatic's got a harpoon."

As befits an old man with a rotting cerebrum, I remember acutely the scene I saw when I looked into the sailors' quarters. The tall boy Alexandrei, Mead's pony handler, stood in the galley area. In his Asian face the mouth stood wide open and gave out a great piercing wail. The right hand, which held the harpoon, looked as if it were about to glide into a fluid and expert throw that would pin one of the sailors against his bunk.

In front of Alexandrei, sitting at the table with his back to his fellow Siberian, sat Nikolai, the small, bullet-headed man who had grieved so loudly out in the blizzard that afternoon. Tonight he seemed more passive, his head hung, there were tears among the stubble of his face. He looked as if he grieved softly because his friend Alexandrei was so distressed. As well, he knew—and we could see—that he was the only other man in the room who was safe from the harpoon. The sailors were all milling quietly at the bunk end of the room, eyes subtly averted from Alexandrei. Only PO Bertram Wallace sat, squinting at the Russians from beneath a split eyebrow. The pony handler had cut his eyebrow open with the butt end of the harpoon. Henson and Jones, men of restless temperament, looked as if they might charge Alexandrei at any second, just to break the hiatus.

Sir Eugene said, "No one move!"

John Troy joined us in the doorway. His eyes, taking in the crisis, were bright beads of canniness in a face that was older than its thirty-three years, hooked, crooked, knowing. He reminded me of druids and those Cornish fishermen who have secret ways of spotting a shoal of halibut.

He murmured in Sir Eugene's ear about breaking out a carbine. Sir Eugene thanked him but declined, asking instead for Warren Mead, who knew some Russian.

Mead was fetched from the stables. He had not heard his handler going berserk in the sailor's quarters. The wind noise, the hiss of the blubber stove, the snuffling of ponies had filled his hearing, and the slight swelling on Tulip's underjaw provided him with his sole horizon.

Before Warren arrived, Steward and Mulroy began their advance on Alexandrei.

I stayed by the door jamb, half protected by it. I wanted to call out about the folly of walking up to Alexandrei, of not shooting him first. I've found out since that only the very brave are able to estimate the quotient of danger in a situation. Like most men, I've spent my life overestimating perils.

But because Sir Eugene and Mulroy made their slow way to Alexandrei—Sir Eugene murmuring the man's name over and over, soothingly—I felt bound to expose half my body to the harpoon, and I cursed not Alexandrei but the knight and the petty officer. I watched the three terrible barbs at the point of the harpoon. I knew it had been deep in the bodies of seals and sea leopards whose blood had dried on it. These weapons were cleaned but never sterilized. The wound would be terrible for that reason, as well as because of the barbs.

As the leader and Mulroy approached him around the end of the mess table, Alexandrei let out an even shriller threnody and threw the harpoon with expert force but at no particular target. It would, in fact, have entered some part of Percy Mulroy's upper body. It seems there are tennis players who can actually *see* a tennis ball, its defined edges, at ninety miles an hour. Likewise baseball batters and batsmen in cricket, a Britannic sport in which some modern Australian bowlers can project a ball at speeds close to a hundred miles an hour. Mulroy must have been one of these high-speed sighters, because he lifted a chair, holding its legs out toward Alexandrei, and fielded the harpoon with it. The barbed point punched into the underside of the seat and impaled it as far as the wooden haft.

His missile released, the Siberian knelt, folding himself up smaller than seemed naturally possible. Then he fell on his side, moaning. He had become too pitiable for anyone to want to punish him. Alec Dryden felt his pulses.

"Is it rabies?" Stewart asked, thinking of the horses and the dogs.

"None of the dogs have rabies," Alec said. "We took swabs from each of them."

When Alexandrei had been sedated, three sailors lifted him onto his bunk. I remembered how they always lifted the weak or injured with a certain tenderness. But that day they had had too many shocks and toted Alexandrei unlovingly.

Nikolai, the dog handler, still sat at the table. In his quiet and absolute grief he didn't even seem to notice what had happened to his friend. Mead had now arrived and sat beside him, murmuring to him in Russian. It seemed that every member of the expedition was around the doorway or milling in the sailors' sleeping area, watching the dialogue. At last Mead seemed satisfied and patted Nikolai's shoulder. Then he came to Stewart.

"They are afraid of the darkness," he told Stewart. "That's basically what it is."

Stewart said, "I think you should explain that to the men. They must be angry."

Mead coughed and instantly obeyed. "Nikolai and Alexandrei were afraid the night would never end. It's as simple as that. I beg for your tolerance and I promise you nothing like this will happen again." He hesitated, half turned back to Stewart, but then began speaking again. "I think we might all be more understanding of the two of them. We lump them together as *the Russians*. In fact, Alexandrei is a Chukchi from the far northeast corner of Siberia. He grew up in a sod shanty, roofed with walrus hide. He didn't hear Russian spoken until he was thirteen. Nikolai is the son of a Russian father and an Evenki mother from near Magadan, far to the south. They both have separate languages—Russian is their second language. They have different songs and dances and customs. They are friends only because no one else is their friend."

Mulroy, who had fielded the harpoon, was going red in the face beside the impaled chair.

"Permission to speak, sir," he said. "The men in here have been very kind to the two Russ— Asiatic persons. Language is a problem, sir."

The way he said it, respectfully aggrieved, you could read a submerged question: If you like them so bloody much why don't you take them in next door?

Mead stared him in the eyes, aloof, not chagrined. "I am sure both men have received consideration from you, Petty Officer Mulroy. But we can all get on better with people if we are aware of their backgrounds."

The emergency had ended. We sauntered to our places in the hut. It seemed the air of our habitation had changed. Until today, the hut had represented an agreeable life. The one quarter acre where your breath, your sentience, the integrity of your skin were all guaranteed. Now we each wondered, would I be safer outside?

Ten minutes later, as I stood bemused by the mess table, Alec Dryden asked me back into the leader's alcove. There I found both Sir Eugene and Warren Mead seated, and Warren began speaking even before the curtain was pulled.

"You have to remember," he began shyly, "these two Siberians are primitives. Until Christianity reached that corner of Siberia, its people were sun worshipers. Naturally enough.

Like most primitives they used to believe that every season was a miracle, that you couldn't depend on the sun returning in strength in the spring unless you performed certain ceremonies." He then seemed to be afraid we might feel superior to Nikolai and Alexandrei. "It used to be exactly the same with peasants in western Europe. In fact some of our popular festivals today have their origins in that kind of belief."

"We understand," Sir Eugene assured him.

"Now, even after Christianity arrived, the priests had to perform certain rites to guarantee the return of the sun. That's a common experience Nikolai and Alexandrei have shared all their life. A priest comes into the village at the beginning of winter. He wears a silken cope and carries a golden disk. It's just what the sun priests used to do centuries ago, except that the golden disk now has Christian symbols engraved on it. The priest blesses the people with the disk, then he conceals it in the folds of his cope and takes it away to the church. The idea is that the strong summer sun is in God's keeping and God will send it back at the proper time."

"Fascinating," said Sir Eugene, his avid face characteristically tilted.

"It's a very important ceremony up where Alexandrei comes from. The polar night is deep, though not quite as deep as this. Just the same, the Chukchi know they will die if the sun doesn't return to them." Now Mead winced as if he'd come to the most painful part of his story. "Victor Henneker was a correspondent with the Russian High Command during the war between Russia and Japan some years back. The war petered out in the summer of 1905, and Victor must have visited Siberia on his way home and obtained a sun disk there, because I've never seen them on the open curio market in England."

"Victor owned one of these disks?"

"You know what Victor was like," said Warren. "He was

a sort of teasing uncle. He liked to have something to tease everyone with. He would have heard about Nikolai and Alexandrei and thought a sun disk would divert or tease them. That was his nature."

My respect for this votary of packhorses was increasing as I listened.

"Nikolai said that about the time the sun was vanishing Victor suddenly produced this disk in front of them. He teased them with it, threatening to drop it down an ice crack. You have to understand, to Nikolai and Alexandrei it was a cosmic threat, even if it might have been no more than a good joke to Victor. Here was the sun in Victor's care and he was threatening to sink it to the bottom of the sound. Anyhow, when Victor was missing, both the Siberians began fearing for the sun. You see, in Siberia, priest passes the sun disk on to priest, but here was this man they considered dubious and he had no one to pass it on to. When he died, the sun was lost forever. I believe, Tony, that fear of that loss set Nikolai wailing this afternoon. They're good men, both of them. They thought the world had changed beyond repair."

"Just to torment them," Sir Eugene murmured. "He did it just to torment them."

"No. It seems a time came—I don't know when the time was—that he wanted certain favors. From Alexandrei."

As he said this, Warren Mead's face, sooty from blubber smoke, managed to take on a supreme pallor. In the alcove there was a silence for ten seconds, and ten seconds are a wide and intimidating time.

"Favors?" Sir Eugene said. But I could see him realize then that it was unfair to make Warren specify further. He filled in the picture himself. "Do you mean homosexual favors?"

"According to Nikolai, sir."

Sir Eugene thought for a while. There was a grunt from him

as if he'd been hit in the stomach. Everyone seemed compelled to comfort him.

Mead said, "This sort of thing can happen anywhere."

Alec Dryden said, "Henneker wasn't exactly chosen by you, sir. He was thrust on you by the expedition's need."

The phrases of comfort did not dent Sir Eugene's bewilderment. It took him some seconds more to drag his mental and moral forces together. When he did he said, "Did any of you have any inkling of this matter?"

"Not of Alexandrei's case," I admitted painfully. "I had heard two rumors of Victor's—tendencies."

"My God, what sort of man would do this to a Russian peasant?" He turned to me. "Why didn't you say something, Tony?"

"One prefers not to believe rumors of that kind, Sir Eugene," I answered, as men did in those days.

"I suppose not. Alec, did you have any intimation?"

"I saw . . . certain indications. Sir Eugene, I refuse to believe the greatest polar expedition of its day could be destroyed by . . . by homosexual undermining."

Such a sentiment would today be considered a line from comedy, from the same sort of comedy that would make a joke of a journey in search of an egg; yet I saw the total belief with which the sentiment was delivered. The consummate British Antarctic expedition could not be harmed by sexual abnormality. God would not permit it. Alec Dryden *knew* God would not permit it.

Mead went back to inspect Tulip's underjaw. If her breathing was congested he would sit up all night with her.

As soon as Mead was gone Sir Eugene asked Alec to search again for the sun disk, and when Alec had gone out of the alcove he turned to me and asked me to specify the rumors I had heard concerning Victor.

I gave him the information about Victor and the Mulroys I had gotten from Barry in his state of sexual grievance. Sir Eugene made notes.

At last Alec returned and put a golden disk on the table. It looked old and was engraved with a Byzantine Christ, a Messiah promising summer from his cross.

"It's exquisite," said Sir Eugene. "Come."

We followed him as he carried the disk through into the men's quarters, more or less concealing it under his sweater. He stopped at the lower bunk where Alexandrei lay, eyes nearly closed. Nikolai leaned over from the upper bunk. We could hear the hiss of breath he let out when Sir Eugene produced the disk. Even the comatose Alexandrei saw it. His eyes grew wide.

"Alexandrei, Nikolai," said Sir Eugene in the English language they could not understand. "I have the disk. I will keep it safe. The sun will return."

Immediately Alexandrei smiled, turned on his side and went instantly to sleep.

FIVE

I woke at 8 A.M. in a severe stillness I could not at first define. After some seconds of frowning I understood that the blizzard had passed. I became aware that Quincy was already sitting on his bunk reading, and I saw Sir Eugene tiptoeing toward him.

"Brian," I heard Sir Eugene say to Quincy, "I would be obliged if you read the memorial service at eleven."

"Around the mess table, Sir Eugene?"

"That would be altogether too homely. In the open I think."

As I made my way to the latrines after breakfast I saw Sir Eugene walk up to Mead in the stable. Mead sat dozing—cold pipe in mouth—on a butter box by the stove. It was a strange atmosphere he worked in, the air narcotically heavy from the blubber heat and the floor of the stable solid permafrost.

"Warren, we're having a memorial service for Victor this morning. I want you to tell the Russians that they are to attend and that their behavior is to be perfect. When that is over we can all settle again."

We can all settle again. Shivering in the latrine, I considered the mandate Sir Eugene and Alec Dryden had given me to raise the question of Forbes-Chalmers, because there might have been many reports of sightings suppressed when Sir Eugene, in the autumn, labeled the vision an illusion of light. I was also to listen to and observe the sailors. I didn't know how to deal with this last duty. It wasn't a problem of class. I wasn't a product of the great public-school system. One of my uncles had been a petty officer in the Royal Navy, and I had no trouble talking to him. But it was the task of speaking to them obliquely, without having them guess the truth.

When I mentioned this to Sir Eugene, he smiled paternally.

"Don't approach anyone if you believe *that* might happen. We're in a unique position. It is far less dangerous to let the criminal escape than to admit the existence of the criminal."

That was his principle. He had stated it to me twice before I went to my bunk.

What a wondrous day-night it was in which we stood officially remembering Victor. As a congregation, we faced that brilliant prospect of the sound and the far Victoria Land Mountains. The starlight was bright as moonlight on those distant glaciers, and the moonlight bright as moonlight in any desert. Unlike yesterday, no aurora fluttered above the sound, but its absence drew our eyes to the volcano called Erebus, rising on our left, three miles high and trailing a spume of smoke above its frozen lip. Closer to our south we could see the convulsed and rugged ice shapes of the Barne Glacier, feeding itself from the higher slopes of Erebus, grinding as a slow and barely plastic river down to the frozen sound. I could talk of the ice shelf beyond that, but I don't want to press your patience. We will come in any case to the ice shelf. Enough to say that to stand in McMurdo Sound in the clear dead of winter was to step beyond the normal laws of perception, to stretch the senses, to threaten perspective. It depended on your temperament whether it enchanted, or frightened the pants off you.

We stood in a semicircle at the base of the weather vane hill to the north of the hut. On the lower slopes of the little rise stood Quincy, the priest, and Sir Eugene, the panegyrist. Quincy prayed that although Victor had fallen subject to the corruption of the grave he would one day rise glorious. I find such hopes hard to share. Even if Victor had not been a seducer of Mulroys and Chukchis, the idea of this waspish journalist rising glorious on Judgment Day would not have seemed plausible.

Besides, Antarctica being what it is, Victor had not become subject to the corruption of the grave. He lay ice-solid and impermeable in a pouch of sailcloth in the ice cave behind the hut. Even in the summer it would be impossible to bury him in the frozen earth around the foreshores, and although I did not know it then, Sir Eugene intended to commit the body ceremonially through an ice hole to the depths of the sound once spring came.

Now that I am close to the last dark cave myself, I think of Antarctica as the consummate burial place. A lot of people aren't afraid of the oblivion of death. A lot are frightened of the awesome choice of subjecting their flesh either to the rot of interment or the blast furnace of cremation. About ten years ago, one of my favorite granddaughters was living with a likable young man, an unemployed pilot who was sniffing about for a way to make a fortune. I got him alone one night at a party.

"Do you know that Antarctica is an ice mass of six million square miles?" I asked him.

"I didn't, sir," he said.

"I suppose, then, you also hadn't realized that seven million cubic miles—miles, mark you—of ice lie atop the six million square miles of continent. There's a fortune to be made in Antarctica, from all that ice."

"I suppose so, sir," he muttered politely, evasive around the eyes in a way that said, all too obviously, *why* don't they can this old ding-a-ling?

"I mean, a fortune for a pilot." I explained to him how some people worry about corruption, although no human should need to have *that* explained to him. "If you offered to drop corpses by parachute into that great ice mass, the wealthy would know that their bodies could ride in the ice for hundreds of years. People would pay a great deal to be dropped in a dignified manner onto the polar ice cap or even onto one of the glaciers. You could initiate a famous service, and as long as you did it well, no one could interfere with you, because all governments have—by the Twelve Nation Treaty of 1959—suspended territorial claims over Antarctica."

"What about Greenland?" he asked. I could tell by the way he said it that he was not taking me seriously. "Greenland has an ice cap."

"It belongs to Denmark," I told him.

I was disappointed. I thought that if I put up the money for this quite serious undertaking, I would be able in my turn to sleep above the Beardmore Glacier or lie in state in Victoria Land.

Despite his belief in the Resurrection, there was a tension of distress in Brian Quincy's voice that morning. That tautness of grief, missing in most parsons at most such ceremonies, was good for all of us. We began to feel it ourselves—the fruitful grief that lies just this side of the moment when you say, yes there has been a death, yes he is gone and we must keep the stove going, mend our long johns, eat our lunch.

Quincy would, before the war began, give up the priestly life, and that morning the vestment hung on him in the manner of clothes hastily donned and about to be hastily taken off. He had spent the first part of the morning unsuccessfully trying to help Byram Hoosick break a hole in the ice of the sound. They had used augers and picks at a point at which they knew the ice was thin, perhaps only five feet thick. For this work they had had to wear windproofs and smear their faces with seal grease against frostbite. Quincy's face still looked greasy above the cassock, stole, and surplice. At the same time, the bulk of windproofs beneath his robes made him thicker, massive, a Druid, a magic priest in the way few Anglican clergymen ever are, and therefore—somehow—an outsider to his profession.

Yet he stepped back so humbly when he had finished, yielding up to the vast sound and to the forces that had terribly shaped it, the spirit of his brother Victor. I had no doubt that he knew nothing of friend Victor's secret tendencies.

Sir Eugene's eulogy was brief. "Victor Henneker," he said, "was a famous figure and a challenging man to work with. Others more eloquent than I will utter panegyrics for him when the wide world hears of his death. If only we could have him back to ask him why he went out alone on such a day. I will not discuss the metaphysics of this event. I think of banal matters—such as that I do not want to repeat this ceremony for any more of my men. Whenever anyone leaves the hut, no matter how benign the weather, he must take someone else with him. I know that is an awkward rule to make. Mr. Webb often has to come out to the dogs; Dr. Warwick often comes out to the weather screen or Lieutenant Beck to ski cross-country. I must make it a rule, however, until further notice."

On that pedestrian phrase, he shook hands with Quincy to show that the ceremony was over.

I was standing near Beck and thought it might be time to begin my duties for the committee of three. "Par-axel!" I called.

He stared at me without smiling. I didn't know whether it was the death or the ban on solo skiing that made him look that way.

"If you need a skiing partner...," I said, just as a way to begin the conversation.

He nodded. "Thank you muchly," he told me, "but Beck is not enjoying the cross-country as he did in the pasts."

"Don't say that." I could feel the false smile on my lips. "You must see so much on a good cross-country run." But I was immediately at a loss to name some of them. "Mountains, ice, even some winter seals perhaps. Old Forbes-Chalmers..."

He shook his head. "I still am doing the repair jobs on skis." It was his continuing complaint, the way we treated our skis. Once he had lectured us: "All the time I ask you all to leave each his skis either in the racks in porches or in the nature room. You can hang them on rafters in there. How else can I keep track of them if you don't put them each in its same place every time. But I find them anywhere—under bunks, in stables, even in latrines find I a pair one damn day."

Now he shook his head and said to me, "If I go, I come and tells you."

As I turned away I was blushing that my small investigative sally had ended so inanely. I walked back to the hut behind Barry Fields and Peter Sullivan, the cinematographer.

"It was a strange speech," I heard Barry say. "I thought the leader liked poor Victor. I thought he thought Victor was a lovable rogue or something. You know puckish or something."

Sullivan's reddish nose sniffed; his ginger mustache jerked. Once he had made a feature film that Victor and a half dozen other columnists had mocked. He muttered wistfully into his scarf, "There was a day in '06 when I spent the whole morning thinking I'd go round to his place in Cheyne Walk and beat the bejesus out of him. However, . . . a nice service of Quincy's, very fine."

Barry said, "Well, of course. Not that that stuff means anything to me. I'm a bloody socialist."

Behind them I groaned. Not at Barry's habitual statement. But I understood that I was a child lost in a garden of complex motivations.

On a shelf above Alec Dryden's bed lay a small mummified seal. Alec had found this dried and incorruptible body some forty miles inland in the Taylor dry valley. He always told us that it was at least two hundred years dead, a little crab eater who took an inland course, driven by an evolutionary impulse or by some short-circuiting of instinct. Once when Alec had had two brandies he toasted the small mummy as either a zoological fool or a hero. Its eyes, however, were glazed and humbled by the decision it had taken one southern autumn in the reign of Queen Anne. In its shrunken face was no quotient of reward for its errant intention to live far from the coast.

I watched it as Alec spoke tactfully to me. "I don't think we should seek each other out," he said. "I don't think we should draw attention to the fact...that we're helping Sir Eugene...that we're ... *serving* together."

It seemed to me that we had drawn attention when the curtain was pulled across Sir Eugene's alcove. But I said nothing. I could not myself understand why, as soon as I entered the hut, I had come to Alec's corner, to his table covered with pages of handwriting and fine naturalist's sketches and zoological works of reference.

"I was wondering," I said, looking about me for an excuse. I picked up a pencil drawing of the organ and blubber areas of an Adélie penguin. "I was wondering..."

The blood in my jaws smoldered.

"It's all right," Alec said. "It's shock, you know. Sit here awhile."

As I lolled, nursing my brow, at Alec Dryden's desk, Norman Coote the tractor man had begun to cross the room toward us, and was about to add further definition to the killing.

I am not the first to comment on the decline of murder as a rational exercise. In the first ten years of the century the world and society seemed well-ordered and reasonable, and murderers, even if acting in passion and on impulse, paid tribute to the rationality of their universe by committing rational murders. Their motives were appreciable and rational, having to do with gain or clear sexual goals or freedom from a real, not a paranoid, threat. No one seemed to climb a steeple and, for reasons the sniper himself could not guess at, snipe at people. You would not, on emerging from a barber shop, say, be shot dead by a stranger for reasons neither the shooter nor you would ever fathom. Murder seemed not haphazard but an outlying planet in a clockwork solar system.

We expected, therefore, that the killing of Victor, even if it was the work of Forbes-Chalmers, partook of the orderliness of the world.

It seemed, when Norman reached Alec's desk, that he was presenting one of the elements of the order of our grand Edwardian polar murder, or even that the crime, being its own animal, was giving us a glimpse of its pervasive organs by sending Norman to us.

He stood above us. His square, dark face was fixed in a frown, and there was a hiss of air between his set teeth. He always hissed somewhat.

"I believe you two gentlemen are more or less Victor's executors."

It was the idea he had picked up from last night's frantic conferences.

"You have his property in hand," he suggested further.

"That's true," said Alec. He invited the tractor man to sit on the bunk.

When Coote found a place to squat, he asked in his lockjawed monotone, "All his documents?"

Alec lifted a folder. "Articles. Letters. Yes."

"You must have seen his gutter-press journal then. And in that case you probably know about my thousand pounds from Cave tractors. But then, I've never made a secret of it. Sir Eugene's aware of it. I don't want Sir Gavin Cave frightened though—frightened by any snide comments in the rags."

We stared at him, comprehending nothing.

"You must know," he stated.

"No, Norman, we don't." Alec handed him the folder. "Look in that, if you want."

But Norman didn't want to. He seemed to be moved by broader purposes than simply to safeguard his connection with Cave the tractor maker. He asked, "You remember the day the ship left?"

It had been in mid-February. The *McMurdo,* not buoyant even when unloaded, wearing sail and putting out steam yet still making slow headway, cruised hooting up the sound. Making for Tasmania, which, by an irony, had once been Britain's farthest convict hell. As I watched the *McMurdo* go, I had a convict hollowness in my bowels. The sound, without that human landscape of forecastles, masts, mesh of rigging, main-deck meathouse, and stubby quarter-deck, seemed deathly vacant.

I remember that Sir Eugene, understanding the state of our souls, issued eight bottles of brandy. This meant a quarter bottle each, enough in most cases to steam out of us our sense of exile.

That clear and sunny evening of late summer, the hut was not quite ready to be occupied and we were camped in tents on the black volcanic scree close by.

Victor and Coote had shared a tent and sat up in their sleeping bags that evening, each with a stomachful of brandy, chatting. And we all knew how badly Victor held his liquor, considering he was a man of the world.

Norman catalyzed Victor's quick tongue by projecting his own success. If the tractors outhauled man, dog and pony, Sir Gavin Cave would pay him a thousand-pound bonus, and with that amount you could start an engineering firm of your own. The pleasure Norman took in this promise of a bonus was childlike and endearing to most of us, and since dragging supplies in man harness, though excellent for the belly muscles, quickly lost its aura, we hoped, yet doubted, the tractors would succeed.

I can imagine, though, how Norman's hopes would have irked Victor. He could tell the boy mechanic how a true professional makes money on the side! The words in which Norman Coote now reported Victor's proposals had the Henneker flavor to them. Victor began in the gutter press, said Victor (said Norman and, now, say I). He never lost sight of how much you could earn from that source. He discovered the scandalous associations of many famous people partly through his contacts in Parliament and the services, partly through the efforts of an inquiry agent who pursued and spied on the famous for him. Albert Dawe was the agent's name; he kept a big office on Tottenham Court Road. And why not a big office, because Victor could make a few thousand out of a good scandal just by selling it anonymously, and Albert Dawe got twenty percent and considered himself a literary collaborator.

Because the expedition was bound to become a "fabulous enterprise" (this was, according to Norman's memory of a conversation now four months old, Victor's phrase), Henneker had employed Mr. Dawe to look into the lives of the expeditionary officers. It wasn't an expensive commission, said Victor. Dawe took a day or so to discover of any London resident more than was known by the man's wife or mother. With country dwellers like Alec Dryden, it took as long as two days, and because country work was harder and more wide-ranging, he often left the more mechanical London inquiries to his senior staff.

Listening to Norman's recital, I began to cough, choking on spittle as I wondered if Albert Dawe's professional expertise had been applied to the days of cyclical lovemaking and wine sipping I had enjoyed with Lady Hurley in Norfolk.

They look like a garden of roses, Victor had said. Our young colleagues, the flowers of youth. (He strove for all the clichés which ten years later would show up on war memorials.)

You'd be surprised, he said. He mentioned a few names. Once the expedition was over and we were all hallowed figures, he could sell us singly or by the brace or set to the right editors.

Norman, to his credit, asked Victor how he could consider letting this sort of information out about his colleagues. "You don't understand journalism," said Victor, "or the popular mind. It's all very well to give the masses heroes; the masses want them. But you've got to remember the masses also *don't* want them. They want to find out that men as ordinary and squalid as themselves could participate in polar heroism; they want to have the heroism rendered normal by reading in the gutter press that in some aspects great men are mean or grasping or lustful. People in authority don't believe such stories, but the clerk from Vauxhall, who is never going to do anything heroic, is titillated and enthralled by scandalous stories of heroes and doesn't think any the worse of the individual hero."

"I asked him," Norman told us, "if he had some sort of dossier on all of us. He said, 'not you.' But even what I'd said to him—about Sir Gavin and the tractors—that could be made into the right kind of story. Of course," he added, "it lacks the element of . . . of adultery and such like." He coughed. "He mentioned the leader's wife," he said under his breath.

"What?"

Norman's teeth bit tighter still, as if he'd set himself a ventriloquist's task. "He mentioned Lady Stewart. No details, but he mentioned her. She was one of his better assets."

Playing strenuously with his pipe and all the varied objects on his desk, Alec gave Norman the obvious assurances, asked for his silence, and sent him back to his garage.

I was still innocent enough to think, if Victor made a log of our sins, no one's would be worse than mine. I didn't want a search made for any supposed journal.

"He was teasing Norman," I said.

Alec showed me his unconvinced eyes.

"Norman's a backward damn mechanic," I said, more desperately, "as naive as Victor's readership. Listen, most of us are men in our twenties. What could he say about us? That once or twice we visited brothels?" My indelicacy caused a small pained flicker of Alec's eyebrows. He believed Norman's story because it had subtleties to it that were beyond Norman's powers of creation. The argument that (Norman said) Victor used to explain how no one was damaged by a press exposé were exactly the reasons a glib and contradictory man like Victor would have touted.

Alec massaged his forehead gently with the tips of his fingers. It was a mannerism of his, a little rite to ensure a clear brain. "I don't want him to know yet. It could be painful to him." He nodded in the direction of Sir Eugene's temporarily vacant alcove.

I could have said, he doesn't need to be coddled. He's forty-three years old and leader of the New British South Polar Expedition. But it didn't suit my purpose to be peevish.

"Watch the stove," said Alec, "though it's hard to burn a journal in a stove without half a dozen people knowing. The burning of a journal is quite a winter incident . . ."

I went back depressed to my auroral painting. But yesterday's vision was stale today, and I didn't want to spoil the work by putting a distracted brush to it. My mixed paints dried in their little pots and still I had not managed a stroke.

While I sat useless at the easel, the neurotic certainty came to me, rapidly taking my body over in the style of a virus. Quincy and the American were making a hole in the ice. Quincy and the American would, for reasons the virus would not specify, slip the journal through the ice.

Light came from something—from the moon low in the north, from stars, perhaps even a minor radiance from the winter sun above New Zealand. We did not need our lanterns;

they lay unlit. Hoosick manned the winch, and Quincy and I lanced ice fragments in the hole we had at last made. If we ceased spiking in the hole new ice would form, thin in one second, impermeable in ten. I was happy however to deal with the stubborn freezing instead of with the persistence of suspicion.

"All right," Hoosick said. The words meant nothing except that he was happier than he ever was in the hut. I suppose he knew what to expect of men, but never knew what biological surprise might come up from under the ice at midwinter.

He began to winch the net and bucket out of the hole. As it came up I saw the flashes of gold in it. In the instant before the water in the bucket froze, he lifted out the fine mesh net and dropped it in a wide-mouth thermos flask held and now capped by the parson, Quincy. Some of the splashings shone golden on his gloves, yet winked and went out as the water turned to ice.

"Diatoms," Quincy explained. "Copepods. The food that krill live off."

"And whales live off krill," I suggested.

"That's right," said the Reverend Quincy. "It's the first time anyone's dug through the ice to find out if krill might still be there at midwinter." He had so much pride in his brother biologist. I looked at him hopelessly. In which colleague could I safely take pride?

"Gentlemen," Hoosick said, "please keep working with the spikes."

For in a few seconds of idle conversation ice inches deep could form in the hole.

Oh, it was cold out there beneath the afternoon stars. When I left the hut just after 2 P.M., Waldo's instruments promised a freezing forenoon. I believe the alcohol thermometer read $-55°$. A breeze had come up and put an edge to that.

"If there are copepods, there are krill," said Quincy. "And

if krill, then perhaps Byram is correct in his surmise that whales may stay in Antarctic waters in the winter. Not by choice, of course, but through a failure of the navigational or mating instincts."

I imagined a vast blue mammal nosing under the thick ice, its instincts jangled.

Quincy coughed, set his face, but continued. He had all at once remembered Victor and so did not want to go on explaining krill and whales to a layman. "Not this far south of course. They have to breathe, you see. At least every hour or so." He harpooned the ice in the hole. "Not this far south. But the presence of the diatoms is, you see, a sort of negative proof ..."

I saw tears start from his eyes and freeze on his cheeks. I was awed by someone who could actually weep for Victor.

After he composed himself he said, "You know, Byram is a fascinating fellow." Byram, five yards away and upwind, could not hear him. "Full of feelings of damnation. Yet such an appetite for the natural world. Yesterday he was concerned with a minuscule parasite out of a fish's gut. Now his mind is on some great blue whale lost under the sea ice."

"Feelings of damnation?" I repeated, for that was the phrase that had taken my attention.

"Well, I mean, hasn't he ever said to you—?"

"No."

"Oh, I thought he said it to everyone. 'I'm going to hell, you know.' He often says it to me. As often as Barry Fields says he's a socialist."

"Why would he say that?"

"Because he's wealthy."

"I thought that in America wealth was a sign of salvation."

"Not to Byram. Of course when he says hell, he doesn't mean a conventional hell. He claims to believe in reincarnation. Perhaps he's afraid he'll come back as a mean little parasite in a fish's gut, whereas he wants to come back as a finback whale."

"All right," Byram called, "I'm lowering the apparatus again, this time to ten fathoms."

I thought of Hoosick's infamous and frail mother, who herself had sought contact with great mammals. Her apogee had occurred on the day she bribed the king's chauffeur in St.-Jean-de-Luz. Oh, the impact of U.S. railroad and stock-market money, that it could corrupt a royal chauffeur! The result was that King Edward had a puncture on the road to Biarritz. I suppose a puncture is, like death, a reminder to the king that certain impassive physical laws are at work. Edward stood in the road waiting for another car to appear. When it came and the equerry had flagged it down, it proved to be the vehicle of the American pursuer, Mrs. Hoosick. All he needed, Edward said, choking but gallant, was to travel with her back to Biarritz. And so, behind her own tight-lipped chauffeur, she rode through the town, the grandest wintering place of Europe, with a king at her side.

Edward said of her rival king-chaser, a Mrs. Moore, "There are three things in life which one cannot escape: *L'amour, la mort,* and La Moore." The name Hoosick, you see, was a little too much for his powers of punning. But an equerry bravely said, "There are four things, Majesty. There is also La Hoosick."

* * *

Hoosick had to poke the bucket down through the chunky ice with a pole. Whenever I stopped spiking I could feel the cold dragging on my heart. The crazy surmise that had brought me out here had now evaporated. These men had better things to do than contribute to the body organic of the murder by slipping journals through the ice.

The net and bucket brought little of visible interest up from its ten-fathom drop, and I was pleased when they decided it was time to go indoors. I toted the crowbars for them, for they needed both their hands for carrying indoors their canisters of marine treasures.

"Are you cold?" I asked.

"It's a cold day," Quincy admitted, but conversationally.

Hoosick shrugged. "It isn't too bad."

The cold hadn't touched their core, because they were still brothers and could not feel the new malice in the wind.

We made for the west door so that they could go straight in past the darkroom and put their thermos of copepods in their biology cubicle. In front of that west door, however, two figures in windproofs stood. Antarctic moonlight is sharp and even men in heavy windproofs have an individual way of carrying themselves. We could tell from thirty yards away that the two men were Sir Eugene and Barry Fields.

Barry said, "But you consider yourself exempt, Sir Eugene."

"That is the nature of rules," Sir Eugene told him. "The legislator isn't bound by his law."

"Well," said Barry, "I don't want to argue with that," though he immediately began to. "But this is a rule that has to do with a measurable good. I broke it but so did you. And so I wonder about the validity or your original ruling."

The phrases "measurable good," "validity" did not surprise us. We could all guess the way he spoke in public—the closing off of all emotion by the false statement that he was a socialist, the efforts to prove he was a redneck—was the fruit of his being a colonial and feeling himself both much better and much worse than we native Britons. Even now that America has been two hundred years self-governing and the pound is lunging down toward a dollar and a half, you can meet some of the same responses in Americans.

In any case, Quincy, Hoosick, and I stood back politely. We could tell Sir Eugene was angry, and it embarrassed us. We tried not to notice how stiff his body was, as it always was during his rare furies, giving you the feeling that he was dreaming of the recourses of eighteenth-century captains—flogging and chaining in the cable hole.

At last he said, "Mr. Fields, sometimes you are a pain. I would like you very much to help me when I give orders by imagining that you are a rating in the Royal Navy and I am your superior officer."

"I don't know," said Barry, "if I'm quite up to stretches of the imagination like that."

He nodded, turning inside, slipping on the iced doorstep, but leaving Sir Eugene unappeased in the open. We still stood back awhile, and I think even Hoosick and the Reverend Quincy were confused at seeing Sir Eugene a little desperate and strident, as mediocre men are when they issue orders. Authority is an unpopular concept now, but in McMurdo Sound we depended as much on a quiet and rational heart of authority as we did on the promise of spring. Sir Eugene was the heart. It seemed from what we had seen that the heart was not secure.

He let Hoosick and Quincy pass through, making merely polite talk.

"An interesting haul?" he asked as Hoosick passed him.

"Lots of copepods, sir," Hoosick said, still awkward.

"At midwinter?" asked Sir Eugene. Usually his interest wouldn't have been so merely polite.

"Yes," said Hoosick. They were as uncomfortable with each other as a stiff schoolmaster and a shy fourth former. I felt angry at Barry for reducing them all to this.

"I wonder, could I see you, Mr. Piers?" Sir Eugene asked.

So the other two, who didn't feel the cold as intimately as I did, were allowed to go through into the warm.

"Tony," the leader said. I could hear Norman hammering something in the motor-sledge garage along the wall, but it was a mere dimple of sound in the imposing silence, and Sir

Eugene's voice was low. "I've just—as Barry pointed out—broken my own rule by going for a solitary walk. I went to look for the place where you and Paul Gabriel found the deceased. Yes, I know. We should have done it earlier."

"No, no," I hurried to say, "I didn't imply that."

"In fact, it was an instinct of mine that someone might go early this morning—an instinct in the good sense of the word, a sort of rational expectancy for which you don't quite know the reasons. I knew the someone might very likely be the assassin or have knowledge of the assassin—otherwise why go alone? In fact—unless you're a morbid personality, and none of the men seem to be—why go at all? That was my intuition."

I was frightened by the frantic nature of his explanations. Did he want my approval?

"I watched them all morning. It's easy to notice absences if you know where men are supposed to be. Harry Webb of course visited the dogs, and men went to read the two weather screens, but no one went as far south as the place where Victor died. I could tell by timing and also, I must confess, by spying on them briefly through the roof hatch in the workshop."

"That was a reasonable thing to do," I reassured him.

"After lunch one of the men came to me and I had a rather distressing interview. Nothing to do with Victor, although it's strange how a death will put people into a confessional mood."

Sir Eugene coughed. His face seemed to dim and then even to shrink, but expanded again after a second.

"I decided to go to the place myself. And Anthony, there's a problem." He coughed, as if what he was going to tell me was a lapse from good taste. "There are only three remains of boot tracks there. Only six feet. Only yours and Paul's and Victor's. To the best of what I can see."

I frowned, considering the lack of an appropriate number of boot prints.

"I prefer not to deal with the question," Sir Eugene told me.

"Some days, however the mind works, it's usually wrong."

This pessimism shocked me. He lived in a place where Barry or Waldo, Harry Kittery or Quincy or Hoosick could lithely harvest a new natural truth or at least a new theory per day. Yet here was the foreman of it all, telling me it was illusion.

"But there would surely have to be a fourth man's boot-prints."

He ignored my crass absorption in the physical world. He stood by and seemed to chew the inner linings of his cheeks.

"I saw Barry Fields," he said. "I saw him march over a hill of moraine near the bottom of the Barne Glacier. He'd actually gone walking out on the Barne alone, which no one has ever done anyhow, given the dangers. You heard the end of our conversation."

I lied. "No," I said.

"Why would he go walking on a glacier? Doesn't he think we've had enough trouble?" He sounded like the tremulous father of a wild family.

At last we went into the porch. It must have been thirty degrees warmer in there. I still could feel my heart as a separate and harshly tried organ, and now it seemed to gape and devour the warmth. Beyond the second door, in the body of the hut, the air would stand at, at least, a sweet, subtropical 40°, and despite my leader's demoralization and mine, I wanted to get through to it.

"There is a point," he told me. "We'll find the killer before the egg journey, because if we are confused, then he also is confused."

We went through the second door then, perhaps both lusting that Forbes-Chalmers was more than a smear on the imagination, was real and homicidal, an outside threat like the threat of frostbite, for frostbite can be dealt with and is not an internal disease.

"Snowshoes, Sir Eugene." I whispered this to him. "The fourth man must have worn snowshoes."

He let his head fall on one side. It fell slackly, so that he looked not avid but tired. "It could be. It could be."

The indoor warmth produced a small elation in me. Under its motive power, I took my windproofs to my bunk. Paul Gabriel stood beside it, talking to Quincy.

"Are you going to move down into the lower bunk now, Brian?"

I saw Quincy blink at the question. The lower bunk had been Victor's until 4 P.M. the day before.

"I think I'll stay in the top one," said the Reverend Quincy.

"I see." Paul sounded buoyant, as if he'd recovered suddenly from the shock and the mourning. He stared at Victor's bunk, the blankets stripped from it now, its palliasse bare. "Would you mind if I put some of my books on it then? We're pushed for space."

I thought, *He can't see: Quincy wants it left bare as a memorial.* But to Paul it was only vacant real estate.

"It won't worry me," lied Quincy, slinging his windproof jacket on the post of the upper bunk. "Unless I bump them climbing up and down in the night."

"I'll keep it all tidy," Paul promised. Quincy and I found each other's eyes, but Quincy turned away from my gaze. The first book Paul deposited on Victor's empty bed was Sir Arthur Gomboy's *Flightless and Primitive Birds.* Out of the enthusiasms Paul had picked up from such volumes, I had been seduced into the emperor-egg journey.

Soon the palliasse was covered with heaps of books and monographs. Like Quincy I could not help feeling that a grave had been desecrated. Yet when he had finished, Paul sat— panting a little, yet pleased with his work—on the edge of his own bunk. "That's good now. Everyone will start to forget."

I didn't tell him grief was more complicated than that. I nodded, but it was myself I was agreeing with. For he was like a child, trying to bury our memories under a heap of books. I thought then and I still think it was because he never had a named father, not even an absent one, from whom to learn, on whom to practice the skills and ceremonies (such as they were) of male respect, male aspiration, and male sorrow.

"It's nice of you to think of us," I told him, and he smiled.

Barry Fields sat at the mess table, a little uneasy (I guessed) from his argument with Sir Eugene or, probably, from having seemed to win it so easily. He held in his hand a mug of tea, perhaps to show he wanted things back the old way, the way they were before Victor fell. And the sign of that was the tea he sipped slowly—tea, the survival drink, the sacrament of normality.

I walked over and sat by him.

"You heard the quarrel?" he said.

"Yes."

"Well, it's bloody ridiculous. Just the same . . . it's shaken him up, hasn't it?"

"You silly bastard," I told him, jovial in a forced way. "What were you doing up on the glacier?"

He hugged his cup. "I just skirted the edge."

"Purpose of journey?" I asked.

"Forbes-Chalmers."

"The illusion."

"The joker himself."

"Come now."

"Listen, the man exists."

"And you went out to interview him?"

"Men like Victor don't fall down and bump their temples. There's too much . . . too much *forward* velocity to their lives for that to happen. Listen, and stop treating me like a bloody mental defective. Belief in Forbes-Chalmers is not equivalent to belief in the evil eye—"

"And you've been speaking to AB Stigworth," I suggested.

"Too bloody right I have. And Sweeper pays testimony to the mess Victor was and wonders how in the hell you get in a mess like that by simply buttering your scone. Come with me."

He led me toward the sailors' quarters and knocked. The door was opened by AB Bernard Mulroy. His fine, pale features and green eyes had a new and disquieting meaning for me now that Victor was dead. I frantically weighed my responses to him, testing for the faintest voltage of desire.

Barry wasted time on no such exercise. He winked at the sailor. "Permission to come aboard, Commodore," he said.

Mulroy did not smile but held the door wide as we entered.

In the galley, Walter O'Reilly, chef to two Antarctic expeditions, sliced onions for a sort of casserole of leftovers from the midwinter feast. When he saw us, he immediately took on the role he liked best, that of music-hall Irishman.

"Evenin' gentlemen," he said to us. "It's after goin' to be a dull ol' meal this evenin'."

"I don't believe it, Walter." Barry came so close to Walter as to inhibit the action of his slicing elbow.

"Walter, do you believe in the holy Catholic Church?"

"Yer know I do in a manner of speakin'. And it's why I were never made a vice-admiral of the blue, yer know. Pure damn religious prejudice."

"Walter, do *you* believe in Forbes-Chalmers?"

"Now Forbes-Chalmers's is a different kettle o' hash, Mr. Barry Fields. I'd say I'd have two separate attitudes to Forbes-Chalmers, given that he constitutes no mystery of faith. In me capacity as a noncommissioned officer, I don't believe in him because he's after bein' a distraction to me labors. In me capacity, however, as a human by name Wally Ignatius O'Reilly, I'd have to say I believed in Forbes-Chalmers, yes, Mr. Barry Fields, indeed sir."

"Well so do I, Wally. Now. Could you give Mr. Piers an indication of the reasons for your belief?"

"Can I go on choppin' here?"

"Of course, Walter."

"I had puddins stolen—eight. Out of a crate I opened in May—a crate of three dozen Swallow and Ariel one-pound plum puddins. We used seven every Sunday for four Sundays, and the last eight weren't there the fifth Sunday I went to fetch 'em. Now, if we happened to be domiciled under the volcano of Vesuvius instead of under the volcano of Erebus, I would guess one of the lads had tea-leafed 'em and sold 'em, one way or another, to the local populace. Or if we were at anchor under Gibraltar, I'd say the lads had snaffled 'em for a picnic or some such shore-leave celebration. But the idea of one of our lads liftin' puddins and takin' 'em up a glacier, where he sits on the lip of a crevasse and has a feast unto himself, *that* idea is entirely laughable, don't yer see? And that aside, Sir Eugene don't skimp on food. He didn' on the last trip, and he don't on this."

This time O'Reilly's long-winded reportage didn't much amuse me. I walked to the door of Walter's storeroom and opened it. The walls of the room were of supply crates and the roof of timber beams and tarpaulins, erected according to the same construction method as the stables. It was far below freezing in there. There was no direct way out, no hatch or door for a pantry thief to escape by. The idea that the mythical creature, the trick of light, had been in here seeking cans of pudding seemed fantastic. Barry and the cook could both sense my resistance to it.

"Of course, that's what a man in his situation," Barry observed, "would go for—something sugary, with raisins in it."

Walter seconded him. "And the lads are sound sleepers. If one of them stirred and saw a feller walkin' about the hut, what would enter his mind except that it was the night watchman comin' in from the weather screen? There ain't much of that insomni-ee in this habitation, praise God. As for me, I sleep deep, yer know, not before—ev'ry evenin'—takin' note of the way things are in me storeroom. Would yer mind closin' that door now, Mr. Piers?"

I obeyed him, for the pantry cold was invading the galley.

"You didn't raise this question with Sir Eugene," I said.

"Bein' in the Royal Navy's after like being Galileo. If the captain of the ship says the earth don't go round the sun, then a man don't argue."

"Thanks Walter," said Barry. "You've brought a lost soul to belief in Forbes-Chalmers."

Walter, dark-haired, handsome, lyrical, laughed and cried over his onions.

"Would you like to talk to Henson?" Barry asked when we stood again in the center of the room. "He had a large piece of sailcloth taken overnight. And PO Mulroy missed some timber. Are you convinced?"

I frowned. The phantom sought sugar, and was a handyman.

"I was looking for some sort of ice burrow," Barry told me. "I was looking for blubber smoke coming up through a piece of stove piping. I didn't find any signs."

I laughed.

"What's funny?"

"The idea of you—looking for a chimney in some ice bank up there."

"Well there's got to be. There's an ice cave where Forbes-Chalmers lives. It's not comfortable by our standards, but you can get used to almost anything. It's heated by a sort of rudimentary blubber oil stove. It might have a paling floor with gutters for melt water from the walls. It would have a crude bunk with blankets and maybe sealskin covers. He's probably got a freeze room full of carcasses of seals and penguins. These are his meat. He must have enjoyed his puddings after all those sugarless years . . ."

I remembered the way the cold had unmanned me that afternoon. "It isn't possible. No one could take the cold for all that time."

"It's possible. I don't mean, Forbes-Chalmers hasn't wept with the cold, hasn't cursed and bloody raged. But you can live, weeping and cursing. Oh yeah, it's possible."

We went back to the officers' mess and to Barry's tepid tea. He tasted it, made a face, put it down.

"All of you seem," he said, "to see his survival as the mystery. But the mystery is why he never lived in Holbrooke's hut—why he didn't eat and make fires and sleep there—because there are no traces, no fire marks, no refuse. Instead, he's lived somewhere in an ice warren for four years—by choice. The basis of the choice, that's the mystery."

Not saying anything, I sauntered to the library shelves by the darkroom and took down the two volumes of Holbrooke's expeditionary journal. Barry followed and looked over my shoulder as I turned the pages, seeking photographs of Forbes and Chalmers. First we saw them posed in a group on the expeditionary ship. Chalmers perhaps twenty-four years old, dark hair parted in the middle, long-mouthed, smooth, an assistant geologist. Afterward, his mother had publicly denounced Holbrooke for losing her son in Antarctica. I remembered how she picketed Holbrooke's testimonial dinner and public lectures, making (to her credit) more noise than the combined motherhood of the world would during the Great War.

Forbes was an older man, perhaps thirty-two, already balding. You noticed his strong throat, standing out from his sweater like a tree trunk. Holbrooke, in speaking their obituary, said they were good friends and bunk mates. Forbes was chief geologist, a position held in our expedition by Fields himself.

We turned up other photographs of the two geologists and studied them as if we could find the ice warren of the one or both of them just from the contours of their faces.

Holbrooke had mourned them and had written his stylish obituaries. His imagery was better than Stewart's. When he at last sent a search party, the autumn blizzards very nearly got them as well.

"Poor sod," Barry said.

"Which one?"

"Whichever one it is."

"Could it be both?"

"There couldn't be both." Barry hit the bookshelf over and over with his index finger, pulsing out the reasoning. "There couldn't be both because they couldn't both be mad in identical ways. Now if there were two, one of them would have been on the ice foot, waving and bloody cheering when we landed. If there were two, one of them would have wanted to live in the luxury of Holbrooke's hut. No, I tell you, it takes one fellow to be mad enough to live in an ice hole and push Victor instead of greeting him."

I exclaimed in the accustomed way about how unlikely it all was, an encounter between Victor and Forbes-Chalmers in the middle of a blizzard. It was all I could say. For Walter O'Reilly's comic evidence had roused in me a desire, a positive taste, for Forbes-Chalmers's existence. In the end I yielded.

"Barry?"

"Yes."

"I'll look with you—for the man, I mean."

"When?"

"Tomorrow, if the light's good."

"I have to do some work in the morning. An article on the geology of the dry valleys, as it happens. If we find Forbes-Chalmers in the afternoon, he might be able to help me with it."

"Please, go in the morning."

"Bloody artists. Painting bloody nudes at irregular hours and complaining about the bloody artistic onus. I can't go in the morning."

"All right then."

He laughed at me. "My guess," he said, "is that he's among the hillocks along the north edge of the Barne—close enough to raid and observe us, close enough to the shore for hunting, yet far enough away for the kind of weird privacy the man seems to want. I'd say a nice snowbank sheltered from the south. Now, it will involve a lot of looking . . ."

But I was already feeling exuberant. A few miles up the Barne were a finite series of promontories sheltering a finite number of snowbanks. Searching them was a task of mere human proportions.

Barry went back to his little desk in the laboratory, and I put Holbrooke's two volumes back on the shelf. I was about to turn away and try to spend the day's scrag end at my easel, but there was an unusual flash of color among the staid bindings. It was a book with a scarlet spine and, when I drew it out, a marbled cover. It was entitled in gold *The Journalist's Yearbook, Gazetteer and Diary, 1909.*

My brain jangled in my head like one of those little bells that you ring when you want the dishes cleared, for it seemed to me that the crime was making terrible impositions on reality. It had taken advantage of the mention of Forbes-Chalmers to make Forbes-Chalmers real. Now it had taken advantage of the mention of the journal and made the journal real, incarnating it on a familiar bookshelf.

I knew before the yearbook opened whose name I would find inside. In fact, I found an inscription: "To Victor from A.H.C. Xmas 1908. Keep your deadliest secrets in here." The opening pages were full of the normal yearbook rubbish—weights, measures, prizes for journalism and their winners, the names, addresses, and editors of all the major newspapers and journals in the British Isles. In my shock, I read a few pages of this handy information. I still remember that the political editor of the *Glasgow Herald* was a Mr. Fergus Ogg.

Before I had leafed through these pages and had even seen a word of Victor's writing, I knew it would be a nightmare book. What it would do would be to show me that my colleagues were nearly as weak and liable to craziness as Anthony Piers was, and that therefore the world was much more dangerous than I had ever thought.

The page marked "Jan 1" bore these words: "Sir Eugene Stewart—See later entry *re:* Lady Stewart." There was nothing written on the "Jan 2" page, but on "Jan 3" began explicit charges against Alec Dryden.

In October 1900, Captain Arnold Jeffrey, Dr. Dryden's brother-in-law, a former officer of the Cape Colony Police and a squadron commander in the Bush Veldt Carabiniers, was wounded in the side during an engagement at Tielerfontein in the Orange Free State. The wound and its treatment were so severe, including cauterizing the injury with molten mercury, that Captain Jeffrey had to be administered dangerous doses of morphine. In 1903, not long before Dr. Dryden's departure on the first Stewart Antarctic expedition, Captain Jeffrey, then a wraith-like guest at Dr. Dryden's home in Devon, stole from the Dr.'s surgery and administered to himself four grains of morphine. Dr. Dryden was persuaded by his wife and by a friend of Captain Jeffrey's to write a death certificate for heart failure. My unwitting source in this matter is Captain Walter Styles, the friend who urged, and approved of, Dr. Dryden's unethical action.

There's no need to tell you I began to sweat. The exactness of the information ("near Tielerfontein," "four grains of morphine"), the naming of sources—it made treachery seem an exact science.

My fingers were cold and stupid as I turned the pages, knowing that if he was exact about me, he was exact about Dryden. Thumbing, I saw that someone's entry, comprising three pages, had been ripped out. I didn't know whose, for if the notes following Sir Eugene's and Alec's were in order, I couldn't see what the order was. At last, on the pages for May, I found my crimes set down.

In 1908, at a dinner at Brenton's, the gallery owner and restauranteur, Anthony Piers was seated beside Lady Anthea Hurley, wife of the Anglo-Irish lawyer, Sir Oscar Hurley, K.C. The results of this juxtaposition are amply provided by a gaggle of society gossips.

The results of this juxtaposition . . .
I remember the dinner and the happy lottery of seating that put me opposite Anthea. When she laughed I had the strange impression that she was seventeen and was glissading up and down the scales of time. Yet her face was also sensual, so that I instantly and deliciously wondered what it would look like in the extremes of lovemaking.

She was a wonderful talker, and Brenton put her opposite me because she went every year to the showing of the Paris Salon, and had just been there and could tell me about it.

When you remember such women you know that even now, in a Laguna Hills nursing home for decaying plutocrats, you are still in love with them. And the nausea felt on seeing her name in Victor's journal ... it was for her, because she was honest and vulnerable. It wasn't a matter of a wink and a feel-up under the table. I was too young and bedazzled for that, and she was too poised and dazzling a woman. The day after the dinner I wrote her an infatuated letter but I never posted it.

It was a second accidental meeting that initiated the affair. A Bond Street gallery on a wet Tuesday afternoon, fortunately uncrowded. I followed her from painting to painting, chattering stupidly, and in the alcoves I couldn't stop myself from touching her.

Lady Hurley and Anthony Piers continued an adulterous liaison for ten weeks. At least two evenings a week she visited the artist's lodgings in Warwick Gardens off Kensington High Street. Mrs. Alise Bailey, housekeeper at No. 47 Warwick Gardens, opposite the artist's lodgings, had employed Sir Oscar Hurley in an unsuccessful inheritance case and therefore recognized Lady Hurley and kept note of her arrivals and departures. Piers and Lady Hurley also spent some weekends at the Clarion Hotel in Norwich, registering separately and taking adjoining rooms ...

"Is that room on the western end free?" I used to ask the clerk. "The one with the view of the cathedral." As if I had come to Norwich for the architecture.

Sir Oscar was fifty-seven years old and I was twenty-three. If Freudian hypotheses had been popular then, I might have asked myself if in making love to Sir Oscar's wife I was trying to kill my father. As it was, I had a simple arrogant certainty that Anthea would marry me. When I mentioned it, the affair ended. "You can fall in love again," she said, "but I am Oscar's last love." She also said something I thought was barbarous at the time: "Marriage isn't a matter of desire. It's a matter of placid companionability." As I begged and raged she promised that I'd be in and out of love at least two times before Christmas.

She was right in spirit, though the Antarctic enterprise arose and forestalled any sustained liaison. Just the same, even in this senile house so far from the Clarion in Norwich in that Edwardian spring, I knew that I loved her and could have married her, and that our marriage would have had a lot to do with desire.

Admittedly, I was always easily infatuated. I realize with a little amazement that the blond and tanned Californian nurses, lusty girls, warn each other about me. One of them once called me a randy old notoriety. My sexuality, which in the Clarion was a divine distillation, is now an antediluvian joke for geriatric nurses.

That aside, I now wanted the entries explained away by someone older, someone fatherly. Yet, as I watched Sir Eugene writing in his alcove, tears came to my eyes. I saw he had to be protected as you might protect a parent. I saw the graying hair, the keen tilt of the head, the baggy cardigan. I saw the cracked suitcase with its yellowed luggage tags. He could have been a failed accountant, or a sacked schoolmaster, writing his apologia in some flop house, hopelessly expecting some redressing of justice. I couldn't tolerate the idea of his reading my entry and the words at the beginning of the book: "Sir Eugene Stewart—See later entry *re:* Lady Stewart."

Carrying the journal, I rushed away across the hut in case my tears became obvious. I might try to burn it immediately, but people would notice if you put a whole book into the stove. I might bury it in a snowbank, but then I wouldn't know what Victor had against the others, and I wanted to know it all, not just as a key to the crime but because I needed, to adjust to my new despair, to know the scope of my brothers' culpability.

Huddled on my bunk, I searched the journal, looking for that later entry Victor had promised on page 1. Names, familiar and strange, cluttered the pages. The quiet and circumstantial accusations dazed me. But I couldn't find a word about Lady Stewart, and decided that she must have been featured in the pages someone had torn out. I trembled, thankful to that someone for this mercy.

And what someone had already done in mercy, I could do also. I could strip out the pages of my entry and Alec's. I had my hands already on the pages concerning Anthea and myself. My thumb was already clamped against Victor's rapid handwriting when I understood the many reasons why I could not do it. Could I prove and pretend that some previous handler had done the ripping? In my loneliness, I wanted the closeness to Alec that mutual knowledge of our crimes would bring. I felt repugnance to reading the journal alone, without Alec's decency to provide me with rails.

I didn't know where Alec was. His unoccupied desk, his bed, his mummified seal stood only a few feet from the shelves. I found him sitting alone in the workshop. He contemplated a heap of food that stood on a square of sailcloth on the floor: Some pounds of pemmican, the dehydrated meat that boiled up into a fine stew we called "hoosh"; a few pounds of rice; canisters of Huntley and Palmer biscuits—hardtack (it blended well with a pemmican stew and gave it body and protein); two pounds of butter; two pounds of tea; two pounds of sugar— the classic diet of Antarctic expeditions, inadequate according to most modern dietitians. Alec, unblessed with the more advanced dietary notions of our age, sat pondering the balance between the items, the proportion of biscuits to pemmican and pemmican to rice, a finite ratio that guaranteed survival.

The proportions, which would receive a rough testing on our

egg journey, had already been debated at length by John Troy and Alec himself. Soon, if the egg journey was to take place, Alec would have to stop pondering and tell Henson, "That's it, Sails!" And Henson would sew the supplies up in sailcloth containers, each one (it was hoped) sufficient to sustain a party of three men for a week of sledge hauling. We would carry three such containers, caching one behind Mount Terror for the return journey.

"Alec?"

"Hello."

"Alec, this is going to be embarrassing. I've found Victor's journal."

"Good." He stood slowly, knocked out his pipe against the edge of the bench.

"Someone's entry has been ripped out, not by me."

"Sir Eugene? Have you told Sir Eugene?"

"No."

"May I see the book?"

I didn't hand it to him, though I already felt more at ease. "There's something in there about Captain Jeffrey."

He closed his eyes. "Is there?"

"There's also something about Lady Anthea— about a lady and myself. For the purposes of this conversation, it happens to be the truth."

He put his hand out for the book. "I know, it's all very painful."

I gave him the book. He read the opening page. Then the story of Captain Jeffrey. He sighed. "He has the details exactly right," he muttered. After a while he began to chuckle. "It's no use being overwhelmed by mutual shame."

"The missing entry . . . ?"

He told me without a pause, "Waldo Warwick's entry is the missing entry. You can see for yourself. In which case the deleter, the expurgator, performed an incomplete service."

Then he turned back to the first page, turned it to me to indicate that it alone was the one that radically distressed him. "Sir Eugene Stewart—See later entry *re:* Lady Stewart." He ripped that one page out and tore it into many neat squares and into twice as many again and dropped them all behind the workbench on which the lathe stood. That workbench would never leave Antarctica. It is still there in the Cape Frye hut, and no doubt, the diced page of Victor's journal still lies behind it, pristine in the air of the ice desert.

Alec returned the book to me. It was a touching gesture of trust, of fearlessness.

"Why was it put there?" he wondered, even before the *Journalist's Yearbook,* now further edited by himself, was back in my hands. "Why was it put where it was put, beside the Holbrooke, which everyone reads? Not by Waldo, though. It wasn't put there by poor old Waldo. I mean, you wouldn't steal it, take out only the entry that damns you, and then put it back on the shelf, would you?"

"Is catatonia associated with madness?" I asked.

Alec coughed and lowered his eyes. I saw the white scalp beneath the parted and impeccably brushed brown hair. His neatness seemed a sign that he wasn't yet unmanned like me.

"Don't be prejudiced," he advised me.

It seemed he thought I was unfair to catatonics. He beckoned to me, and I followed him into the meteorology room, where Waldo was still working. When we entered the room, we found him sitting at a desk making pencil marks on a sheet of hydrography paper that he had just taken from one of his self-recording instruments. On the paper were the lines that told how the marginal humidity of that polar desert had risen and fallen in the past ten days, and Waldo's pencil marks pointed to the patterns of moisture. Perhaps in the Libyan desert, perhaps in the Atacama or the Rub'al Khali, some heat-crazed colleague of Waldo's recorded humidity readings akin to those Waldo now took. "We're desert dwellers," he would sometimes tell us, smiling broadly.

Bent over the roll of paper, Waldo resembled a Pre-Raphaelite knight—intent, sensitive, unsoiled. A William Morris apparition. I began to feel nervous.

He indicated with a wave of his pencil that we were welcome, but could we wait a little while? He finished work on the roll of paper, glancing at us occasionally. As we waited, we could hear AB Stigworth setting the table in the main quarters.

"Gentlemen," he said solemnly, looking straight at us. The bowed head and oblique look, which normally persisted for days after his fits, were not in evidence today.

Alec asked him had he heard any rumors of a journal. Details of peccadillos and so forth.

Waldo smiled a little, as if the idea made Victor more endearing. "I'd heard gossip," he admitted.

"He had something to tell about all of us."

Waldo said, "He was that sort of man. He didn't intend any harm."

"I can't agree with that," I said.

"The journal has turned up," Alec announced.

I frowned at him. I wanted the journal, especially the section concerning Anthea Hurley, to remain secret or, at the very least, confined within the knowledge of our little committee. Only after a while did I notice that Waldo himself was suffering, his eyes blanking and then seeming to travel inward, his pallor more intense than was decent even for a man who suffered fits and had lived two months under the moon. If you'd told me then that he would live till eighty-three, become burly and jovial, hold a chair at Stanford, and go through three wives, I wouldn't have believed you.

Yet I was about to have an intimation of how he would achieve this. If pain and grief became too much for him, he was capable of dumping them entirely upon another creature and could walk away lightly from the new sufferer he had, so to speak, infected.

Alec said, "When Tony found the journal, there were entries for every member of the officers' mess, except for you and Sir Eugene Stewart. Both those entries had been torn out. Sit down again if you like, Waldo. In fact it would be a good idea."

He held Waldo's elbow as Waldo sat again at his desk. "This is painful, I know."

"What are you expecting to hear, Alec?" Waldo muttered. "What *are* you expecting?"

"Well," said Alec. "Well . . . you know, Waldo. I . . . I saw the two of you once."

"Oh Holy Jesus!" said Waldo.

Alec took Waldo's wrist as if to soothe his pulse. "Come now," he murmured. "Come now." And, after a pause, "Lady Stewart and yourself—you had a liaison." I never understood why he should say it with me there, or even why I was there at all. Was it for some therapeutic reason, or was he honoring the committee of which I was a limp and dazed limb? Any pernicious reason is out of the question. He always consciously forbade himself to act for pernicious reasons.

"I know that because of the Stewarts' cook. She's an Irish woman called Miss Maggie Tierney, and she must be close on seventy years of age. She knew, I don't understand how."

"I don't understand how," Waldo repeated. "Lady Stewart would never meet me anywhere at all public. She never came to my place in case my neighbors noticed her, in case my man-servant noticed. She used to tell me, 'Don't worry about Maggie; she doesn't know about physical passion.' "

Alec said, "Miss Tierney came to see me while I was staying

at the Cadogan Arms. She wanted me to speak to Sir Eugene or to Lady Stewart herself. Since it's confession time, I don't mind confessing that I've always been awed by Lady Stewart, and I certainly didn't want to distress Sir Eugene, who was fundraising up and down the country."

"She used to say to me," Waldo reminisced, "that I was an innocent particle, thrown this way and that by some electric tension between herself and Sir Eugene and the continent of Antarctica."

"It's a way of looking at the situation," said Alec, coughing. "But, of course, it begs the question. In any case, the next time I visited Sir Eugene at his place—"

"Oakley Gardens," said Waldo, uttering the address with nostalgia as well as abhorrence.

"—I went down to the kitchen and asked Miss Tierney if it was still necessary to talk to either of the Stewarts. She said no, the phase had passed."

"I . . . *met* with her five times. I entered and left by the mews and no one saw me that I know of; yet you've known, Alec, all this time."

Alec tried to de-charge the memory, to rid it of its Oedipal reverberations. He didn't want Waldo to display his symptoms again. "It's always the way," he said. "I had an uncle who visited a mistress three times a week for thirty years, yet no one knew till his will was read. It's we occasional sinners who have all the bad luck."

I admired Alec for the use of that personal pronoun, for the decency of listing himself in the brotherhood of adulterers to which Waldo and I belonged. Here was a man who had loved one woman only, who saw the immanence of God in the aurora, a compulsive father to all other men. When his private journal was published in 1958, it was a song of passion for his wife, of mystical sexuality, a statement of wholeness. It did not sell well in that soulless decade, but it proved to my satisfaction that he had never had to lie to reception clerks or creep past resident cooks.

"It began," Waldo said, "at my insistence. It was broken off against my insistence."

Alec nodded, accepting this statement as a gallantry. There was a silence, during which my mind progressed as far as an image of Victor's Mr. Dawe working on the Irish housekeeper. No doubt Alec considered questions of more point.

Waldo was recovering nicely from the brief discomfort of having to talk about sleeping with Lady Stewart. He had stood up again and even, like a busy man temporarily distracted, moved a meteorology log from the center of the desk to a more suitable place to his left. "I spoke to Sir Eugene after lunch today."

"You spoke to him?"

"I told him . . ."

Alec covered his own mouth with his hand. It was his turn to be pallid. "Waldo, were you trying to kill him?"

But Waldo couldn't admit this. Confessing had done him so much good. He couldn't believe it hadn't done Sir Eugene good also. "No. I was . . . I suppose I was . . . trying to do right by the two of us."

"Yourself and Lady Stewart?"

"Myself and Sir Eugene," he said, shaking his head, canceling Lady Stewart. I wondered how she could have wanted this child? I suppose I was also asking why, if she wanted a child, she didn't choose me that night at Brenton's.

Waldo coughed sharply. "I was rather low after yesterday's fit. I'm not supposed to have them. It's inappropriate. It's inconvenient for others. I *haven't* had any since I was thirteen. I had no idea they would recur. As for Sir Eugene, he *ought* to know; he'll be happier for knowing. I realize he can't speak to Lady Stewart for fifteen months yet, perhaps eighteen. Perhaps that's a good thing. In any case, I couldn't go on meeting him every day and not telling him."

The next words spoken were the kind that surfaced in some of the psychiatric melodramas I designed in Hollywood in the 1940s and 1950s. It shows you that one generation's solemnities become the melodrama of the succeeding generation and the comedy of the next.

"You saw the fits," Alec suggested, "as arising from a sense of culpability—of culpability unconfessed?"

"Oh yes," admitted Waldo. "Oh yes, there's no doubt." He began to tell us how they had started in the first place. He was ten years old and his parents had taken him and his brother and sister to the coast of Dorset, in the area of Portland Bill. There is a sort of cratered bay there, almost a lake, but the sea entered it through a narrow mouth. Waldo and his tough twelve-year-old brother, Simon, had hiked to this strange bay, called Devil's Hole, and hired a rowboat. As schoolboys will, they tossed a coin to see who would take the boat out first. Waldo was allowed to toss and catch the coin but when he had it in his hand he did something that was contrary to their code, something he had nonetheless been trying to do whenever he tossed but which his brother always spotted. He turned the coin over twice instead of the prescribed once. His brother did not notice this time, and Waldo won the first half hour in the boat. His brother waited on the shingle for his turn. After the agreed period, Waldo brought the boat in. He was not as comfortable as he pretended, because there was a surf running, as there often was in Devil's Hole. Waldo was happy to be on the wet shingle again and to hold the bucking rowboat as Simon climbed in. A thundercloud covered the sun; the surf got imperceptibly higher. After the rowboat capsized Simon should have been able to swim ashore, but locals, who always know these things but don't say them until after the event, said that some sort of circular rip occasionally set up in the Hole, that it was futile swimming against it as Simon probably tried to do. Yes, the rip would have taken him out through the gap. Waldo's fits began soon after, and he knew why: If he hadn't broken the code by turning the coin twice, he would have had the second turn and the rip would have taken him, not Simon.

At thirteen he got the idea that the fits would cease if he confessed to any authority. He told the school doctor, who went to the trouble of getting the popular school chaplain to inform Waldo on the Deity's behalf that Waldo was not culpable for a silly thing like the turn of a coin.

It was ridiculous, said Waldo, now, a man of twenty-six, but he was following the same cure as when he was thirteen. Without blinking, he asked us to believe he had considered suicide, but that would have left the expedition without a meteorologist.

We were understandably silent for a good ten seconds after Waldo had finished his recital. Alec spoke first.

"After you told him . . . how was he?"

Waldo flinched. "He said of course he was devastated. He was very honest with me. He said that for the moment he didn't quite know how he could go on managing the expedition, but he suspected that in a little while he would have found a place in his system for what I'd told him—it would become mere baggage."

"Which it never really can be, Waldo. Can it?"

I remembered Sir Eugene's confrontation with Barry that afternoon, the lack of his normal primacy, and Barry's uneasy belligerence.

"He thanked me," said Waldo, "for my honesty. That's too kind of him. But I believed his ignorance would have . . . would have affected the whole enterprise."

We thought about this, and reached our separate conclusions but did not voice them.

"I have a favor to ask you," Alec told Waldo. "I would like you to pass the word around that the journal has been found, that Sir Eugene and I have it."

It wasn't I who was being asked, but I couldn't help objecting. "Pass the word *around?*" I said.

Alec did not seem to hear me.

"I would like you to do that, Waldo."

"It will bring people to us," Alec told me in explanation as we reentered the main part of the hut. AB Stigworth was serving sherry around the room, a ritual of gentility that always went strangely wrong because most of the men had nowhere to drink it but sitting and standing around their bunks. "Men will come to us and ask us what Victor knew about them. We can interview them without summoning them, without our having to admit that Victor's death was an inflicted one."

We stood in front of the leader's alcove. The curtain was drawn but we could hear him speaking evenly. "Of course," he was saying, "if you don't care for my reasonable instructions, you can always move down the coast to Holbrooke's hut. It doesn't have the comforts, but if your independence is so important to you—"

I heard a mutter of words. It sounded like Barry.

"Very well, Mr. Fields," I heard Sir Eugene say. "If you see Stigworth, will you please tell him to put my sherry beside my place at table?"

The curtain opened. Barry came through, saw us, grinned awkwardly. From his desk, Sir Eugene also saw us.

"Gentlemen," he said. It was clear he had made a quick recovery.

We went in and Alec put the journal on the desk. "That is the rumored journal Victor kept."

"Rumored?"

"Some of us had heard a rumor. You'll see, Sir Eugene, that Victor knew things very prejudicial to Anthony Piers and myself."

Sir Eugene looked at us. I can remember blushing and hating myself for it.

He turned the pages. "Victor was morally defective," said Alec. "All news was news as far as Victor was concerned."

After studying the journal for three minutes, Sir Eugene looked at us again.

"There are two conspicuous omissions. They seem to have been ripped out."

"They were already missing when Anthony found the journal on the bookshelves."

"I suppose," Sir Eugene said, "someone was trying to be sensitive toward Dr. Warwick or me—or to the both of us."

It was said offhand. He was admitting no connection with Waldo Warwick.

It was to me they came, knowing I was involved yet sensing I had none of the true committee-of-judges stature that Alec and Sir Eugene (if "enjoy" is the word) enjoyed.

Par-axel's was a typical approach. He leaned over me as I finished my meal. He was wary; he was simultaneously apologetic and angry. Seeing him and others like this, stooped as if the one public shame of their lives were now a physical drag on their shoulders, I felt some of that hatred of Victor that must have gone into his strangulation.

This was an age when people liked to seem infallible as popes. No one frets about his reputation now as men like Par-axel did then: *Pure* shame could almost kill men then the way getting caught and being made to pay can very nearly kill men now. Therefore, the contrast between Par-axel's anxiety and his tortured English was pitiable.

"I hear," he said in a highly audible whisper, "you find a little book of nasty pages belongs to Victor? Is it so?"

"Yes, Par-axel."

"Sir Eugene has it?"

"Yes."

"He is going to keep it?"

"I don't know. I really don't."

"What does it say of me?"

"I saw only what it said of *me*. That was bad enough."

"Oh." He laughed a second. "Women?"

"More or less."

He began frowning. The hint of illicit love hadn't distracted him for long. "Whatever Victor said of me, truth or falsities, I want each and every one of the pages for burning."

"Of course. We should tell Sir Eugene that."

Together we went to Sir Eugene's alcove. Although we were two apparent petitioners, I was in fact the decoy, leading Par-axel in.

Alec and Sir Eugene were both working at Sir Eugene's desk, as they often did in the evenings. I rapped on the bookcase and they looked up.

"Par-axel wants to speak to you, Sir Eugene."

"On the book belonging with Victor," Par-axel amplified in his stage whisper.

So the curtain was closed and we sat, Par-axel and myself, on Sir Eugene's bed.

Sir Eugene lifted the *Journalist's Yearbook 1909* and dropped it back on his desk. "It contains some awkward information about all of us."

"My share of awkward information." Par-axel began. "Does it say Beck loses six men in the mountains?"

Sir Eugene opened the journal to Beck's place and read a little of what was written there.

"Beyond the Lapp Gateway," he muttered aloud. "The

Kjölen Mountains in Norrbotten. The iron-ore railway. Does that sound right, Par-axel?"

Par-axel's face contorted, as if in preparation for tears. "Sufficient is sufficient," he said. It was a saying he had. It meant, why can't people leave things alone?

"You don't have to explain, Par-axel."

"But did you know about, Sir Eugene?" Beck wanted to know. "Did *you* know about Par-axel?"

He worried for his expeditionary reputation, worried that Sir Eugene would now think him unfit to inhabit the Antarctic.

"I'd heard something, Par-axel," said Stewart. "You don't have to explain . . ."

But Par-axel could not be prevented from explaining. For the second time that day I found myself listening to a story about responsibility and guilt—of the iron-ore railway from the Swedish Arctic town of Kiruna through the wilderness of the Kjölen Mountains that gave on to the long fiords running down to Narvik, the iron-ore port in the infant state of Norway. In the early spring of 1908 a dozen avalanches obliterated the line on the Swedish side of the border and overturned and buried an ore train. The Swedes reopened the line for the summer, but wanted to survey another and safer route for the rail bed. Par-axel, commissioned only a year but accustomed from boyhood to the mountains beyond the Lapp Gateway near Sweden's northwestern border, was serving with one of the two companies of Alpine troops garrisoned in Kiruna. He didn't like Kiruna, he said, telling us why briefly. His views on small-town life in Scandinavia were similar to those of Ibsen and Strindberg, which would later become commonplace to theater goers. Kiruna's melancholy was even more stifling because, being one hundred miles north of the Circle, it suffered nearly two months of total darkness. And the mountains beyond, said Par-axel, were like God's teeth.

Par-axel liked it best when he was on patrol or guiding

survey teams in the mountains. He was in the mountains of Norbotten province during the first week of September. He had a group of soldiers with him and was guiding a squad of railroad surveyors. Some of the soldiers and surveyors got sick, a high fever. Beck and the others believed it was something they had picked up in the muskeg swamps between Kiruna and the Lapp Gateway. One morning, said Par-axel, he had an argument with the head of the survey team. They had five men sick. They should all, said Beck, stay in camp and nurse them, and rest, and watch for the outbreak of the symptoms in themselves. The head of the survey team, a man in his fifties, refused to obey a subaltern and said it was urgent that the survey team complete a certain series of triangulations in a nearby pass. Beck, himself unwell, sent his sergeant and another soldier to guide the four surveyors on a short excursion.

In the afternoon, a furious April blizzard rolled in from the west. Beck did not worry too much about the surveyors and his two men, for they were all sensible, and they had some food with them and two flimsy tents adequate in such emergencies for three men each.

When the blizzard ended on the second morning, Beck skied out to meet them, but they did not come back, and only two bodies were found. Despite all their training and mountain experience, they had behaved like novices. They had not pitched the tents, which were found in the private's backpack. They had tried to get back to their base camp and had lost touch with each other, calling uselessly in competition with the wind. The court of inquiry, Par-axel said, found their blizzard madness inexplicable.

"Now," he said, "now, Par-axel cannot show you he is not the Holbrooke kind of creature." He meant, not as negligent, not as stupid, not as culpable. Today a computer would assess Par-axel under all these headings, but Par-axel on Cape Frye could not hope for electronic exoneration.

In response to the tale, Sir Eugene tore out the Beck pages and handed them to him. "Burn them, Mr. Beck," he said.

I foresaw a time when there would be nothing but covers left to Victor's book of scandals.

For a second, Par-axel inspected the pages. "Ashes, they aren't enough," he said, a perfect sentence. "No. Ashes are never the end for any trouble."

But he nodded and went, leaving me with Alec and the leader.

Sir Eugene said, "Well, is it him?"

"I don't know," I said. "No, it can't be."

"Can't it?" Alec asked me. He seemed melancholy, a pained convert to the idea that the assassin was within the hut society. "I think of how the journal got on its bookshelf. I think of the likelihoods. Both depressing. A man who thinks he is shameful takes it from Victor's belongings and finds by reading it that we are all more or less shameful. You see, to put the journal on the shelf might be an act of pathetic despair. And the other likelihood is less comforting still: That an assassin put it there. In which case the despair is even more pitiable."

"Forbes-Chalmers?" asked Sir Eugene. "You were devoted to the Forbes-Chalmers hypothesis last night."

Alec put a limp hand on the desk, closed his eyes, and spoke in a still voice. "I wish it were still tenable," he said.

Against his crisp analysis, the theories of Barry Fields and Walter O'Reilly—positing a plum-pudding fiend who enters a pantry from which there is no simple exit, yet does not raid the ice cave farther up the hill where frozen carcasses are kept—seemed like village gossip.

Sir Eugene tore out Alec's share of Victor's journal and gave it to him. Then he tore out mine for me. The lights went out. "Is it eleven?" I asked in the dark.

"It is," said Sir Eugene softly. "Good night, gentlemen."

We said our good nights, and Alec stumbled off to find a

candle to light him to the latrines and to bed. I had farther to travel and was further delayed by the small accident of ramming my shoulder against the bookcase.

"Anthony," said Sir Eugene.

It was not totally dark. The storm lantern for use by night watchmen was lit and threw some small indirect light into the alcove.

"Anthony," said Sir Eugene, "the ... er ... the liaison between yourself and the ... the lady—the ... the liaison of which Victor writes ..."

"Yes, Sir Eugene?" I was alarmed. There was no air of Socratic elucidation about the way his shoulders hunched, about the uncertainty of his diction.

"You mustn't think it indelicate of me, but ..." He chuckled, doing his best to show he didn't blame me. "You know, when I was your age, pretty older women never approached me—"

"I'm afraid, Sir Eugene, the approaching was all from my side," I said, deliberately defending Anthea, and though he did not know it, Lady Stewart.

"Of course, of course, it happens—more than we think. The younger man, the older woman. I think of the husband though."

My face was burning in the dark. "So do I, Sir Eugene." I managed to confess.

"I'm not trying to cause you discomfort," he said, increasing my profound unease. "My experience of these matters is not as extensive, for example, as my experience of the navy." He waited. I heard his lips squeak as if he was bunching his face, one eye closed, the other focused on the unequal bulks of the two sets of knowledge: Knowledge of women, knowledge of ships and the society of sailors. I stood in the dark, promising myself he would not ask me about the inner life of an adulterer. No man could be so transparent, so much like a hurt child.

He asked me! He said, "Tell me ... the lovers ... do they ... mention the husband? Do you perhaps tend to ... to mock him?"

I wondered if I could end the conversation by mockery—by asking, You want to know what Waldo and your wife said about you while they lay together? I also considered shaking him, telling him, You're forty-three and a great captain. You shouldn't ask a boy these questions. Did he believe a woman of his wife's stature or Anthea's would compare bodies or mannerisms?

My answer was out of my lips before I knew I had spoken. "I believe, Sir Eugene, that most decent women can make mistakes, but they would consider the sort of thing you mention to be the worst infidelity."

He said, "That's what my sense and experience tells me. Thank you, Anthony, for allowing me to raise this delicate matter."

Rather than grope across the room and search for a stump of candle by my bunk, I borrowed one from Alec. The stables were half warm and gently lit by the radiance of Warren Mead's blubber stove. Warren himself was no longer there. The threat of glanders must have passed. The upright ponies snuffled, standing asleep.

Only one of the latrines was occupied, the farthest of the five. I entered a middle stall, closed the door, and fixed the candle on the spike provided. I bared my haunches and sat shivering, welcoming the minor animal warmth left in the seat by a recent occupant. In a week, I thought, I'll be bedding down in a tent on the weather side of Ross Island. But I could not believe it. It was a surreal proposition to me.

I coughed. "Must be minus fifty-five outside," I said aloud—trying to achieve some old-fashioned, premurder, prejournal small talk.

There was a brisk answer from the end stall. "At least, Anthony."

Quincy.

"What are your plans for tomorrow?" I asked, just to make a noise in the near dark.

"I? . . . Well, Mr. Hoosick and I might try some ice trolling."

The "Mr. Hoosick" was very strange, and the voice cold and still brisk. I had been half expecting this—that men could resent my knowledge of them, or of Victor's version of them. What was his news of Quincy? I knew that the English press loved a ripe parsonical scandal.

"Trolling?" I said. "Again?"

Quincy coughed. "Today's haul is not quite adequate. Good night, Anthony."

I heard him open the cubicle door and go.

I had a similar experience as I crossed the main room. Troy rushed to my side from his corner bunk. "I suppose," he said, "the leader's told you all about my crimes as a quartermaster. I mean, usually a sailor's record is the concern of sailors, a fraternal secret, but it seems that you and Alec have been admitted to some kind of all-knowing triumvirate—"

"I . . . I know very few details," I muttered, not very appeasingly. I had in fact seen fragments of John Troy's story each time I thumbed the journal. A story about a cruiser, the *HMS Monmouth* and the Kiplingesque haven Port Said. Goods from the ship's stores sold to merchants ashore. A board of inquiry brought together by the cruiser's captain to hear charges against Troy and certain petty officers.

I blinked, sorting the elements of John Troy's near tragedy while he lectured me too loudly. Did anyone—Victor, Sir Eugene—bother to record that the court of inquiry led on to the court-martial, fining, and reprimand of the captain? Had anyone ever explained to me, Anthony Piers, what it was like for some officers in the navy, the ones whose background was not genteel, who were allowed to quartermaster or to spend their careers in the engine room, who rarely joined the gentry on the bridge other than by exceptional invitation, "and who are available as convenient victims in the event of explosion or alienation of stores?" he concluded.

I tried to manage a tone of brotherly sensitivity I had never quite felt for John Troy, "Why don't you speak to Sir Eugene about it? We can talk to each other, you know. All of us can talk to each other. We're not strangers."

"That's open to debate," John Troy murmured. "I make no apologies about it. I want to go to the Pole. It's the road up from below decks. There, I've said it. I don't want Sir Eugene to be talked out of taking John Troy to the Pole."

"Honest ambition," I said, not telling him that for some reason I was repelled by it in him. "But you should sleep easy, John. Victor didn't accuse all of us of lifting a few ship's cheeses. Some of us are accused of lechery and murder."

"Does *he* say it was cheeses—?"

"Good night, John."

As I walked away, he became remorseful. "Listen, I don't mean to imply any of it is your fault."

By my bunk, I stripped to my thermal underwear and lay back among the blankets. But the haranguing wasn't over. Above me I could hear Paul settling down. "This time next week," he murmured, "we'll be two nights out towards Cape Crozier." The idea, obviously and for the moment, made him exultant.

"It's going to be cold," I said, almost whimpering.

"Of course, but we'll be out in the open, away from memories of Victor, away from routine."

I could understand that: The hut had suddenly become claustrophobic.

"Paul?"

"Yes."

"You're over the disappointment? About the Pole party, I mean."

"Oh yes. Of course it was my eyes. You can't take a chap whose glasses ice up. You can't take him all the way to the Pole."

My head found the pillow and I was warmly comatose when another voice, close to me, roused me. "Tony." I sat up. Isaac Goodman.

"Tony, if Victor says the London Zionists put him on a death list, he's a liar."

I sat down early at the main table. Harry Kittery, the night watchman during the period of deeper darkness just passed, had left some of his night's work by his empty teacup. It was a scientific memo to Sir Eugene, of the kind Harry often asked me to read so that I would know and tell others that Sir Eugene did not have him beaten, either as a scientist or a man.

Dear Sir Eugene [I read],
An examination of my notes, sketches and observations of sea ice both in McMurdo Sound and during the voyage south leads me to propose the following series of events in the formation of sea ice. Firstly, I have observed that sea water of normal salt content freezes at about $-2°C$. Small crystals or platelets of ice, usually square or hexagonal in shape, form just beneath the surface of the water. The Norwegians have called these crystals *frazil ice*. Their density at this point is still at least 0.985 that of water and so they do not float as buoyantly as ice at its normal density (0.917 that of water). Their density and the nature of the formation of these crystals, I suggest, indicates conclusively that water commences to ice internally and that icing is not initiated by precipitation from the air. . . .

I felt again that sense of unsafeness that passed through me when Sir Eugene asked me his simple-minded questions about adulterers. How could a great and stable leader push strange and incorrect ideas so stubbornly. I comforted myself by remembering Dr. Samuel Johnson's berserk theory on where swallows went in winter. They flew, said the doctor, in decreasing circles until they coalesced and sank to the bottoms of the rivers of Europe, where they hibernated in a glutinous ball of feathers.

Harry returned from washing himself in one of the communal water basins AB Stigworth set about the hut in the mornings. He couldn't see who it was reading his memo, but got his glasses on and could make me out better. He smiled. He claimed not to be as nearsighted as Paul, but sometimes I wondered.

"This is very well put together," I said.

He grinned again and sat down, a towel over his shoulder. His boyishness diminished my sense of the moment. As I looked at the rest of the paper and saw the stages entitled "grease ice," "pancake," "new ice," "old ice," "hummocking," "rafting," "brash ice," "fast ice," I did not suspect that this was the first time a scientist had delineated correctly the stages by which sea ice grows and decays. A nearsighted boy who, as he said, "had been to Norway once on an excursion," and who, for the rest, knew only Derbyshire and Oxford, had been able to do it more exactly than the Norwegians, who had lived so long with the reality of ice.

When I had finished reading, Harry squinted directly at me.

"Does Victor mention my uncle?"

"What?"

"I had an uncle who was charged with stealing lingerie. Does Victor mention that?"

"Oh no." I lowered my eyes from his bright lenses. "He didn't write about you."

"Oh?"

"Your page said, 'Harry Kittery, physicist, age twenty-seven years.' Little else. He wouldn't mention uncles, Harry. With most of us he could strike closer to home than that."

"Oh God," Harry murmured. "It can only mean I've led an awfully dull life."

In this newly fallible world, I wondered was this true.

For even John Troy, in his anger and frankness, had mentioned only one court, and that the lesser in human complexity. He had, in fact, come before two courts. The first, the one about which he had made his protests by candlelight, had been exactly as he said. The captain of the *HMS Monmouth* brought charges against Lieutenant Troy for having misappropriated the ship's stores for the sake of someone ashore. Because John Troy was full of native wit and had good counsel, it was shown that the captain had been guilty of the misappropriations. Admittedly, Lieutenant Troy's lenient bookkeeping had enabled the captain to draw ship's stores at will and Lieutenant Troy was asked to be more stringent in the future, an urging he had certainly obeyed among us in Antarctica. Perhaps, in fact, this was the case that had distressed Troy more. If that were so, it told something of Troy: that his talents were mainly for keeping stores, whatever the navy caste system had forced on him.

The second case had involved a court-martial and arose from a charge of assault brought by a young midshipman called Bennett. Victor's journal made this case into a homosexual triangle drama, a reading that on the basis of Troy's behavior with the maidens of Christchurch was not very probable. Bennett accused Troy of striking him regularly and using abusive language. Troy said that the only time there had been contact between them was once when they bumped into each other in a corridor. The ship's surgeon (whom Victor cast as the third point of the triangle) gave evidence that after a passageway collision with Troy, midshipman Bennett had come to the sick bay, had said that Troy had attacked him, and had displayed a real panic fear that Troy had injured him mortally. That Troy was acquitted was considered by Victor the result of the surgeon's partisan evidence. That Bennett was put in an asylum within six weeks of the court-martial showed, to Victor's satisfaction, the extent to which Troy had tormented the boy. And the import of the event was that officers (those genteel officers of whom Troy had complained) would cover up for Caligula if he happened to be a brother officer.

Victor then contradicted himself by adding a note something like this:

Anxious that his superiors might believe a naval officer is not normally court-martialled twice unless there is a basis for it in the naval officer, John Troy is twice as busy as any other man. This, he feels, will earn him a place on the polar team, and in the background of a British hero who has been to the Pole, two minor court-martials pale away to nothing. He is boyishly and innocently unaware that when he is a polar god, he will be twice as vulnerable.

Still unsatisfied, Victor ended his entry on John Troy by calling him "a mother's boy." The image the phrase creates, of a mother pretty if overblown, bosomy, sweet, and dominant, was far different from the picture of the wizened and beak-nosed Cornish woman which Troy kept by his bed.

Yet in spite of Victor's clear malice against Troy, in spite of my knowing that John Troy did not bastardize other men, I did not feel easy with a man who felt more at risk over lost cheeses than the lost sanity of a hapless midshipman, Bennett by name.

During the rest of that morning, I became acquainted with the background grievances and histories of half my colleagues, either through meetings with Alec and Sir Eugene or because the men themselves came up to me while I was trying to get on with the auroral paintings.

In this way I discovered from Isaac Goodman that in 1906, during a rebellion in the Ukraine, Victor had been attached to the staff of General Gorochow, the czarist enforcer. His journeys with Gorochow had been what is now called a spin-off from his time with Russian generals during the war with Japan. He had liked Gorochow and described him as "the reincarnation of the Cossacks who harried Napoleon westwards across Europe ... etc." Elsewhere he wrote of him as a "splendid savage, reminiscent of the Tartars." Before this phrase appeared in the London press, a number of Jewish families, including Isaac Goodman's, learned that relatives of theirs had been slaughtered in one of the worst pogroms in czarist history, at Krivoy Rog, an ancient merchant city in the eastern Ukraine. This pogrom had been carried out by troops under the command of the "splendid savage." When London Zionists wrote to the editor of the *Mail* concerning Victor's blatant admiration for Gorochow's style, a style that had, for example, removed Isaac's uncle's entire family from the earth, Victor replied that he didn't approve of everything the general had ever done. But the general had always been kind in his personal dealings, said Victor. It was reports of mutiny in the Jewish quarter of Krivoy Rog that had caused the problem, and although Victor did not approve of slaughter on the mere grounds of prejudice, he felt he had to observe that it was often the stubborn unconformity of people that created trouble. Two

weeks later Victor told a number of London newspapers that
the London Zionists had threatened his life, an accusation he
repeated in his journal entry about Isaac.

"A heresy trial," said Quincy. He smiled at the cup of tea
he held and then raised his eye to my face. "You'd think a
heresy trial would distress a clergyman. Perhaps I'm a bad
clergyman ..."

It was true that beside the other crimes Victor had listed,
Quincy's scandal had a sunny Edwardian madness to it.

"I am beginning to wonder if the concept of heresy has any
meaning in this age. I did not ... no, I did not ... say so at the
trial. I imitated the style of Joan of Arc at her trial. She knew
bishops can be as deadly as all solemn men."

He was chatting. Pleasant and open. I now found it hard
to understand the cause of his gruffness in the latrines the
night before. It occurred to me that by speaking to him in the
latrines, I might have offended his sense of modesty.

"When I was young and mystical," he said, "I instituted
confession in St. Thomas's, Putney. I had studied the church
fathers and there seemed no good reason not to introduce the
practice on a voluntary basis. My rector didn't mind; he was
one of those sporting parsons and had been opening batsman
for Surrey. As long as I didn't interfere with his rowing and
his rugby, I think he would have let me ... well, hold Black
Masses with the Mothers' Club."

"How you would have delighted Victor if you had," I mused.

He told me of armed camps inside the one Anglican church,
alignments of which—as an uninstructed though instinctive
unbeliever—I knew nothing. At one end were the Evangelicals,
who tended to see a papist under every bed the way an extreme Republican might see a Communist in every liberal. At
the other end of the Anglican prismatic coloration were the

aesthetic and mystical young men who found some of the rituals of Rome appealing, though the concept of papal infallibility repelled them.

The Evangelicals were powerful in Westminster and Southwark and in the end would bully the Parliament of England into instituting a royal commission to investigate papist infiltration of that good and pallid institution, the Church of England. One of the first moves of the Southwark Evangelicals in their attack on papist infiltration was to arraign the curate of Putney before the bishop's court on a charge of heresy.

Quincy's rector, the rugby man, on his way out to play tennis at the Hurlingham Club, said, "You're no heretic. You understand the knock-on rule." (The knock-on rule is a fumble rule in rugby.)

"In the end," said Quincy, "I was not condemned for heresy, but I was reprimanded as a witless tool of papism and was told not to hear confessions. The strange thing is, I think they were right. I wouldn't do that now—offer to hear confessions of honest people. It's arrogant and morbid. I think so, anyhow. In the end, I broke with that bishop and moved to Yorkshire and settled down . . . settled down to the study of parasites." He snorted, a little ashamed despite himself that his old confession-hearing passion had died.

"It doesn't sound like a really succulent outrage to me," I said.

He laughed. "Compared to what some vicars do? No, it isn't." Somewhere he had learned to see all things in proportion: Ecclesiastical bun fights and small creatures from the guts of fish.

"You should have read," he told me, "the poisonous letters those Evangelicals wrote me, especially the parsons' wives. They would have thought better of me if I'd kept a mistress on curate's pay."

*　*　*

I remember Peter Sullivan, perhaps because unlike Troy and Beck and Quincy, he neither spoke to anyone about Victor's opinion of him, nor did he look as if he would ever ask. He knew what to expect of Henneker and had more experience of press barbarity than most of us. He did his work and neither hated nor forgave the renowned journalist.

We all knew their disagreement grew from a long moving picture Peter had made two years before. It is very likely that Peter's film was one of the first dramatic features in the modern mold. It was certainly the most expensive to that date, because Peter had gone to the trouble of hiring some of the most noted West End actors and actresses. The film, when cut and edited, ran fifty minutes, a great length for those days. Its birth as (perhaps) the first of a new genre, coincided with the birth of another art form—the film review. Victor's review in the *Sketch* was devastating, and combined with the unprecedented length and the Edwardian artiness of the frame compositions, it meant that Peter failed to get a wide distribution for this, the first (as far as I know) art film.

The journal worked on these facts from Victor's angle, including mention of a threatening letter to the critic from the director and Peter's entanglement with an actress. The lady, however, if Peter's placid busyness around the hut was as authentic as it seemed, did not seem to be on Peter's mind to the extent Anthea was on mine.

By lunchtime all we knew was that the journal had bruised us, had even entered and stained our view of the earth, yet had been no help to Sir Eugene, to Alec Dryden, to myself, as committee members. We had admitted a measured dose of toxin into the body of the hut and found it unprofitable.

As for the rest, the yearbook mocked Barry as a redneck and bumpkin. It damned Hoosick's abstracted scientific air by detailing Hoosick senior's career as a stock manipulator and plunderer of railroads. Unprofitably it derided Warren Mead for his pony love and Harry Webb for his love of dogs. Unprofitably it delineated the strong reasons some of us might have for desiring Victor's silence, for bringing (as somebody had) his silence about. Even Norman Coote had, as he suspected, his place there. Perhaps, wrote Victor, Norman would poison all the dogs one night to ensure the tractors had no competition.

Once I made the mistake [wrote Victor] of mentioning that I was unimpressed with tractor-power and intended to write a feature comparing the mechanical uncertainty of machines with the assured spunk and muscle-power of huskies. As I spoke, Norman saw his dream of owning his own modest engineering works fade. He said, *why not wait for the spring? No sense jumping to conclusions.*

These days Victor would be called a moral defective. He was charming in the way that he gave you the sense that you were the one person in a crooked world whom he respected. And all the time you thought, "Is this the dreaded Victor Henneker?" It was just that he could see no reason not to sell you in the end. Betrayal was his medium and he couldn't help that. I think, even in those days, we all understood that. There was no communal pulse of anger in the hut. Victor had been Victor, that was all.

When we were all at the lunch table that day, Sir Eugene came from his alcove to join us. We saw him stuff the yearbook through the small gateway of the stove. We saw the lick of flames. None of us smiled.

I remember Victor had written only one generous thing in the whole damn book: "Paul Gabriel, naturalist, age twenty-three. Myopic. Have recommended Dr. Philip Sorel's eye exercises."

SIX

"There," said Barry, as if he owned the volcano. We had just crossed the icy hollow three hundred yards from the hut where in summer the Adélie penguins made their rowdy nests. From a small rise cluttered with black rock, the volcano's Jurassic gift to McMurdo Sound, we could see Mount Erebus luminous in the dark, breathing a luminous smoke. Closer, we could see the Barne Glacier running among the shallow hills where, by Barry's reckoning, Forbes-Chalmers lived.

Barry stood still, dramatically, a man making a vow. "Next summer, whenever we can find the time, Beck and me—we're going to climb it."

Six months ago I might have said, let me come too. But today the mountain looked dominant and worshipful in all of its two and a half miles of height. Like the two Siberians, I doubted if summer would ever come and transform the peak.

Barry ran down a snowbank, gave a yell, and jumped to touch an imaginary point in the air above him. "It's great to be out of that bloody hut," he said, landing. "Forbes-Chalmers, guard your loins."

I suppose I was a somber companion. After a time I said— hardly knowing I was doing so—"John Forbes, dead in Christ."

"What?"

"Alec Dryden saw that. On the wall in Holbrooke's hut."

"John Forbes, dead in Christ?"

"I believe it was written in charcoal."

"I'll be damned."

Barry continued briskly over the hummocks toward the glacier.

My shorter-legged attempt to keep level with him reminded

me yet again of the problems I'd be facing within a week. As Barry hiked, he talked compulsively of the stones of Antarctica. The previous summer there had been little time, and he, with Isaac, Kittery, and PO Wallace, had been lucky to manage a journey across the sound to a glacier that Shackleton had named the David a year or two before. Barry's professional passions, not to mention Isaac's, had been roused by the evidence they'd found there. Now the geologists awaited a new summer and the chance to move through the country more widely and deeply. "We came to this great rock wall on the mouth of the glacier," Barry was telling me now. "There was Devonian sandstone on the bottom, four hundred million years old. And above it a great wall of rubble compacted to a single mass by pressure from a glacier—not the David, a glacier older than that, a glacier that moved during Antarctica's last ice age—and then above this nine-hundred-feet thick layer of rubble there was more recent Permian rock, say two hundred and fifty million years old. Now—this is the best bit—in the Permian rock, Isaac and me, we found fossils that contained the petrified leaves of *Glossopteris*. It's a fern leaf, not unlike the leaf of a gum tree in general configuration."

"Amazing," I said, though I didn't yet see the full significance.

"Now, later in the same journey, Isaac examined other Devonian rock just like the Devonian rock at the bottom of the rubble, and found in it fossils of snails and various kinds of lichen. So, you see, Antarctica at one time supported basic life, then it had an ice age, then a period when ferns grew and, maybe, animals wandered."

I looked around me. Had bear and deer and pheasant ever populated this shore? Barry continued, speaking rapidly in time with his stride.

"Now Isaac—who's a really bright bastard, I mean, really

bright—has been corresponding with this German scientist, Wegener, Alfred Wegener, who touts the theory that all the major continents once belonged to one great continent, Pangeia, and that Australia, Antarctica, the Americas, Africa, Eurasia drifted to their present distances from each other. Wegener's laughed at by other experts and finds it hard to get his views published, but Isaac believes that what we found on the David last summer backs up the Wegener hypothesis."

"How dull art is," I said with some genuine envy. "How dull art is compared to that."

"I dunno," said Barry. "I couldn't paint a barn. But I can't wait to get out there with my mate Isaac and with some strong bastard like Wallace. One of those glaciers up on the ice shelf— the Mulock, say. Jesus, we'll give its lower reaches a going over, a royal going over!"

In that moment I pitifully envied Goodman and Fields and their geological obsessions. They had too powerful a sense of purpose to waste their fury on Victor. Theirs to prove Pangeia. Theirs to conjure from Permian rock an Antarctica verdant, subtropical, favored by prehistoric lizards and mammals. No one sacrifices a purpose like that just to punish a journalist.

Now we were among steeper hills. From the top of one I saw the face of the glacier. The Barne itself was riddled with ice holes, but they were too unstable to provide a habitation for man.

We went uphill another two miles, taking fifty minutes to do it. The higher we got, the more noticeably Mount Terror thrust its summit over Erebus's shoulder. On the egg journey we would travel on the other side of Terror. The improbability of the idea depressed me anew.

Seeing the garbage heap, I suspected it was a third mountain. People often had depth problems when they looked at objects in Antarctica. Once, up on the ice shelf, Sir Eugene saw a shred of black biscuit paper just beyond the doorway of his tent and mistook it for a dog team miles away. I looked at the garbage heap (it was slightly above my eye level) and saw a mountain, a sister to Erebus and Terror. It had the configuration of a peak, dusted at the top with last night's small amount of drift on the north side and, seemingly, bare on the south. I did not run to it, because one does not run up to mountains. Barry seeing it more truly, ran up to it and began uncovering its details with his gloved hands.

We would never have seen this midden, short of tripping over it, if it hadn't been for the half-sled lying on top—one sawn-off half of an old sled, now showing a splintered runner, and with all its bindings loose.

"This is a Holbrooke sled," Barry told me. It was an intuitive statement. He was no specialist in comparative sleds. "Forbes-Chalmers must have used it to get carcasses of seals and penguins up here. Now it's broken. I wonder what he'll do?"

I took hold of a strip of broken binding and tugged it, laughing. It could be no one else's garbage dump but Forbes-Chalmers's. I was weeping with elation, and goddamn it if the tears didn't freeze to my cheeks!

"Hey," Barry said, taking a clumsy mittened hold of my shoulder. "Hey. What's got *you*, Tony?"

I couldn't tell him, though I knew. I wept because the garbage indicated the threat might be external to the hut, and external threats can, as Eugene had said, be dealt with. I was already believing that the owner of the dump had struck Victor down insensately as would ice or wind. We dug beneath the half-sled, finding bones and feathers and Swallow and Ariel pudding cans. I sat back in the snow, holding one of these, laughing still, reading its tattered label. I felt wonderful and renewed.

"Not so loud, Tony," said Barry.

"Why?" I laughed. "Why?"

"His hole must be close by. Have you thought of that?"

I stuffed one of the cans inside my windproofs. Through three layers of wool I felt its freezing rim.

Barry dropped the can he himself was holding. "Poor bastard," he said. "Poor loveless bastard."

We searched for two hours. Every near and substantial snowbank. We placed ourselves so that their contours showed up against the sharp night sky, but saw no smoke. We struck the faces of drifts with our boots, hoping to break some artificial barrier that gave on to Forbes-Chalmers's lobby.

"Shall we call to him?" I asked in the end.

"Call? If he wanted to meet us, he could have met us last January."

Some obscure memory of childhood shyness made me say, "It isn't the same thing."

"What?"

"Not wanting to meet people yet answering when they call. It isn't the same thing. In fact," I added, my brain lithe again, "I think he wants contact."

But Barry was beginning to panic. Soon we'd have to turn home. He ran to the top of a snowbank. "If we don't find him this time, he'll move his hutch somewhere else."

"Perhaps he hasn't seen us. Perhaps he's away."

"Away? Away where? He'll see our boot marks. For God's sake, Tony, we've got to find him *this* time."

We hunted and kicked another forty minutes. At the end of that time I insisted on calling. "Why not?" said Barry, dropping on his haunches. "Our tracks . . . our tracks are a dead giveaway anyhow."

I called, "John Forbes." I called, "Malcolm Chalmers." The sound bounced from the sharp snow to the dry air. If he was listening—if, perhaps, *they* were listening—the names must have resounded in his brain—must have taken his legs from under him.

I got no answer. We had to begin the hike downhill.

"Maybe," Barry murmured, "we should dig a pit. Maybe we should set traps."

"He'll show himself," I said. I believed it. The dump had been built to tease us. A man who did not somehow want to meet others would use more discretion in disposing of his trash. I felt some communion with the shy, lonely, homicidal Forbes-Chalmers.

Barry grew aggressive. As on that night in Christchurch, he did not take frustrations well. "Why? Why in the hell would he show himself?"

"It occurs to me," I said, "that he chooses not to take quarters of New Zealand mutton from the ice cave. That would be easy for him, and he would enjoy the meat after all his meals of penguin and Weddell seal. Instead of that, though, he comes in through the porch, walks through the sailors' quarters if not ours. Anytime on the journey to the pantry and back to the porch he could be discovered. Yet he does it. Why?"

"Because he's got scurvy and most of his teeth are gone. He can manage pudding. He can't manage meat."

I laughed. "I hadn't thought of that." Half the struts had been knocked out from beneath my hypothesis, but I didn't care. "I thought it might have been this. He wants to move amongst his fellow men. He keeps away when we're conscious. A shy child keeps away from children he really wants to play with. A shy man won't speak for years to a girl he wants."

"I don't know," Barry said.

Everything had changed for me. Even by moonlight, Erebus now looked like a companion. In the space of perhaps a mile's walk, a dazzling blue drapery aurora defined itself over the Victoria Land Mountains. I imagined Paul and Alec and myself hauling our light sleds to Cape Crozier beneath such wonders. I could feel the shape of the pudding can growing blood-warm inside my clothes.

"Mind you," said Barry, who, untouched by my elation, was still thinking away, "I have posited a Forbes-Chalmers who beats Victor up and leaves him there, down by the hut, then finds his way back to his hutch, two miles in a blizzard."

I had overlooked this obvious question, as people in ecstasy do overlook the obvious. I stopped and noticed the cold again. It felt as if it were falling into the minus sixties. I could feel the air burning as it entered my sinuses. All that was needed now to make us stagger crabwise, wincing, our faces averted northward, was a fifteen-knot wind. Barry kept strolling and spinning theories.

"No worry," he said, "no worry. He must have an ice hole down near the beach for emergencies, somewhere down at the mouth of the Barne. In fact, he'd have to. Imagine if he's out clubbing a Weddell seal and one of those winds comes down off the plateau. We get some kind of warning about these things from Waldo's instruments. But Forbes-Chalmers gets none at all. He has to have some hole down there. I didn't find it yesterday. But then we didn't find his main residence today. Positing"—it was becoming his favorite word—"a beach hole, let me paint the scene as it happens. He meets Victor in the middle of the blizzard. I mean, the middle of the blizzard is no tough time of rendezvous to a man who's lived here alone for four years. And Victor's one of those crazy journalists who would love to be able to tell the world how he interviewed an Antarctic castaway in the middle of a bloody storm. Real Stanley and bloody Livingston stuff. Forbes-Chalmers does Victor all that damage—the damages you say were all frostbite but Sweep Stigworth thought were genuine bottled-in-bond punishment. Forbes-Chalmers crawls back to his coastal hole. He doesn't even hear our search parties. And when the blizzard starts to die early the next morning, he traipses back to his main residence before we've finished breakfast."

"Yes," I said to him, regenerated. "Yes."

"Otherwise..." he pursued, "otherwise...do you think loneliness could endow man with a strong directional instinct, like a whale's?"

SEVEN

Half the things the members of the New British South Polar Expedition learned in Antarctica they learned at the mess table. Now they had discovered from Sir Eugene, over dinner, that it seemed Forbes-Chalmers was not a chimera. The sailors, who had eaten a little earlier, had been asked in so that they could hear too. I saw the Russians smiling at each other. Although they barely understood the speech, they knew it was all benign talk. They trusted God and Eugene Stewart to bring the sun back.

"So, Lieutenant Troy," Sir Eugene said, turning toward Troy's place at the table, "your puddings are accounted for."

There was a stutter of pointed laughter from the sailors, who had to work with Troy and suffer the sharp edge of his fear that stores would be missing by the gross and he would again be blamed.

Sir Eugene held up the tin I had retrieved from Forbes-Chalmers's dump. He turned it in his hand as I had earlier in the day—as if to read its label. "We mustn't seek him too keenly," he said (I suppose "seek him too keenly" was a bashful synonym for bring him back alive), "not only because he may react with blows, but because it might drive him further and further up the slopes of Erebus, where, no matter how successfully he has survived so far, he could not hope to outlive a blizzard. All we can do is watch for him and, should he appear, call to him in as welcoming a way as we can. And if he runs, and we think we can catch him, call at least one friend and go in pursuit. But if we know he's too far away to catch, let the poor man run. Let him run."

He sat and called for another cup of tea. I could see Barry across the table, making angry faces over Sir Eugene's coyness.

As soon as the meal ended and while some of the sailors were still in his end of the hut, Fields went and spoke to Walter O'Reilly. Walter had rigged a device that told him when his bread was baked. It involved two terminals inside the oven attached to batteries outside. One terminal was fixed at the desired height for the loaf, the other rose on the crust. The two terminals united when the crust was high enough, and the bell rang.

Now Barry wanted Walter to rig that device to a sled, then leave the sled outside the door. For if the garbage dump was any sign, Forbes-Chalmers needed a sled. Would there be a way, Barry asked, of making two terminals meet and ring a bell if Forbes-Chalmers tried to take a sled?

Watching the conference, I felt a brief depression. I wondered, would the crime and Forbes-Chalmers, the elected criminal, yield to minor battery-operated mechanisms?

I had been standing by the table in the end-of-dinner scrimmage. As everyone edged and squeezed to get to the location of their work or leisure, and while AB Stigworth already whisked at the floor beneath our feet with his broom, Alec took my elbow.

"Sir Eugene," he said yet again. It was like a replay of the beginning of one of those sickening interviews of the past two days—and the alcove and the suitcase, and Sir Eugene in his cardigan, taking me in with his bright, wistful eyes. There was a difference tonight. Bernard Mulroy, AB Mulroy, storeman, stand-by cook, stood by the desk, and in the corner by the bed stood his brother, PO Percy Mulroy.

When the curtain was again closed we were very crowded in there. Impishly I patted the bed beside me. "Care for a seat, Petty Officer?" I asked the senior Mulroy.

"No thank you, Mr. Piers," he said.

His young brother was ethereal, Pre-Raphaelite, but Percy

had the same features stamped more heavily on a broad, slightly brutal face.

Sir Eugene promised the brothers they could trust Dr. Dryden and Mr. Piers. Elated with finding Forbes-Chalmers's dump, I did feel—very nearly—trustworthy.

"Now," Sir Eugene continued. "Now, AB Mulroy, you say you fed Forbes-Chalmers the puddings."

AB Bernard Mulroy looked solely at his clasped hands while he spoke. "I left them out for him at night."

"Why?"

"Mr. Henneker asked me to." A lover's favor, I thought.

Sir Eugene shook his head, a little impatient with this piecemeal information. "Tell us everything," he said.

"Mr. Henneker told me he saw the man two nights running. The first night Mr. Henneker sighted him down on the beach—stumbling along, he told me, near the tide crack. It was while Mr. Henneker was night watchman. Mr. Henneker was so excited he decided to go night watchman twice in a row, and I think Dr. Warwick had been sick, so Mr. Henneker stood Dr. Warwick's watch. Well, this time he saw him again. He says he saw him down at the dog lines, and the man had a knife and looked like he was going to slaughter a dog and take it away for meat. So Mr. Henneker yelled at the feller, and of course the feller ran. Mr. Henneker was very excited. He wanted to attract that man back, but he didn't want that man to go slaughtering dogs—because Mr. Henneker believed the dogs would be needed later; he didn't much believe in tractors. Mr. Henneker, therefore, asked me to leave food out there on clear nights—anything I could come by, leave it out there near the dog lines. I used to wrap it up in little bits of sailcloth I found around the place. So I suppose I left food out there, in sight of the dog lines, about seven or eight times. It was no sense putting it out there if there was any snow at all because drift would just cover it. The last half-dozen times I left out food I saved from my own rations, because after I'd set out the puddings I didn't want to take any more."

He looked a second at his brother, impassive in the corner. I recognized what the boy was doing, calling in his elder brother to correct or humiliate him, a cringe he had probably practiced since babyhood. Percy Mulroy said nothing, so his brother continued. "The truth is, Percy—PO Mulroy—caught me trying to nick some tinned beef for Mr. Henneker's visitor and he prevented me."

"I punished you," said PO Mulroy, mentally considering whatever the punishment had been and approving it all over again. "I punished you."

"Punished?" asked Sir Eugene. "Punished your brother?"

"The way, sir, a brother does punish a brother."

"What way is that?"

"Chastisement, sir."

"Do you mean *beat* your brother, PO Mulroy?"

"I chastised my brother the way I have always chastised him."

For the first time the story had made Sir Eugene angry. "Were you aware that no commissioned or noncommissioned officer has the right to strike a rating?"

"Sir, I was obeying a higher authority so to speak."

"Who might that be, PO Mulroy? God?"

"I was obeying my mother, sir."

"Your mother told you to beat up your brother?"

"To look after him, sir. She got me to make a solemn promise. 'Look after him,' she said." The memory made him talkative, and he smiled a little, as if inviting us all to consider the quaint and amiable woman his mother had been. "She didn't know how big the navy was, or how hard it was for a brother on one of His Majesty's vessels to look after a brother on another."

"By what logic, PO Mulroy, does 'look after' become physical blows?"

I know Mulroy could have told Sir Eugene that in the Merseyside slums the brothers came from, the terms were synonymous, but Mulroy could sense he would not win this argument. His throat was red as if from the pressure of all the answers he had never been allowed to give.

"It is not to happen again," Sir Eugene told him, as if fraternal punishment were the cause of the meeting.

When the massive sledder was sent away, there instantly seemed to be more air to breathe. Even Bernard Mulroy, of the shamed rating, lifted his face a little toward us. I hated being there, part of the landscape of a humiliation he would remember all his life. For there was a shift of focus in the room now. Sir Eugene and Alec and myself all exhaled and took up a stance to consider the phenomenon before us. It must have been painful for the boy.

"Tell me, Mulroy," Sir Eugene said quietly, "were Victor Henneker and yourself friends?"

"I suppose so, sir."

"In a way that most men are never friends with each other?"

"I . . . yes, sir, although it's common enough on the lower deck, sir, that kind of friendship."

"Is that the truth?" asked Sir Eugene. He did not want an answer. "Men treating other men," he went on, in a small voice, "as if they were women, is that it?"

"You . . . you could say so, sir."

"And your brother, Percy, knew about your friendship with Victor?"

"It upset him more than anything. That's why he talked Lieutenant Troy into choosing me as his storeman. Percy thought I'd be out of that kind of thing down here."

"I see." Sir Eugene looked at us with a half smile. "The expedition had a purpose I was not aware of."

The boy did not answer.

"Your brother beat you then. Would he have decided to beat up Mr. Henneker?"

"Oh no." The concept shocked AB Mulroy. "I was his brother, like. He didn't do that to gentlemen. Percy said he knew better than coming in here talking to Mr. Henneker. In Percy's eyes it was my fault. He kept telling me I could stop it if I wanted—the friendship, I mean. And then it stopped anyhow."

"It stopped?"

"Mr. Henneker got . . . got sick of it." The boy began weeping. At the time and in innocence I thought, why it's just like *real* love. "I couldn't make the sort of conversation he was used to. If he told me a story about famous people, he had to explain what they were famous for. It used to make him angry."

Again I asked myself, do they *really* couple and split apart for the same reasons as men and women? My God! I thought. I had never been to the sort of school where older boys fell in love with younger ones. In my part of the country acts of bestiality, farm boys and heifers, featured dominantly in the sexual lore of my boyhood, and in ignorance I had considered that homosexuality was of the same level of aberration as those shocking barnyard acts.

Meanwhile, Sir Eugene let the boy weep awhile. I thought the leader was doing better work with the younger Mulroy than with the elder. Although the idea of male love so appalled him that he could not utter the word, he had somehow caused Bernard Mulroy to talk about his affection for Henneker freely, from within a homosexual context.

"You must have been upset when Mr. Henneker stopped being your friend?"

"For a day or so, but then Percy made such a fuss about being proud of me."

Alec, who in his surgery had obviously been presented with this problem by anxious parents, asked the question that was going begging. "Do you think Victor found another friend?"

"Yes, someone he could talk with more," said Bernard flatly. There was a wealth of self-contempt in him.

"In the sailors' quarters or in the gentlemen's?"

"Someone in the gentlemen's—a conversationalist, like."

Sir Eugene thanked him and told him he could go.

Getting up, he nearly fell over. He must have been sitting stiff as a recruit in that chair. He went out sideways, to hide his stricken face from the gentlemen. No doubt he would go back to the sailors' quarters by way of the stables, probably hiding in the sailors' latrines until his face was composed.

After AB Mulroy had gone, Sir Eugene motioned Alec to sit in his place. They did not speak for a long time. In the end Sir Eugene spoke softly.

"Of course, it wasn't the Mulroys who hurt Victor. They had no community of purpose. While Victor maintained the relationship with Bernard, Percy had cause to punish him but Bernard did not. When Victor terminated the relationship, Bernard had cause but Percy didn't."

I groaned from my place on the bed. I felt irrationally as if Sir Eugene had insulted the gift we had brought him that afternoon—the palpable refuse of Forbes-Chalmers.

I said, "Please. We know what happened now. We don't have to go on looking for motivations amongst ourselves."

Sir Eugene did his impassive thinking for a second, his eyes closed. No wonder, I thought at that time, Lady Stewart went looking for someone more volatile. He said, "No. It's too big a leap to say that because Forbes-Chalmers exists, as he does, he is mad, and because he is mad, he throttled Victor. There are gaps between all those propositions, and naked hope. I'm afraid, Tony, you will not span them."

I stared at him, for his eyes had opened now. I thought he was being perverse. I looked at Alec.

"Of course Sir Eugene's right," said Alec.

It annoyed me that they were both behaving like logic tutors, when I could tell with the pores of my skin that Forbes-Chalmers had finished Victor that crazy way.

"We'll bring you Forbes-Chalmers," I said. "We'll find him and get his confidence and bring him here, and he can tell you himself."

"I hope you do, Tony," Sir Eugene assured me. "In the meantime we should consider who might have been Victor's new friend."

"These people," said Alec, meaning homosexuals, "move with amazing secrecy. I suppose that's something the rest of society has enforced on them."

But none of us, not even Alec, had the expertise required for spotting new alliances of that nature.

Barry Fields, who was night watchman that night, woke me from my finest sleep of the week. I had been slumbering vacantly, with no undecided questions lying about my brain to fester into dreams. I didn't give a damn who Victor's new intimate might have been; I knew the Mulroys hadn't harmed him. I did not even dream of actresses and Lady Anthea Hurley. Then, from the vegetable innocence of my sleep, Barry, dressed in a greatcoat—for the stove was allowed to burn down a little at night—woke me by shining his storm lantern in my face.

The sleep had been so cleansing that I woke as I had slept, with a blank mind. I didn't know who I was, who Barry was, what the dark place might be in which he shone his lantern. Then I thought it was England, and that I was being roused early for farm work.

He said, "The bastard's been foxing us."

"What?"

"He might be mad, but he's been watching us watch him."

My brain had begun to light up in the manner of a stage set: Hut, Erebus, dog lines, sound, mountains.

"He saw us looking for him. He's mad, but that isn't always the same as being a fool. That midden, it was a sort of stage designer's garbage dump. He put it there to make us believe he lived way up the glacier. It was a place we couldn't miss. I mean we thought we were bloody clever to find it, but really we couldn't have missed it, right there in a hollow. He kept it dusted clear of snow, and he even put in a few pudding tins, which was a touch of some kind of genius. When I think of how pleased we were with ourselves. You can't help admiring the bastard. Because he doesn't live up there at all."

I was now myself excited. I could feel, as if they were partly inside me, the complexities of Forbes-Chalmers's approach to us. He sets a beacon of refuse in our path, but it is in the wrong direction, for perhaps he does not say aloud, even inside his head, that he wants a meeting. Yet somehow or other he hopes we'll take a second thought, like the thought we now had.

I began getting up from my bunk. "We can bring him back for breakfast." I was casting about for my pants and my windproofs.

"No," he said, "I can't go now." He was night watchman. He could not go chasing recluses.

I remembered I myself had a meeting in the morning. Alec and Paul Gabriel. It had to do with the emperor-egg journey.

Barry laughed, his teeth prominent in the lantern light. "It's like fishing. We can feel that electric presence at the far end of the line. After the egg meeting'll do fine. He's been here forty-two months and he isn't going away at this late hour."

Barry picked up his lantern from the floor.

"Listen, don't die in your sleep," he told me, as he often did last thing at night.

EIGHT

If you are to understand the egg journey and even the expedition in general, I shall have to draw you a few rough maps. You see, where we were—on Cape Frye, which juts into McMurdo Sound—was an island called Ross Island—after Sir James Clark Ross, who discovered the sound in 1841. Here is the first rough map:

The mountain marked 1 is Erebus; 2 is Terror; 3 is Bird. Both the latter are extinct volcanoes. 4 is Cape Crozier, where the emperor penguins hatch their eggs in the infernal cold. The crosshatched area? Well, let us open our picture up a little:

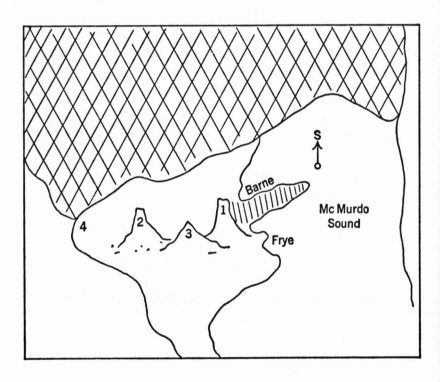

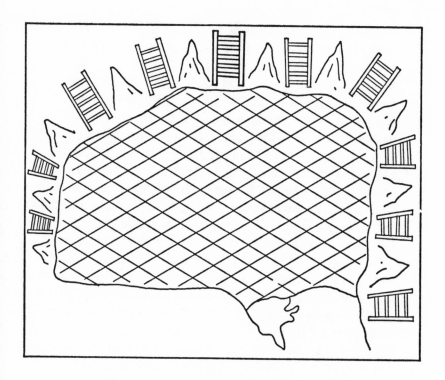

The crosshatched area is a great fixed bay of fast ice, fed continuously by glaciers flowing from the high polar plateau. The glaciers are represented here as crude ladders, for the plateau is very high. The South Pole itself is ten thousand feet above the level of the sea, and when, in my status as living fossil, the American navy flew me there ten years ago, I suffered severe nausea and giddiness from the altitude. I suppose I may have been suffering the shock of reaching the Pole, that trigonometrical siren of the Edwardian age, to find it an ice plain without character, staffed by disconsolate young sailors who would rather have been in Vietnam. In other words, the Pole was no longer a mythical place.

That aside, the fixed bay of ice that welds Ross Island (and in the Cape Frye days welded us) to the great body of Antarctica is somewhat larger than France. The ice shelf was what those classic McMurdo Sound expeditions called it, and the name stuck. If you went to the Pole, you had to cross it, using manpower, dogs, ponies, and laying depots as you went—depots stocked with food and paraffin oil you could use on your way back. Sometimes hills and mountains ("nunataks" was the name explorers gave them, and who was I to argue?) stuck up out of the ice barrier, but mainly it was featureless and flat. Nonetheless, the winds cut ice waves in it, ridges running south-north, so that it was sometimes hard to prevent sleds falling over sideways as you traveled toward the glaciers and the Pole.

The most direct glacier route to the Pole from Cape Frye was up the Beardmore Glacier, marked more heavily than the others on my elegant map. Ice fall, ice Amazon, it figured in all the agonies of Shackleton and Scott—and Stewart—and totally defeated Holbrooke.

To return to the smaller enterprise of the egg journey. You can see that our route was around the back of Ross Island, across the hind slopes of Bird and Terror to the rookery—only eighty-two miles but crevassed with the ice rivers Bird and Terror themselves bred, with volcanoes on one side of us and the ice shelf funneling the sharper winds to us on the other. In a pitted valley, where, against the wind and the wildly seamed surface, we would have to be happy some days to make a mile and on others to sit, knees up, in our tent while all the ice accumulated in our clothing melted in the flesh warmth of our sleeping bags, our skin climate was itchy, clammy, enervating. And hanging from the tent peak, our finnesköe froze as solidly as metal sculpture. In Antarctica now they would never let people hike eighty miles in midwinter. If anyone moves, it is in a convoy of tracked vehicles. It is not that the present occupants are less tough than us. It is just that Antarctica is no longer a zone of crazy effort.

It seemed to me that the hut had once again become a place where ordinary committees could meet and compound the ordinary zaniness of their members.

For example:

"One thing I think we should do," said Paul, "I think we should cease washing our faces at least for four days before we leave. I mean, it will let our natural oils accumulate."

Alec Dryden, acting as chairman, nodded. "The others might find us hard to live with," he assented, "but no one else has ever been exposed to midwinter wind for the length of time we intend. We need every coating—"

"Perhaps," I fatuously suggested, "we could sit over Warren Mead's blubber stove in the stables. If we want coating—"

"Excellent," Alec cried. "Blubber fat would be better still. You see, Tony, you only thought you were being whimsical."

"My God!"

"We will all three of us spend at least an hour a day sitting over Warren's blubber stove during the four days we don't wash. Now, if there are no more questions . . ."

Alec turned to the Admirality map for the south side of the island. I watched Paul Gabriel's eyes gleam as he took in its details. It was a map people he knew had created—Scott and Stewart during their respective first expeditions. As for the Admiralty, it considered the permanent ice shelf to be part of the waves that Britannia ruled in those days.

Alec pointed to the landmarks. First, Hut Point, a small peninsula miles down the sound. Scott had built a hut there in the summer of 1903–4, after working his ship farther along the sound than anyone else would manage to do until recent times. The hut he left was not much more favored by us than was Holbrooke's. Something happened to Antarctic huts once they were left, once the fires burned out. They never became habitable again.

At Pram Point we would turn the corner, drag the sleds onto the ice shelf, and travel east to Cape Crozier. Fifteen miles from the corner, we would leave a small depot. He thought we should make six miles a day on the way out and eight on the way back. We would carry rations for four weeks, though we would be back in three. Three hundred pounds of food. Ten gallons of paraffin weighing ten pounds per gallon.

In the mornings it would take us as long as two hours, wearing wolf-skin mitts and being careful of sudden numbness in the extremities, to take down the tent and pack the sleds. One of us would be frostbitten every morning, and was to be attended to instantly, delay or not. The area behind Ross Island was hectically crevassed, and therefore we would take two medium sleds and place half the rations, oil, and other gear on each. In that case, if one sled went down a crevasse, we would still have the essentials to crawl back home with. We would also carry certain self-recording instruments that Waldo wanted us to leave at Cape Crozier—among the penguins—for retrieval the next summer.

And Alec went on enumerating further burdens—medical kits, ropes, clothing, boots, barometers and wind gauges, a padded crate for the eggs—minor objects that yet added their discrete poundage to the load.

Altogether our burden would be seven hundred pounds on the two sleds. Some of that we would leave at the depot placed fifteen miles east of Pram Point, and the weight would go on diminishing as we ate the supplies and after we had left Waldo's equipment at Cape Crozier. To drag the sleds we would wear man harnesses of leather and canvas that fitted the armpits and around the waist. Two weeks in them left your belly trim and rock-hard, and they (like Antarctic burials) were always something I thought of patenting and marketing in this land of opulence and obesity.

At the end of the meeting, Paul and I moved away from Alec's end of the room together, Paul carrying the book he'd brought to the meeting with him. I was surprised to see that it was not some work on ornithology but Shakespeare's tragedies. The committee, which had endowed the expedition with books, had seen to it that we did not go into Antarctica without the backing of the Bard and the Bible.

"Improving yourself, Paul?" I idly asked.

He opened the volume where his marker was. The page was somewhere in Act III of *Hamlet*. I saw a few lines marked with pencil by Paul or an earlier reader. They were the lines in which Hamlet decides to face his mother and accuse her of her insensitivity in marrying Uncle Claudius so soon after her husband's death.

> ... Soft! now to my mother!
> O heart, lose not thy nature; let not ever
> The soul of Nero enter this firm bosom.
> Let me be cruel, not unnatural;
> I will speak daggers to her, but use none.

I did not read these words one by one, but saw them at a glance, knowing them from my performances as Hamlet in the sixth-form play at a Midlands grammar school.

"Of course," said Paul, "you don't realize when you're a schoolboy how strange a play it is. The ghost of Hamlet's father tells Hamlet that Claudius killed him and Hamlet must avenge the murder. But Hamlet's the only one throughout the play who actually hears the ghost speak, and so he could be quite deluded about what the ghost said; the ghost's message could have arisen purely out of Hamlet's deranged mind."

"I suppose so," I said, not very interested.

"And on the basis of that message all those deaths take place. Hamlet's mother, Laertes, Ophelia, Polonius, Horatio, the King, Rosencrantz and Guildenstern. And I ask myself how such a mad young man as Hamlet can be a universal hero. And as an orphan—a more or less fatherless child—I think I have the answer. Hamlet expresses all the resentment men have against their fathers. And he doesn't do it shamefully. He does it with the sanction of a ghost."

I laughed. "You make enjoying Hamlet sound like an act of father hatred."

"For all but fatherless sons," he said.

Barry saw him first, a stone's throw to our right, atop a low ridge. In the soft darkness his figure gave off a slight electrical luminosity, as if he had somehow inhaled the aurora.

We were now a few miles north of the hut, the shore line to our left, and Forbes-Chalmers displaying himself on our right like a man who wanted to be forced into introductions. I saw him only in the instant before he turned to run, taking a direction a little to our rear, toward the high flue of Erebus. In the second before he disappeared I had the impression that he ran crookedly, with a shuffle. Excited by the sight of him, I did not ask myself any rational questions. I coiled myself for pursuit and was already taking my first stride when Barry pulled me back.

"Not that way," he insisted. "This way." And he pointed down the sound in a direction opposite to the one Forbes-Chalmers had taken. I don't know why I obeyed Barry, but found myself sprinting with him round a wide bay, heading away from the line of Forbes-Chalmers's departure. We were moving fast for men so heavily clothed. The hope and excitement inherent in sighting Forbes-Chalmers for the first time had made me an athlete again. The black sides of volcanic boulders, which, facing the south wind, gathered no snow, showed up in my jolting vision as points of reference. When we were near them I turned inland, running up the ridge to my right. Barry turned a second after me. We could sense there was a defile beyond the ridge where Forbes-Chalmers, having tried to give us a wrong direction in the first place, was now creeping homeward.

It was a very shallow defile we saw from the ridge, more a small open valley, and for a second it was easy to see Forbes-Chalmers jogging along its far slope. Then he saw us, that we were ahead of him. He jumped behind one of those mounds of volcanic rubble that are half snowed up, half bared by the wind. We ran slantwise across the valley to find him there. Because we were so eager to see his face, because we wanted to read his eremite's history in it, we ran direct and together. One of us with surer instinct for pursuit should have mounted the far side of the depression and come down on the mound from above. When we got to the place there was no one there. The mound provided a line of concealment Forbes-Chalmers had used to mount the far rise, to vanish farther inland. We were dealing with a native.

Barry began kicking a frozen heap of rubble and slanging his intelligence. There was now no clear way to go.

"North," I told him, taking the onus as if I were certain.

"D'you reckon?"

I nodded. "North."

We turned again and mounted the rise by which Forbes-Chalmers had slithered away. I think Barry was depressed, but I had more strongly than ever the sense of a game, a child's game in which ultimately even the fastest and most cunning child wishes to be caught so then he can be praised by the chasers.

From the top of the new ridge we could see Mount Bird, minor relative of Erebus and Terror, and the gentle slopes of a wide beach. On its upper edge Forbes-Chalmers shuffled along, delineated by the moon glow from the north. There was something about the shape and the amble of the body that disturbed me, but I did not ask myself about it; I suppressed the question.

He did to us twice more what he had done in the defile. He must have accustomed himself to the contours of that shore so well that he could hide himself without having to think. He threw himself behind boulders, and even though we moved on them from two directions, he was not there when we arrived. We jogged inland a little and saw him again, moving north and looking as tired as we were ourselves. The sweat had frozen on our faces and felt not so cold as itchy. We took off our outer gloves and scratched our cheeks with our mittened hands as we jogged after the shape. He disappeared again in a small depression but could be seen on yet another beach, making for a small, low cape at the far end. We followed him, no more than a sprint behind him but not confident of catching him. I wondered if his strange, crooked walk was an element of the game, a mime of our clumsiness. He got to the line of the cape and rushed ten yards up its side. Although we got to the point ourselves within twenty seconds, he was not in sight. I put my hand out to stop Barry from sprinting any farther.

"This is it!" I told Barry.

"What?"

"This is the place. Otherwise he'd show himself. He hasn't shown himself because he's home."

"What if it isn't a *bloody* game?" Barry asked, rather loudly.

"If it isn't a game, we're never going to catch him anyhow."

Instantly I saw a small cliff on the far side of the cape. Beneath the cliff lay a large accumulation of ice.

"There," I said.

"Perhaps," said Barry.

Soon we were walking along the face of this ice heap. I had no doubt it was the place, permanent, sheltered from south winds, close to the creatures of the seashore. We looked for a vent or chimney and a spume of blubber smoke. We tested the face of the ice with our hands and our boots.

At the far end the toe of my boot struck no resisting surface. I dropped onto my knees and found a small hole, six inches square. As I pulled snow away from it I saw a crude entryway constructed of timber and canvas.

"Here!" I whispered as if I were in church. I was so elated at this material evidence, I could have dug the whole hill away.

Barry came, squatted, and began digging with me. We worked madly but clumsily with our gloved hands. I heard the voice first. "Not in there," it said. I stopped digging and nudged Barry to stop. We heard the voice clearly, though it was muffled.

"Not in there. That's the meat store."

Ten yards away a furry-gloved hand had emerged from the ice embankment. It held back a flap of canvas and so revealed a second hole.

"Come in," the voice said, "since that's what you want."

It occurred to me that he might wish to poleaxe us both as we traveled on hands and knees into his cave. I hung back, reluctant to go first; but Barry apparently had no fear of narrow places or death at the far end of tunnels and was already dropping to his knees for the journey. Crazily, I felt bound to push in front of him. "I found the place," I told him.

The tunnel was an arm's length high and scarcely any longer, and as soon as I bent my head to enter it I could see an interior, poorly lit, and knew that my host had lifted an inner flap of canvas to let us through. As I emerged from the tunnel to the main chamber, he would be standing over me, someone who had already easily fractured Victor's skull-base.

"Come on," he said. As if we were delaying him from an important task. "Come on."

When I was through he let me rise to my full height. The

room must have been six feet high, for I could easily stand. Forbes-Chalmers himself had to stoop slightly beneath the ceiling of timber he had constructed in here. The floor too was of boards, probably lumber Holbrooke had left behind. The walls, of course, were of ice. The whole place measured perhaps eight feet long and six wide.

A storm lantern primed with seal oil shed light, and by it I looked at Forbes-Chalmers. He grinned at me almost toothlessly from a mess of auburn and gray whiskers. His face seemed tanned, even though the sun had not shone for two months. His eyes seemed very bright. His breath stank.

"Of course you're welcome," he said—his voice had a Scottish edge—"you and your friend."

Barry stood beside me now, looking very shy and stooping awkwardly.

"Sit, sit, sit," said Forbes-Chalmers. "Over there, by the stove."

He pointed to a wooden crate that stood against the far wall. A few feet from it was an unlit blubber stove, just like Warren Mead's. Forbes-Chalmers had probably had it on overnight, and the ice walls, wondrous insulators, kept the heat in.

"Sit on it," said Forbes-Chalmers, meaning sit on the crate. He himself sat on a bunk opposite us.

"It isn't a bad place," he said. He did not take off his coat, for it was not much above the freezing point in here, but he dragged his gloves off his hands. "Is it?"

"Very fine," I said.

"I'm Barry Fields," said Barry.

"And I'm Anthony Piers."

"Delighted. Now first I excavated this room as a pit, six feet by eight. I then laid down some wooden roofing. I forgot the weight of accumulated snow would bow it and now I pay the price of that omission, since I can't quite stand up in here. I suppose in that I'm characteristic of mankind."

Barry said, "Were you with Holbrooke's expedition?"

"I try to keep the temperature just a few degrees above freezing so there's no melt water running off the walls. But you'll notice that I've provided ice gutters either side of the floor where any water running off the walls can collect and refreeze during the night. I'm very snug here."

He patted his bunk.

"Why don't you live in Holbrooke's hut?" I asked him.

"I don't trust the carpentry," he said. "How can you trust the carpentry of a man like that? Besides, no one wants to live with memories. And the hut—it's replete with unpleasant memories. It's a better thing to leave home, to make your own little hutch. I don't complain. My name's Malcolm Chalmers. I'm twenty-eight years old. Last winter most of my teeth fell out."

He opened his mouth to show us and we could smell him again. I saw Barry bow his head, blinking away the stench.

"I thought it was scurvy," said the man who was now suddenly Chalmers, "but I didn't get depressed as men do with scurvy, and I can get around, you know, though I'm not as strong as I was."

"Did you hurt your arm?" Barry asked. For Chalmers kept his right arm close to his side, even when he sat, and it was this that had given him his crooked gait as he ran ahead of us.

"Oh yes," he said. "That was 1908, the day after New Year's. I killed a seal, put it on the sled, was dragging it when the sled stuck on an incline, over there. I mean, the runners jammed. I was working it free, I suppose, when the struts cracked and the superstructure fell on my arm. I wept, I can tell you."

As he told the story he took his windproof coat off, and a sweater and a yellowed thermal shirt, and at last showed us the arm. The upper biceps was full and strong, but below it was a cruel crush mark. The lower arm was dead white and withered. There was no power in it—you could tell by the way it hung, by its lack of tone.

"I wept, I can tell you," said Chalmers. "But it's funny how you can live with one arm. Things are a little slower to do. That's all."

"We had a friend who died," Barry said. "His name was Victor. He was a bit of a bastard. Did you know him?"

I heard the question but sat in my own fog of disappointment. The murder had achieved a particular Edwardian ripeness, in that Chalmers could not have imposed those symmetrical bruises on Victor's throat.

Chalmers was thinking of Victors he had known. "There was a Victor in Edinburgh. McGlashen. A medical student. When you say a friend, you mean a colleague. From your hut? I mean to say, I had colleagues but they weren't all friends. John Forbes was my friend and I . . ."

"What happened to John Forbes?" I asked.

"Why didn't you go back to your colleagues?" Barry asked. "I mean Holbrooke was still here, all that autumn, the whole winter and most of the summer—just four miles down the coast."

"Oh the questions," Chalmers said with a little laugh. "I didn't *like* Holbrooke. I didn't *trust* Holbrooke. I didn't trust his carpentry. I didn't want his questions, questions." Chalmers began tugging at his whiskers.

I could see he might order us out and we would have the painful choice then of obeying him or trying to control him in that small cell of ice. "I'm sorry. We're pestering you," I said.

"No, no. I don't mind you two. You're like John Forbes or Stuart Clift. Honest men. Tough." He coughed. "I noticed when you built that hut last summer, there was a priest there, dedicating it or something. There was a priest wearing all the priestly gear. He prayed for the hut and all of you stood around in a semicircle."

"That's right, Malcolm," said Barry, struggling for familiarity but sounding like a salesman. Forbes-Chalmers noticed as much.

"*Malcolm.* It sounds unfamiliar. Of course, it's a good few years since I talked with anyone. I was wondering if that priest was still with you?"

"He is. His name is Brian Quincy."

"A good man, is he?"

"Yes," said Barry, "very . . . very compassionate."

"Could you bring that parson . . . Quincy . . . here to me?"

"I'm sure he'd be very pleased to meet you, Malcolm."

"Mind you, he should bring all his books with him and all his powers to bind and loose." Chalmers stood up and paced the length of the chamber, stooped but moving energetically, as if he often walked back and forth here, in this space two inches too short for him. His one good arm was held behind his back, but its weak brother couldn't clasp it. "I didn't think I could ask in visitors or tell them things. I didn't want to go near Holbrooke's crowd, because I didn't want their questions, questions. You're different, you fellows. I should have known. I should have come and met you early. Is it a happy expedition, yours?"

"It has been," I said, like a husband telling lies about a marriage.

"I mean I could almost *talk* to you two, but *you* don't have power to bind and loose."

Inspired, Barry said, "No, I don't think you should talk to us."

Chalmers had reached the end of the cell. He faced about, paused, took his good hand from behind his back, inspected his knuckles, chewed one for some reason, and said, "I ate John Forbes. John Forbes went to his sleeping bag one night. He was like me, still talking about living. But we didn't have much food left. Two ounces of pemmican, two of biscuit, one of rice, a scoop of butter—that was our daily ration. It had to be. We didn't know when the blizzard would end. Just the same, seven ounces of anything isn't enough in this climate, when you're eighty miles from home and no one knows where you are. So John went to bed talking of survival. In the morning he didn't wake. A coma. He stayed that way for two days, and then the blizzard ended, but I couldn't leave him. I didn't even touch his rations—you can believe me or not. I thought he'd wake up, but he died. God knows what it was. God knows. So I started to get the tent down and pack the sled, but before I'd even started it began blowing again. I put the tent up again, over John and myself. After a few hours I felt a wave of recklessness in me. I got out half the remaining supplies, about a pound and a half of food, and boiled up a wonderful hoosh. The next day the blizzard was still blowing, so I brewed up the rest of the food. The next day the blizzard was still there and there was no food. I thought I'd fall asleep and die like John. The next day the blizzard was still there and there was no food. The next day the blizzard was still there and there was no food. . . ."

Chalmers repeated that sentence at least six or seven times. We were not sure whether his brain had stuck or whether each time he uttered the sentence signified another day of hunger.

"In the end," he said at last, speaking very quickly, "I had to eat John. If the position had been reversed, I would have wanted the same behavior from him. It's not a crime to do it. I know that because I did it and I'm no criminal, you see. And I don't think the legislative powers of Westminster have ever been applied to the problem of one eating a colleague. But once you've done it, you can't go back to the world of clubs and churches and railway stations and lecture halls—and puddings. You can't go back to that world. I said to myself, Chalmers, you wanted to live, but you can't live in the old way, anymore than a man can who's suddenly crippled or blinded. You see, it's a . . . a . . . *an* unclean practice, what I've done. It needs very special acts of purification." He looked at us narrowly, suspicious all at once. "He's the sort of man who can perform acts of purification?"

"Oh yes," Barry assured him. "No risk."

Chalmers smiled and returned to his bunk. "I'd ask you to stay to tea, but I haven't tasted tea for many years. Could you bring me some, when you bring the priest? Do you want to use my convenience? It's that covered bucket by the far wall, or if you like, an outdoor one further along past the meat store. Do you have cans of peaches, too, in that expedition? I could really make a meal of tea and peaches."

"We'll bring them," I said.

"Don't delay," he told us. "Don't delay. Time for you to run."

Both Barry and I were slow to rise. Having found him, we wondered if we should leave him so easily, but it seemed we could guarantee he'd be waiting here for us simply by promising tea and peaches and Quincy's absolution. It was also possible to believe that he liked us, that by being there we had broken his hermetic seal.

If I had still thought he was the killer, I wouldn't easily have left him.

"We'll be back sometime today," I told him.

We walked home over the ice, the quicker way, and into a gusting wind. But the stars still shone in all quarters of the sky. Barry was joyful. He would sprint and jump and let out a whoop in midair. As the wind cut at my face I felt an almost personal grudge against Chalmers. He was in existence; he was mad, and if he'd but had two workable hands, we could have believed he was the assassin.

Of course, Barry's theory was unaffected by Chalmers's withered arm. "A big bastard like that could've hit Victor a good one. Even with one arm he could have hit him a beauty."

"I don't think so," I said dazedly. "I don't think it's possible. I don't think he's so strong. His diet—"

"I wonder why he said he was Chalmers?"

"What?"

"I wonder why he said he was Chalmers. He wasn't Chalmers. He was Forbes."

I stopped walking. I fumbled with the mental negatives I had taken from a study of Holbrooke's journal. I thought of throats and head shapes.

Barry said, "He claims to be Chalmers. He claims he ate Forbes. But he's Forbes, and if he ate anyone it was Chalmers. I mean, he's more than twenty-eight years old. I know if your hair turns gray and your teeth rot you can look old at twenty-eight—but not as old or ageless as he does. He's John Forbes and yet he says he's Malcolm Chalmers. Is he just mucking us around?"

"I think perhaps he really believes it," I said.

"A man becomes his meal," Barry muttered flippantly.

I stared at him. I didn't like him for remarks like that.

"I'm sorry," he said. "You don't have a bloody monopoly on good taste. I can imagine the bloody torment that would make a man believe he was someone else."

Ambling behind him, I didn't particularly want to get home. As Forbes-Chalmers would have said, "I didn't quite trust its carpentry."

NINE

When we arrived at Cape Frye our different moods dictated different ways of telling our story. Barry went inside yelling and telling the population of the hut indiscriminately that he had found Forbes-Chalmers, that Forbes-Chalmers was misinformed or cunning on the question of who he was, that he lived in an ice embankment and wanted canned peaches.

I went to Stewart and beckoned Alec across from his desk and told them the news that, for me, was all bitterness. By the time I had finished my sober account, the main area beyond the alcove was full of laughter and questions and excitement at Barry's triumphant story.

"We're left with that," Sir Eugene said against a background of celebration. "It's our house ... *ours* ... in disorder."

"Of course," Alec said, as if he'd always believed as much.

For some reason of temperament, the leader smiled. "Let's join the others."

Sir Eugene and Alec stood about anonymously, listening to Barry and Troy argue about tea and peaches and Quincy, while Waldo made peripheral statements about the weather, falling barometric pressure, and other signs of blizzard. Waldo was not inhibited in Sir Eugene's presence. In Waldo's view, a crime confessed was a crime expiated.

"They should go," Sir Eugene said, intervening without warning. "We have the problem of his possibly outrageous behavior. Perhaps in the end we should supply him with comforts and let him stay in his ice hutch until the *McMurdo* returns. But in the meantime, he *should* visit us."

John Troy said, "Does this mean, sir, you want a three-man pack and a tent and sled?" A stranger might have thought Troy had been asked to give away a daughter.

"And all accoutrements. Exactly," said Sir Eugene.

So the excursion to bring Forbes-Chalmers back was hastily arranged. A little more than an hour later, Quincy and Barry in double harness dragged the sled down Cape Frye over the tide crack and onto the ice while I followed, steadying the load if necessary. I had won this easier task by a toss of the coin; yet I would have enjoyed the mindless job of hauling.

It was a fast journey. When Forbes-Chalmers's cape was in sight, I looked behind me. The wind was blowing more wildly now, which had helped Fields and Quincy on this part of the journey, but would slow us on the way back. To the south the night was smudged as it would be if a great thumb had smeared the stars out. If that smudge enveloped us we would camp with Forbes-Chalmers, pitching our tent on his door step.

My colleagues snorted in harness, savoring the brute labor, as we slid around the far side of the small cape. Where the frozen sound and frozen shore met, slabs of ice lay upheaved and cluttered like marble in a mason's yard. To land on the cape we had to nurse the sled over this ice ridge. Once that had been done, Barry stood still in his traces and pointed to Forbes-Chalmers's ice embankment.

"There," he said. His pride was like that of a landlord pointing out desirable properties. "And listen, call him Malcolm."

I could see Quincy frowning, and understood his ambiguous feeling. How could he know what Forbes-Chalmers might ask of him?

Barry found the entryway first. He dropped on his knees and stuck his head into it.

"There's no light in there," he reported after a while.

"Are you sure you're not looking in the meat store?"

"No. The meat store's further down."

As it was. Deprived of Forbes-Chalmers's clear invitation, Barry became as irresolute as I had been on the first visit. He stood upright again. "This is serious. He might be going to harpoon us or something, in the dark, one by one."

"Here," Quincy said. He handed Barry a torch. In those days torches were nearly, but not quite, still in their experimental era. "Or else I can go," Quincy offered.

Barry considered handing him back the torch. "You're supposed to be always ready to meet your God," he suggested.

"Supposed to be," said Quincy.

At last Barry wiped his nose on the icy skin of his glove and asked us to pull him out with all speed should he scream.

I bent to do that. He passed without damage, however, right through into Forbes-Chalmers's living space. I could see torchlight bouncing around in there.

"He might be out for a while," I called woodenly.

"Oh yes. Probably dashed down to the corner pub."

It didn't seem the right thing for us to invade Forbes-Chalmers's house when he wasn't at home. Barry emerged from the hole, and we mounted the spur of the cape and looked inland and out across the sea. But there was nothing to be seen except the moonscape of Ross Island now turning dark and indefinite as the blizzard murk touched the moon.

"We can always come back another day," said Quincy when we met back on the high ground after an hour of searching and calling.

Barry had been biting his lips and snorting. "I'm not going to leave this place without him."

Quincy merely nodded at the blizzard murk to the south. Barry came to my side. "We're supposed to be the sane ones," he said. "He talked us into leaving him. We wouldn't know enough to scratch ourselves in a flea market, and that's the bloody truth."

"Is everything inside?" I asked. "His bunk? His stove?"

"Of course."

"Then we can expect him back, can't we?"

While I spoke to him, Barry looked around frantically to all points of the compass. "You two are free to go home. Take the tent and the supplies. I insist on that. I can eat with the man himself."

Quincy shrugged. I walked to the top of the cape. Every few paces the wind blew me backward one step. I could see nothing to the south. As I stood there that peculiar blizzard screech, made by a great blast of air on the fluted sides of glaciers and the contours of the coast, rose so loudly that I had to turn and call to them. "It's too late!"

We were lucky to have a hollow to pitch the tent in. By the time we had it up I could no longer see the facade of Forbes-Chalmers's ice hole. Inside the bell of canvas we sat disgruntled, hunched on our sleeping bags. The wind drummed so strenuously on the canvas that from the aspect of noise, we might as well have camped in the path of oncoming locomotives.

Quincy was the most active of the three of us. He took his outer gloves off and lighted the storm lantern, lifting it to the peak of the tent pole with his palm, clumsily, in case his fingers stuck to the frozen metal. Next he ignited the heater, slipped it under the frame of the cooker, and, still avoiding contact with fingers, lifted two pans of snow onto the frame. Watching him, we knew that tonight we could not have been so awkwardly deft.

As Quincy opened our pemmican bag and mixed the brownish lumps of dried meat into the melting snow on the stove, as he handed out our hard-tack and our few ounces of raisins and our four lumps of sugar, Barry went on mourning the loss of Forbes-Chalmers.

"I can't understand it. He wanted a priest. He wanted peaches and so on. I would have sworn he'd wait."

"Perhaps he changed his mind," I muttered. I meant about

contact. Perhaps, having had his meeting with the race, he never wanted to meet any of us again.

"Oh my God," said Barry justifiably. "The great mind speaks and it manages perspicaciously to announce that since the man isn't here he must have changed his bloody mind."

"Please, Barry!" Quincy begged him.

I said, "We should have known he wouldn't wait for us. We would have said to him, no you're not Malcolm Chalmers. You're John Forbes. And for some reason he doesn't want us saying it."

"Perhaps because," said Quincy, "Forbes is a cannibal, which this man doesn't want to be."

If we had come from an age in which Freudian principles were the commonplaces of conversation and people presumed unconscious motives for all strange behavior, we might have been able to explain the man's disappearance, to our satisfaction at least. For Edwardians, there was no key for interpreting madness.

* * *

The hoosh we ate was full of fur fibers from our coats, gloves, finneskoe and sleeping bags. That was the way meals always came out when you were sledding. But the hairiness of the stew seemed twice as annoying that night. Over all of us, even Quincy, lay the suspicion that we had lost Forbes-Chalmers because of a moral or mental failure of our own.

Later that evening Barry took the risk and groped his way out to the ice embankment. It was as far as we could hope to go in our search for Forbes-Chalmers. The hermit's bunk was still made up quite neatly with its blankets and furs, Barry said on his return. When he had crawled back into his sleeping bag, I think he was weeping, whether from the cold or for the hermit I do not know.

We slept badly. If one of us dozed the others would begin

a conversation about survival. Did Forbes-Chalmers have a second hole—a den for emergencies?

"If not, can a man survive by digging himself into the snow and sleeping the blizzard out?"

"The dogs do it that way."

"We know the dogs do it that way."

We would refer to the lore of earlier expeditions. "I knew a man," said Barry. "Hoar was his name, or Hare, or O'Hare." His uncertainty about the name didn't say much for the accuracy of the story. "A fellow countryman of mine."

"A socialist?" I asked ironically, but the irony was ignored.

"He was lost for a day and a half during a blizzard down on Hut Point during Scott's expedition some years ago. He did that, dug himself in. Now he's back in Queensland growing pineapples. But that was midsummer. This is midwinter."

Quincy spoke of the shepherds of Yorkshire who wrapped themselves in a blanket, then in canvas, and slept well in the rain.

By way of epitaph, Barry said. "He may have stank, but the room was tidy." And then: "They say at first it's fierce and then it becomes a pleasure. I believe drowning's something like that."

Soon after, I fell asleep and the pummeling of the blizzard on the tent surface became a narcotic throb in my brain. I did not wake for seven hours. When I sat up and checked the time, I noticed that both Quincy's sleeping bag and Barry's were empty. In such circumstances, when there is infinite blackness beyond the double walls of canvas and only the fragile nimbus of lantern light for company, the feeling of being the last man on earth becomes a morbid conviction.

At once I needed to know if the others were close by; yet first I had to beat my frozen finnesköe until they were malleable enough to go on my feet. Once I had them on, I loosened the lanyard at the mouth of the tent. As I crouched, half in, half out, it seemed to me that visibility had improved to a full handspan.

However metaphysically isolated I felt, I staggered to my left a little, overcome by the necessity to urinate. After a step or two I could not see the cone of the tent, but very nearly collided with a shape. I could make out by the stance of the shape, or rather by the outline of its shoulder, that it too was relieving its bladder.

"Barry?" I roared. "Brian!"

The prosaic names, from the world of trains and town-clerks and daily newspapers, were erased by the wind. But further peculiarities of the shape before me convinced me that it was Quincy.

"Tony?" he called, but he stepped one foot farther north. It was an unconscious gesture of clerical modesty that made him turn his back to me like that, for I could barely see him in the first place. Now I could not sight him at all. I hoped his old-fashioned personal reticence did not carry him too far north and lose him in the storm.

I shrugged and began attending to myself. Once I had dinner with Admiral Byrd, the Antarctic hero of the 1930s. He told me when the dessert wine had been served that he considered the greatest problem of Antarctic exploration was how to extract half an inch of frozen organ from three inches of protective clothing. I dealt with this problem and idly considered the ridiculousness of natural functions in the open in this place, and then again the shyness of the Reverend Quincy. And it was while my mind idled in this way that I deduced, without fully knowing I had done it, who had broken Victor's skull and throttled him, how it had been achieved to the confusion of all parties, and when and where.

When I found what I had done, I had no joy but stood dazed and unbuttoned. Only when I began to feel in my genitals the sting that precedes frostbite did I remember where I was.

Quincy found me in the dark and passed me and crawled into the tent. When I followed I found him already breaking out the biscuits for breakfast. I should have taken over, since he had cooked last night. But I was too dispirited to offer.

"Barry's over in the ice hole," Quincy told me. "He went over there at five this morning. He got the feeling that the man would come back. Of course, it hasn't happened."

"It isn't going to happen," I said a little brutally. "The man couldn't leave us alone; yet he can't live with us."

"You think he's given himself up to the blizzard?" Quincy asked. The niceness of the image annoyed me.

"If you want to put it that way."

Quincy stared at me but uttered none of the parsonic exclamations that you'd expect of clergymen when the question of suicide arises. I was grateful for that.

"Brian," I asked, "that day—the day Victor just walked out in the blizzard—you said you went looking for him about mid-afternoon, and found him in the latrines?"

"Yes."

"You didn't open the door and actually see him?"

"No, a man's entitled to his privacy."

I thought of Petty Officer Henson. A full-blown Edwardian crime, something as opulent and amply limbed as an Edwardian demimondaine, would incorporate elements such as PO Henson. The number of times I had found him among the sailors impersonating Sir Eugene or Alec or Troy. His part in the organism of the crime was to me rationally tenuous. Yet a scientist can define the nature of certain acid in the nucleus of a living cell, say, by his constant failure to discover it by test. Similarly I could define Henson's part by its apparent absence. It would not be the first intuitive leap I had made in my confused study of the crime, but it was the first correct one.

"One of the petty officers—Henson: He's a mimic and a practical joker. He could have been in the officers' latrines that day. I mean, it's exactly the sort of joke he loves to play. And if he's sitting there enjoying his little escapade and someone comes and calls 'Victor,' he might decide to take the joke further and answer in Victor's name, especially if Warren Mead isn't in the stables and he can scamper back to the sailors' quarters as soon as you turn away."

"No. It was Victor. It was exactly Victor. The use of the phrase 'dear boy.' 'I'll be right along, dear boy. Hang on to your curious fish for me.' That sort of thing. No one can imitate it."

"You just did. Though Henson is better."

"It *was* Victor!" Quincy insisted. My grin must have been the annoying grin of impenetrable certainty. Henson had answered Qunicy. For Victor had already left the hut, and at a reasonable time, before the blizzard was more than a rising wind. "Henson, of course, has no sense of guilt about playing this little joke on you. He has no idea how much rational weight Alec and Sir Eugene place on your conference with Victor in the latrines. Sir Eugene doesn't tell the sailors these things. They're innocents to him, and knowledge will spoil them."

I then asked the question that would rout the Reverend Quincy. "Brian, a few nights ago, did I speak with you in the latrines?"

"Yes," he said.

But I laughed, he was so mistaken.

"Brian, this is serious. Please answer truthfully."

"Yes."

"Did you mention trolling to me?"

"The other night you spoke to me in the latrines, and I told you I might be trolling the next day."

Quincy had just put an ax to the roots of my theorem. I should have been pleased because the original deduction had stunned me to the point where I began to suffer frostbite of the body. Yet I still believed in the tree of my reasoning; Quincy's refusal to make his contribution to it had only convinced me of its intricacy, its specialness.

By the time he had the breakfast stew bubbling I had explained to myself exactly how he had been misled. Fueled by the small, perverse elation of this further step of reason, I crawled out into the storm to fetch Barry for breakfast.

Once outside I remained on my hands and knees. Crawling, it was harder to move in a semicircle, easier to keep straight and find the ice embankment, easier then to find the hole and Barry.

I knew that it was no use talking further to Quincy. I must get back home to Cape Frye and talk to Henson. I could think of Cape Frye as home now. The killer was known and was now merely a pitiable item of the household.

Inside the hole, Barry had discovered Forbes-Chalmers's library. None of the books had an inscription in it except for a rubber-stamp mark in each saying that it was provided by the Library Fund Committee of the British South Polar Plateau Expedition. They had entertained the world's ultimate castaway for nearly four years. There was a Bible, Rider Haggard's *She,* Kipling's *Jungle Books, The Old Curiosity Shop, The Deerslayer* of Fenimore Cooper, *Murders at Brostwick Abbey* by Bernard Higgins, *The St. Meryn Cricket Club Murders* by E. C. Halsey, *Through the First Antarctic Night, 1898–1899* by Frederick A. Cook, and *The Botany of the Antarctic Voyage of Erebus and Terror in the Years 1839–1843,* volumes 1 and 2, by Joseph Dalton Hooker. There was no book of geological survey notes and no geological reference book. There were no navigational or geological instruments or tools.

Perhaps Forbes-Chalmers had dumped them all somewhere when his new life began. To be a hermit is probably an all-consuming occupation.

The blizzard lasted a full two days. Barry spent most of the time in Forbes-Chalmers's ice house, accustoming himself to the disappearance of the owner. There was, as a result, more room in the tent for Qunicy and me. We read and talked and were more or less comfortable.

When the wind dropped it did so slowly, but by five o'clock on our third afternoon you could see the ice embankment dimly from the tent's entrance. Immediately the three of us did our duty and went looking for Forbes-Chalmers. We traveled five yards apart from each other and moved inland. Our guide was a small hand compass specially adjusted to take account of our closeness to the magnetic pole. We encountered, after a mile, some broken ice ridges that not even Forbes-Chalmers would have tried to travel over in a blizzard. We searched northward two miles along the foreshores, calling all the time. We searched southward as far as the defile where Forbes-Chalmers had made fools of us. The cold was, of course, unspeakable, especially in that three-mile beat southward, facing the wind.

So we were staggering when we found Forbes-Chalmers's cape again. We lay on sleeping bags waiting for our hoosh to cook and there was little conversation. Each man lost himself in an obsession over the savor of the cooking food. After the meal, Barry got ready to spend another night of eccentric vigil in the ice hole. Before he left he turned to us.

"I was so bloody hungry tonight," he confessed, "I think I can understand cannibalism."

"Oh yes, oh yes," said Quincy.

"But of course he's right, that Forbes-Chalmers, you couldn't go on living the same way afterwards."

The next day we hiked fifteen miles, calling for the man in a variety of directions. The lack of an answer did not surprise me.

TEN

As Cape Frye came into sight that afternoon, we could see also the shapes of men and ponies exercising each other on the ice of the sound. Closer to them, we could identify Mead in front walking the convalescent mare, Tulip. Then Stewart with Larry, Alec with Shylock, Troy with Sally, and so on. I noticed that Norman Coote led Igor, the brute who usually led me. It was good to see them, to come out of a great vacancy and find them at their daily routine.

One of them spotted us in the distance and waved, and passed the word along the line. The horse-walking stopped. Everyone stood still to count us and wonder why there weren't four. Stewart hurried Larry back toward the shore to intercept us before we reached the hut.

Once he found out that Forbes-Chalmers had vanished he turned to other questions. That was his nature, to pretend to be more interested in the periphery than in the center. As if his mother had told him it was bad manners *ever* to utter his disappointments.

He asked how fast the sled journey over the ice had been, how long we had spent searching yesterday and the distance covered, how tired we'd been, how far we'd walked and sledded today, how tired we were at the moment. Did we think the balance of fats and carbohydrates was correct? Did we think, if the blizzard had lasted a week, the sledding rations in the three-man pack would have been adequate for us to stay healthy and sled home? I suppose we knew what he was doing and answered him dully.

We had been gone a mere three and a half days, but the refinements of the hut dazzled us as the Savoy might dazzle a farm laborer. We sat for a long time with hot mugs of cocoa in our hands. The flesh of our palms gratefully took in the heat, while AB Stigworth, as a concession to our small winter journey, set the table around us. If I hadn't been surrounded by colleagues, I would have groaned like someone sexually aroused as the heat of indoors took over my extremities and crept toward my core.

Despite the warm air and the warm food that followed, I spent two hours in the latrines that night. I went heavily clothed for comfort and carried a novel called *The Courage of Captain Plum* by James Oliver Curwood, and a pocketful of candle stubs. I kept a conversation going with every visitor. They were short and undemanding conversations because no one stayed in the cold latrines longer than they needed.

In this way I spoke with Mead and Goodman, with a drowsy Barry Fields, with Peter Sullivan, Hoosick, Norman Coote, Harry Kittery, and even with Sir Eugene. Close to eleven, when Captain Plum had ceased to entertain and I was beginning to doze, I knew by the opening and shutting of a door two stalls away that I had a late visitor.

"Cold night," I called.

"It certainly is," said Paul Gabriel.

"Have you been busy the past few days?"

"Moderately. Dr. Dryden and I have been dissecting a seal."

Dr. Dryden? I let the latch loose on my door, crept to the occupied stall, dragged its door open. PO Henson was there, half standing, his trousers around his knees. I told him to come out.

"It's just my hobby," he said, pulling his pants up. "Go easy on me, Mr. Piers."

"Come with me, Ernie." He was chewing his lips, imagining how little Sir Eugene would laugh about a puckish sailor whose best joke was using the gentlemen's latrines and conversing with them in their own voices.

I led him to the blubber stove in the stable, and we sat on the boxes where Warren Mead and Alexandrei spent half their day.

"The first thing, Ernie: Quincy doesn't call Hoosick Mr. Hoosick. He always calls him Byram. Paul Gabriel likewise calls Dr. Dryden Alec. The titles are just a front they put on when they're with the sailors."

"I always started with first names," he said, defending his art from a critic, "but after a while it would sound so wrong, I'd always go back to surnames. If it was a wrong move, I seemed to get away with it. People do seem to talk a bit stiffer when they're in an outhouse."

"You can get in practice by calling me Tony."

"I did, the other night, didn't I?"

"So you did."

"I like to do him," Henson admitted. "I like to do the Reverend Quincy."

"I believe you're very good at me too, Ernie."

"Yes, Mr. . . . Tony."

This conversation, the performance advice I was giving PO Henson, might seem improbable to anyone born after 1940. But in those days people spent their entire life stuck like flies in amber in a particular level of society and had no way of discovering how people in another class *really* spoke to each other or behaved privately. There were no movies to intimate these things, and the theater and music all dealt mainly in caricatures. So, what I was telling Ernie Henson, my next-door neighbor, was all news to him. Apparently even a twice-daily visit to the officers' latrines hadn't been an adequate education.

"I must say, you were good," I told him.

He tried to bite off his grin. "All the lads say that. They say I ought to go on the stage."

"You did Victor once. It was the day of Victor's accident."

But he shook his head. He wouldn't do that to a man. He wouldn't mock a man the day of his accident.

"I understand it must be hard to remember all your individual triumphs, but it was the time Reverend Quincy came and said that he was about to do an interesting experiment with the blood of an Antarctic cod."

"I remember that. Oh yes. I remember. He said, 'Are you there, Henneker?' And I thought, what the hell. 'Yes, dear boy,' I said, 'yes, dear boy.'"

I did not want Henson to dwell on the indecency of imitating the voices of the fated.

"And you must remember," I told him, "a special success you enjoyed four nights ago. When the Reverend Quincy came to the latrines and spoke to you."

"The lights went out and he said, 'Oh, lights out already.' And then I . . . well, I started doing *you*. He left after a while and the next one in was you. So I . . . I did the Reverend Quincy with you."

"A tour de force," I said.

"What?"

"It's what the press will very likely say when you go professional, Ernie. It's a polite way of saying, 'bloody brilliant.'"

"Thank you, Mr. Piers."

"Sleep tight, Ernie."

"Are you going to say anything to Sir Eugene?"

"You'll hear nothing, Ernie. Nothing. For all I care you can continue latrine-crashing."

In the bunk area Victor had named the Cloisters, Paul Gabriel was already abed, and reading a book entitled *Miss Ravenel's Conversion from Secession to Loyalty* by a New Haven Yankee called John William de Forest. It was said to be a classic of the American Civil War, and traced a Louisiana girl's rise to a Yankee rectitude of thought.

"Enjoying it, Paul?" I asked.

"Oh yes," he said, without taking his eyes from the print. "If I'm not finished with it the day after tomorrow, I must take it on the egg journey."

He thought of the egg journey as a frontier. Once he was started on it he would be safe; Victor would be history and all culpability a historical question, like the question of blame for the death of Abraham Lincoln or Mary, Queen of Scots.

Weariness came down on me, indefinite but enervating. "I would like a long talk with you sometime, Paul, but not tonight."

"Certainly," he said absently. He turned a page and a new chapter heading could be seen: It said: "Colonel Carter Makes an Astronomical Expedition with a Dangerous Fellow Traveller."

"Don't forget," Paul muttered, deep in Colonel Carter's dangerous expedition, "you have to sit over the blubber fire every day."

"As a matter of fact," I said, "I've just been doing that."

I considered him. The myopic assassin. I wondered how I could save him from suicide or execution. From his radical madness it was already too late to rescue him.

I presumed that Paul's crime had arisen from some homosexual crisis involving Victor, even suspecting that Paul was the new companion of whom AB Mulroy had told us, the lover who didn't need to have famous names explained to him.

Thinking that way, I went walking with Alec and Paul, a walk that was a toning exercise for our coming journey. If I abstracted from the question of Paul, I could almost have said I was strong, content, and confident. That morning I had managed a successful water color of the aurora. Men had crowded around my easel to admire it. They seemed to feel that now I had halfway expressed the inexpressible, they would never be as awed and frightened again. It had been a week since I'd worked. I was glad to have the potency back.

Now, as we walked, I listened to Alec and Paul arguing about the ancient race of penguins. It was as soothing as when Barry talked geology. The towering mists of rock and penguin history imposed on me a calming sense of my context, my ultimate paltriness. For the moment my ultimate paltriness was a comfort to me.

"They were never birds of flight," Paul was saying. "I used to think they had been, but the study of the latest work convinced me otherwise. Consider the case of those Argentinian geologists on the Palmer peninsula who found the fossil of a sixty-million-year-old penguin tall as a man."

"Five and a half feet long in the taller instance," Alec said, correcting the poetic inexactitude of "tall as a man." "Only four feet ten inches in the other."

And in these fossils no indications of a structure appropriate to winged flight!"

"Yet the flippers more elongated, proportionate to the structure, than in the current forms of penguin."

"No indication of keel bones!"

"But what if they're in the embryos we find—keel bones or wing quills in the embryo, which develop out by the time the chick is born?"

"I suppose we *must* depend on this journey to put paid to all your speculations, Alec," said Paul dismissively.

Alec smiled at me and we walked in silence, except for the strange squeak of our boots on the snowed-up surface of the sound.

"Sometimes," Alec said at last, "I pity the emperors. In the spring, when the chicks are hatched, it's like a battlefield at Cape Crozier. Sudden cold spells will kill the young. Petrels will drop down from the sky and rip open the infants' stomachs to get to the fish inside. Parents who have lost a chick will try to pick up a stray one and, in the fight for possession, the chick is invariably trampled to death. It seemed to me that young cadavers were everywhere."

Paul said nothing in reply to this. Alec possessed some ultimate authority: He had been to Cape Crozier one spring during Stewart's first expedition. He had seen the chicks perhaps six weeks after they ceased being embryos and cracked their way out of their eggs.

"Yet when you consider," he continued, "the price at which this is done." He coughed. "There are probably six thousand adults in the Cape Crozier rookery. Six thousand males astride their eggs. They'll have been starving six weeks when we arrive. And even with their blubber for insulation they pay a savage price in terms of cold for the biological privilege of breeding. Consider what they might do if they all turned on us in rage."

"So," said Paul, "they await their first clan chieftain, eh? Their first organizing king? That's poetry, Alec, but scarcely zoology."

We stopped far out on the sound. The silence was that kind of Antarctic silence in which you can hear a dog bark eight miles away.

"Shall we jog back?" Alec suggested.

I excused myself quickly. "I have some residual soreness."

Alec cantered away and Paul was tensed to follow. I restrained him with a hand. He looked at me, half smiling.

When Alec was more than a hundred yards ahead, I said, "Paul, I think you must have killed Victor."

He looked straight at me, biting his bottom lip. Then he turned his eyes, the frosty lenses of his spectacles, to the ice surface and began to nudge it with the blunt toe of his finnesköe.

"That's right, Tony, as Hamlet must have killed Claudius, I suppose."

I watched Alec diminishing in size ahead of us. "What?" I asked. "Hamlet? Claudius?"

"I hope," said Paul, "it won't interfere with the Cape Crozier journey. That means so much to me."

I put a hand on his shoulder, just to support myself. I started weeping in front of him. "Oh, Paul," I said.

"I had more sanction than Hamlet. I had better authority than a ghost. That man . . ." He began to lose control of his lips. "That man told me himself. He had . . . he had an actual letter from her."

There was only one *her* in Paul's canon. "Your mother? A letter from your mother, Paul?"

"I don't blame him for coming. I suppose he'd already made his arrangements and he couldn't change them just because I was chosen, just because my eyesight made me a late selection."

He looked at me, but I could not see his eyes for the rime on the lenses. "But I blame him for bringing the letter from her. He had something in his baggage to maim everyone with. And for me he had a letter that said, 'Dearest Victor, Our son . . . *our* son . . . is well and sucks from his mother and will never be importunate with his father.' "

The whole great crime lay before me on McMurdo ice. It was all tentacles. It was more livid and purple, more glutinously, more heinously limbed than anything Hoosick and Quincy would ever bring up from beneath the ice. It was the grandest and worst cancer and might yet devour our crude society and stain the primal landscape.

"It isn't her fault," Paul assured me. "She thought I was a child of love. She told me whenever I asked. She would say, 'I can't tell you who he is, because you might visit him and see he's not interested. But I tell you this, you're a child of love.' 'Love,' she said, 'love is the only legitimacy.' "

He shook his head at the memory, like a good son remembering little domestic eccentricities.

"You know mother," he continued indulgently, "her opinions of marriage! Of family life . . ."

At last I could speak. "The rumor always was . . . that you were the son of that confectioner. Who was he? Howard . . . Howard Middleton."

"Mother," said Paul, "would never have given herself to such a vulgar man, to a man who gives gifts of real estate!"

Yet she'd given herself to the young Henneker, who could not have been a *gentil and parfait* knight.

We began to walk. Alec was now a black spot in the dazzle of moonlight on ice. "She lived by her concepts. She wanted no one else to be enslaved by them, not even me. She would be hurt to know what Victor thought of her. But men like him —they never come to an honest view of women."

"You always trusted Sir Eugene," I said. Paul had, in fact, edited the journal in a rudimentary way to save Sir Eugene pain. "Do you think you could speak to him?"

"I'd rather wait till we got back from our journey."

I sliced the air with my arm. His ease about the killing, his ease about my knowing, made me desperate. "Paul, if you don't tell him I'll have to."

What was pitiable was that Paul didn't even think of threatening me. Patricide was his only strength as a criminal.

"But the egg journey . . ." he said. "It's my project . . ."

When I began to groan he laughed uneasily, in disquiet at causing me grief.

"All right," he said, "into the leader's alcove!"

I couldn't speak now. I thought of his options, believing it likely that they would try to talk him into suicide, offering him a weapon butt first, asking him to be an honorable chap and end their anguish, their quandary. Otherwise there was always exile in the Forbes-Chalmers manner, or an ultimate British hanging.

Unless he was forgiven, simply forgiven by Sir Eugene—like that. This unbalanced hope operated on everything I did in the next two days.

I remembered as we walked how he had found the tracks that evening, how his insistence had brought us to Victor. About this I questioned him.

"I wanted to make sure, of course, that it had been done. Things done in a rage are like dreams. You can't believe them once you're awake." He stopped a second, remembering apologies owed. "And might I say, while we're talking about passions, how much I regretted having to let that account of your friendship with Lady Hurley stand in Victor's evil little book. I considered taking it out. But I felt that if I spared you, I would have to spare everyone, because I like them all. The only exception was one made for the leader's sake. And we all depend on the leader."

I asked him about Victor's letter from Thea Gabriel beginning "Dearest Victor, Our son..." Had he destroyed that? "Oh," he said, with a light gesture of the hand, "I let the wind take it."

I wondered whether the absence of the document would ultimately help him in a court of justice, if he lasted long enough to face one.

"We might as well jog now," he said then. "We can't have Alec out on his own. It's contrary to a very wise rule."

Paul's confession to Sir Eugene was very simple. I was still pulling at the curtain to close us off from the rest of the hut when Paul spoke.

"I wanted to tell you that I killed Victor Henneker. It was done in a just rage. I'm very sorry for the anxiety it gave you all, but there's no answer to a just rage."

Sir Eugene nodded, as if Paul were merely confessing the loss of a zoological specimen.

"Why did it happen, Paul?" he asked. As you would expect, he sounded conversational.

"My reasons were akin to Hamlet's," said Paul, very nearly with a smile. He kept insisting on the literary precedents for his act, as if they would save him. "You may be in a better position to understand if I tell you I am Henneker's natural son."

Stewart's face was no longer inclined in its normal Socratic way. He had raised it full height, and now it stared at the ceiling, as if the staggering statement could only be understood against a blank surface.

"Is this true?" he asked.

"I wouldn't boast about such a painful genealogy," Paul said. His lips quivered. "I can say only that the victim worked harder than I did at accomplishing his end."

It was a statement so apt that Stewart mumbled, "Of course, of course."

"I want only to go to Cape Crozier. I want to have made that contribution to the corpus—to the corpus of Zoology."

Stewart asked me, "What do *you* say to that, Tony?"

"I don't fear him," I said. "I want him to have that right, to make the journey."

Yet my speech seemed rarefied, unreal.

Stewart said, "Very well. But you are not to speak to anyone of this, neither of you."

He rose himself to open the curtain for us. "I appreciate these admissions, Paul," he murmured. But he rammed a piece of paper into my left hand as well. When he had written it I didn't know.

As we went out into the body of the hut he called to us, companionably, for anyone to hear who wanted to. He had asked Dr. Dryden if we would like a support party to travel with us the first day or so to lay our depot behind Erebus. He would take Quincy along as his fellow sledder.

It was such ordinary polar talk, so offhandedly said, that I thought everything would be ordinary from then on. He has decided to forget Paul's aberration and knows that killing your father *is* something you can do only once.

We nodded. Sir Eugene withdrew again. Paul thanked me and went through into the naturalist's hut. Sitting at the table, I opened my fist slowly. It had been clenched around the note so firmly that now the individual fingers shook.

Stewart's message asked me to meet him in the meat store in fifteen minutes.

I couldn't refuse him, yet thought of pretending to be sick as an alternative to a conference among the frozen sides of meat.

Our meat store was of the same polar design as Forbes-Chalmers's house, but its entry tunnel was much higher to allow passage to a stooped man with a side of New Zealand lamb on his back. Because Sir Eugene was there before me and had brought a storm lantern, I could see the floor plan of the place at a glance. At one end, sides of lamb and quarters of pork, fine New Zealand produce, lay piled. Along the wall opposite the door stood a steel rack from which hung quarters of beef. Behind the door the carcasses of Weddell seals were heaped. They resembled discarded luggage—dusty carpetbags, say. Along the free wall, Victor's sailcloth-shrouded corpse could easily be seen in a specially hacked alcove. It had been considered irreverent to heap a human body indiscriminately with the meat supplies.

In the middle of the floor space, on a butter crate, sat Sir Eugene, heavily clothed and wearing a Navy greatcoat over everything else.

"You can share the crate, Tony," Sir Eugene told me, moving over for me.

"No thank you."

"Do you really think it's reasonable?"

"I beg your pardon, Sir Eugene."

"To allow him to walk about, to Cape Crozier and back, God knows where else?"

"He isn't a danger," I said.

Sir Eugene gestured, with an open-palmed mitt, toward the alcove. "Why of course he is. Tell me, did he simply offer the information?"

"I asked him—a friend asking a friend."

"You simply—?"

"And he said yes."

He grew accusatory. "It can't have been a sudden enlightenment," he said. He suspected I had withheld stages of reasoning from Alec and himself.

I began my explanations. A classic crime imposes pontifically its own version of truth upon the votaries, the servants of its flame. *Our* picture of Victor's murder, our accepted version, had involved awkward timetables which we had no more questioned than would a Christian question the established timetable of the death and resurrection of Jesus.

Our timetable had Victor leaving the hut at two o'clock, traveling through the naturalist's room going and coming. In this version, only Paul saw him on his return. In this version also, Victor noted the readings in the log on the desk in the weather room. John Troy had been absent at the time but had come back half an hour later and found the readings entered in the log. No one saw Victor until Quincy spoke to him in the latrines.

A mannerism of the Reverend Quincy's had made me understand; I told Sir Eugene that our picture of the afternoon was based on Paul's word and, on top of that, the gratuitous performance of PO Henson as a mimic.

We had promised ourselves—Sir Eugene, Alec, myself—that first night we met, that we would mistrust everyone and question everything, but we were not equipped for that. We did not question Paul or Quincy, or look at the log entries that Paul must have made in a panic hurry after the murder.

While he listened to me, Sir Eugene rubbed with his finger a little hole in the hoarfrost on the crate. "You know everything then—all the details?"

"I didn't ask him for that this morning," I admitted, implying I would tomorrow morning or someday soon. "It wasn't simply a matter of that afternoon. I think it began when his mother . . . the great Thea . . . decided he ought to become an English gentleman and sent him to Eton. She told him she despised everything such schools stood for, yet still bound him to their ethos by sending him there. I suppose she saw it was his chance of survival—he couldn't very well grow up to be an erotic dancer. I don't think she realized, despite all her public criticism of public institutions, just how cruel and conforming boys at places like Eton can be. They scoffed at him because of his mother's reputation, because he was a frankly proclaimed bastard. And when he asked her who his father was, she'd never say. Yet she always told him that he was a child of love. When boys taunted him he could comfort himself with that. He wasn't a child of a conventional marriage; he wasn't a child of bored hostility and habit. He was a child of love. He once stressed the same idea to me, I remember."

"My God!" said Sir Eugene. His happy childhood had deprived him of a lot of knowledge. "How startling," he said.

I was, in fact, becoming more embarrassed; my speech was growing more stilted as I tried to explain these matters to Sir Eugene, who greeted them as if they were anthropological data about some lost race.

I began to diarize for him a more credible time scheme.

"When Paul joined the expedition, Henneker already knew he was Thea Gabriel's son. In the years before Victor decided to . . ." (I didn't know what phrase to use—"to renounce women," I finally decided on.) ". . . to renounce women, he had known Thea and had a letter from her . . . one of those letters from notorieties Victor carried everywhere . . . telling him she considered Paul to be his child. Then Victor saw Paul perform during the early days of the expedition, and grew a little sentimental about his paternity and somewhat proud of the boy."

I projected that Victor had shown the boy the letter on a midwinter's evening, when sentiment and blood alcohol had been high in the hut. I didn't know what the letter actually said—Sir Eugene could find out from Paul, and I myself never wanted to know—but on the basis of Thea Gabriel's theories, I guessed it very likely said: He is our son. . . . I simply wanted you to know so that we can both secretly rejoice.

"You know something of Thea Gabriel's theories?" Eugene asked me at the end of this exposition.

"I was an admirer," I told him, and *blushed*. "Of course, I don't know how much you could . . . you could trust the judgment of Miss Gabriel in this matter. By her own admission, she's always been promiscuous . . ."

I paused, now definitely ashamed of my formal presentation and my reflections on the breathtaking Thea's morals. I was at a loss to talk any other way to Sir Eugene

"Paul was devastated, of course, to have this strange man claiming to be his father. I don't know if he knew anything of Victor's unusual leanings or whether he could simply tell that Victor was clearly not the sort of man who begets children of love. The following morning, when we—Paul and I—went to the weather screen, I thought he was depressed about not being included in the Pole party. In fact, the root of the depression was that he all at once had a father—the wrong kind, a despicable one."

I was aware now of the third presence, Victor's meat in its alcove. The meat of a man who had been reckless with his documentation.

The killing went in this way, I told Sir Eugene: On the way out to the weather screen that afternoon—he could verify the details by talking to Paul—Victor came through the naturalist's hut. Some conversation began. I believed it probably ended with Victor saying, "*You?* A child of love? Your mother was a . . . harlot," or words to that effect. Paul struck him with whatever was at hand. I thought it was very likely a frozen skua gull he was thawing. Victor probably turned from the blow, and it hit him on the base of the skull and, because he didn't have his hood up, he was struck full force. Next Paul strangled him. Thea's child of love had grown up shortsighted but thick in the limb. "Yon boy wi' glesses," PO Wallace had muttered early in the expedition, "is a fearsome sledder, man." That afternoon, having so quickly cracked Victor's head and throttled him, Paul continued to move quickly and in great fear. And he too was thinking in terms of classic Edwardian murders, in which footprints were always significant. So, while lumping Victor away, he very likely wore Victor's finnesköe while carrying his own jammed inside his windproofs. Frightened but very rational, he envisaged some professional investigation and put Victor's boots back on the corpse only when he had dumped it beyond the weather screen. Although he would now have had to put his own finnesköe on immediately to avoid being crippled by the cold, he probably walked on his knees or rolled barrel-wise for a distance. This action had been labored and unnecessary, but in his care, he showed that he too had been a victim of the concepts and conventions of his great crime.

He believed now that he had created an adequate mystery.

Why did Victor wander beyond the weather screen as if undertaking a journey with a blizzard threatening? And how had he died? A divine accident? Involving no other pair of boots.

Later, when he heard that Quincy had spoken to Victor in the latrines long after the event, his confusion must have been an agony. But then he came to believe either that God or the gods were protecting him or that Quincy was saving him as one would save that other justifiable homicide, Prince Hamlet.

In the meantime, by half past two he had been through Victor's belongings and taken Thea Gabriel's letter and the journal. He found that his own entry was safe and referred only to his myopia. He destroyed the letter and a certain section of the journal and, in the end, put it on the shelf. Did he want to fog our insane perceptions further? Did he want to show more fully the moral deficiencies of the man he had killed?

When I finished, Sir Eugene joined his hands in his lap and sniffed. His eyes looked bleak and badly focused as he stared at me. He didn't want to speak yet. Therefore I continued.

"Paul saw himself as parallel to Hamlet, as I said. Everyone forgave Hamlet his crimes because, as Paul said just an hour ago, the victims connived at their own murders, and because Hamlet was doing something that had a profound meaning for the human soul. He was killing a false father . . ."

"Oh God," muttered Sir Eugene. It was certainly a cry for help.

He gave up the crate and got slowly to his feet, an involuntary action, like that of a man seeking more air.

"What am I supposed to do with all this? I have a man who confesses to killing one of the thirty human occupants of this continent. If he did it, he's mad. If he didn't do it, he's mad. I lose on both arms of the proposition. And what can I do with the mad? And what can I do with the guilty?"

I rushed forward with suggestions. "In the short term," I

said, "a journey to Cape Crozier is as effective as imprisonment. It might even be the equivalent of . . . of a capital sentence for all three of us."

"Is that a funny remark, Tony?"

"Forgive me." I began to plead that the committee be made responsible for Paul. If his behavior was not strange or troublesome, he could be returned to England when the *McMurdo* came back in January. If Paul was kept from the journey, he would certainly become bitter. I think I was arguing crazily for an absolute pardon. Paul would recover from the act of strangulation and cease reading *Hamlet*.

Sir Eugene held his hand up, halting me. "You don't understand. I hope to be on the polar plateau by the time the *McMurdo* comes back and no more than two hundred miles from the Pole. Besides, *ordinary* men change in six months. Their behavior and morale can alter beyond recognition. And stranger temperaments deteriorate more quickly still." He went on trying to persuade me that the idea of a pardon, which I had not mentioned and he would not, was impossible.

As he spoke he would now and then fiercely pinch the bridge of his nose. My arms twitched as the electric anger ran through them. I wanted to cross the few feet to Victor's meat and punish it with my hands and spit on it like a Sicilian. In my Mediterranean fervor I had even forgotten that the corpse would be approximately as yielding as granite, that my spit would freeze before it stuck.

"I'll watch him," I promised. "I'll watch him every second of the day."

After giving this offer ten seconds' thought, Sir Eugene picked his lantern up, implying we should leave the meat store. "Very well," he told me. It was not consent. He was just giving up for the moment. "And thank you."

When we were in the open and walking side by side past the

dog lines, the dogs yelping at us in the hope of exercise, he began to talk again.

"I want you to remember, Tony, that circumstances like these can endow me with powers over the people involved in the expedition, powers that are as absolute as a Pharaoh's. If ever I decide to use them, I expect your obedience."

I know now that I must have understood the meaning of this satrapal statement as soon as it was uttered.

ELEVEN

Paul remained exemplary the rest of that day. He washed and dried his two sets of thermal underwear. He neatly darned an elbow hole in one of his nautical sweaters. He sewed a button, I remember, back on the left breast pocket of his woolen jacket. I remember also that he lost himself in the last hundred pages of *Miss Ravenel* at afternoon tea and sherry time, finished it with a sigh, and after dinner, chose a new book from the library for use in the tent. It was Jack London's *The Sea Wolf*, an undemanding story about a Dutchman who is thrown overboard by a collision at sea, and is picked up and pressed into service by a brutal sealing captain.

Paul's eyes met mine as he came back to his bunk with the brightly covered book. He showed a few seconds' awkwardness, as if he was guilty at being found with a best seller in his hands so soon after strangling Victor.

"Immortal literature isn't much use in some circumstances," he said apologetically.

"No, of course not," I told him.

At dinner, Sir Eugene began a conversation about penguins, perhaps so that he could watch Paul's reactions. Alec and Paul refought the argument of the morning. Paul seemed restrained and well informed.

Afterward I wrote a letter to my parents. Since I felt uneasy and alone, I did not want to go on a winter journey without leaving behind a letter that in the long run would reach some handsome woman.

Dear Lady Hurley,
    Tomorrow three of us go on a midwinter excursion to find of all things an emperor penguin egg. I do not look

forward to the cold of that excursion with any confidence and anticipation. But I thought that this was a good opportunity to say how wise I think your decision was in our regard last year . . .

Memory of her spiked not only my mood but the blood in my groin. Yet I couldn't write of apposite things—breasts and white flesh and green eyes—without embarrassing her and forcing her to burn the letter, and I didn't want her to burn it. I wanted her to preserve it. I gave way to a second's daydream of how she would finger it and hide it from her not too intrusive husband, taking it out every spring, or whenever it was she went through her most private papers.

At the same time Alec wrote to his wife and Paul to his mother. When we had all finished, we delivered the letters to Stewart's office. They would arrive in England in the European spring of the following year. The long-delayed delivery, the idea that we might all freeze behind Ross Island, suited my feverish mood.

During those last twenty minutes before lights out I sat on the edge of my bunk listening to Paul scuttering around me, and watching Quincy stow spare clothing and a few personal things in a small seabag. What *I* felt was the sort of eve-of-battle paranoia I was to see in some soldiers in a few years' time. What I saw in Paul, however, was eve-of-battle euphoria, and in Quincy, a friendly soberness. When Quincy put *The Book of Common Prayer* into his bag, I resented him for the first time. Why did he want to utter blessings? Why did he want to put ritual frills on the raw task?

He saw me looking at him. "Tools of trade," he said, shamefaced.

There was no easy sleep to be had, but superficially unconscious, I saw an image of Alec and Paul staring over the black lip of a crevasse into which I had fallen and now dangled, spinning in my harness. My one thought was a sort of complaint to the gods—if someone had to dangle, it must be Paul.

I opened my eyes, understanding in a rush that I felt at risk traveling with him. Yet I was his advocate. My fear of him had to be sat on, bitten off, whatever else, in case it crossed the living space and entered Sir Eugene and Alec.

It was, I remember, a night for unquiet sleep. Two hours after the lights went out, while I still lay awake, I heard an open-throated scream from the far side of the room. Mead was night watchman, and I saw him shining his lantern in the corner where Barry Fields slept.

For an instant Barry sat upright in his bunk, his eyes stark, his mouth still opened for shrieking even though the shriek had died. Then his face composed itself. He looked at Mead and correctly understood that he had woken the whole room and possibly the sailors too.

"Sorry everyone," he called. "I dreamed I was at my wedding."

AB Stigworth woke me early. It was easy to rise instantly, without drowsiness. There was a feeling of flux and momentum in the hut, even though all but five of us were sleeping still. We began our breakfast, talking quietly, but the others rose early anyhow, and we all began to drink tea.

There was a forced brightness in all the faces, the sort of aching smile I would see on officers new to the front in the coming and unexpected catastrophe. After we'd been to the latrines a robing of ritual proportions took place. I took off the trousers and old cardigan in which I always slept and put on first the new thermal underwear I had warmed by the stove, then a woolen shirt and ditto trousers, next two woolen sweaters (we carried two extra on the sleds), a woolen jacket with a hood, windproof fur-headed top, and windproof trousers. Two woolen socks on each foot inside a felt undershoe and a finnesköe of fur. For our hands, mittens inside woolen overgloves inside wolf's fur gauntlets.

The others were all outdoors to cheer when Paul and I dragged on the harness of our sleds at nine o'clock. Quincy, behind us, harnessed himself to the lighter load on a half sled, holding his and Sir Eugene's small tent and rations and the supplies they would depot for us fifteen miles on the far side of Pram Point. Sir Eugene and Alec walked beside us, inspecting the loads for incipient instability.

Our well wishers sang the anthem of the king, who (they did not know) had already died. They sang then *Why Were They Born So Beautiful?* Men of their age—sublime and ridiculous.

By the standards of the summer, we were dragging small burdens and using three sleds to do it. But before we had got them over the tide crack and onto the ice, I could tell with gratitude that it would be brutally hard, that I would not have time for thinking in the next few weeks, that I would exist on a level of sinew and belly muscles and basic thirsts, terms that involved no dangers with Paul.

What can I say about the climate and geography of that day? −67° F. Wind fifteen knots out of the eternal south. Little Inaccessible Island growing out of the sea ice on our right and the shore on our left. Humidity? There was no need to state a percentage. If you let the dry air in your mouth, it instantly stole moisture from your tongue and palate and fused them to each other. Continually I wanted to drink. We stopped on the hour and scooped up snow into our mouths and smiled at each other.

We had agreed, for some reason, to do without the noon meal that day. It was a plausible decision because a meal meant the raising of the tents, the lighting of cookers. But, in the breaks from sledding, I craved food; I felt it was merely humane to feed up someone as uncertain as I. There was little to distract me from hunger. There was no aurora that day; the light did not extend as far as the grand mountains of Victoria Land or even far up the slopes of Erebus. The landscape did not absorb you, as it could, by the hour. After a while I diverted myself by insisting on taking over Quincy's sled and becoming thirst-crazed as well.

In the matter of geography: We found ourselves off Hut Point by midafternoon. We could see Scott's old hut and the crude wooden Celtic cross Scott had left on the point to honor the first man lost in McMurdo Sound, an able-bodied seaman called Vince, the victim of a summer blizzard in 1904. Seeing that cross there so close to the hut, seeing the hut itself, was a strain of the imagination. You felt that perhaps just around the point you might find shops and tram depots.

The hut was to have been our first night's camp, but we had reached it too early. We could see in front of us the cliffs of the ice shelf, quite luminous, quite dominant, in the moonlight. Beneath their dazzle I did not realize that someone had been forcing the pace.

So I innocently dragged Quincy's sled behind the others around the line of Pram Point and up and among the broken ridges of ice on its far side. By such jumbled routes we made a slow way to the ice shelf, heaving the sleds up one side and down the other of great and luminous white slabs.

Now the terrain changed for us. The ice shelf was level though secretly pitted and crevassed. A giant and careless fracas between the ice of the land and the ice of the shelf had made abysmal fissures in the surface, across whose mouths there always lay a thin bridge of brittle ice, which might or might not collapse as you crossed. An expert, such as some of the canny dogs, could sometimes tell the bridge from the solid surface. Most of the time nobody could.

It happened that, like the dogs, Quincy had an eye for minor changes in the surface. Perhaps it should have been some kind of symbolic warning to me when Paul and I had to wait in our traces while Sir Eugene, with the parson's help, probed and tested the surface ahead of us.

I could barely see the leader's hand when he raised it in the dark, calling a halt. Later I would be amazed to remember that he announced, consulting the bicycle-wheel tachometer on the back of my sled, "That's excellent, thirteen miles in this weather."

He seemed to be saying there was a future in the journey, for all of us.

It was while Alec and Paul were putting up our tent and I was getting the cooker and supplies from our sled that Sir Eugene came to me. As he spoke he looked at Quincy, who had been sent a few hundred yards ahead to detect crevasses, so that tomorrow's journey would not suffer an early disaster.

"You realize," he said—his breath was still a little short from the march and his words thick from his sledding thirst—"you understand that we can't travel with Paul any further?"

"I don't understand," I said. In fact, I understood instantly.

"In bluntest terms, he can't live with us anymore. I don't like the term execution—"

I began to laugh but in anger.

"What else can I do?" he asked. "Imprisonment? Supervision? Give him the option of suicide? I don't believe in suicide." He coughed and scraped some caked slime from his lips. "I warned you yesterday. I tried to talk you round. I mentioned powers to you. Yet it's strange, I'm not commanding. I ask you to concur in my using them."

What I said was, "When?" If I said "When?" it was because I knew what Stewart would attempt. Could I have been begging for a mere delay?

"Now," he said.

"No. Of course not."

"Don't speak loudly."

"You'll have to do it to me too."

"I don't think so, Tony. Please understand our situation."

I tried to be contemptuous, satirical. "Is it going to be a gallows job?"

He took a large revolver from inside his shirt and turned it over, displaying the means of extermination. Its barrel and revolving mechanism shone like wet sealskin.

"Quincy won't let you," I told him, "and I won't let you."

He had already packed the revolver away inside his windproofs, as if worried about the effect the cold might have on its working.

"I've spoken to Quincy."

I remembered Quincy packing *The Book of Common Prayer*. "I suppose you want his help in the traditional priestly roles?"

"I asked him an hour ago."

"And he said yes."

"He told me to go to hell."

"There you are!" I said; yet I whispered. There was a sort of impetus to everything Sir Eugene said now, and I feared that Paul would become aware of it and be terrified.

"Of course there ought to be no loud and careless talk. It wouldn't help the boy. It would be punishment. And I am not interested in punishment."

I shook my head in a way that still implied the leader's harmless lunacy. "You're a perfect bloody madman—talking quietly to a scientist, a parson, an artist, asking them to help you in an assassination."

The polar knight blinked a little at my rhetoric and looked away to his right, where Quincy, an earshot away, stood probing the ice surface tenderly with the butt end of an ice ax.

"Quincy will help. I know he's over there looking for crevasses and hoping it will all blow away. So do I for that matter. But Quincy will help. He accepted my explanations, even though he was shocked. I hope you do too." He turned half away from me and called, not very loudly, to Quincy. The parson stumped back toward the camp. A tired man, a miner coming home. Ten yards away from us he stopped and tensed, somehow seeing the solid intention in Sir Eugene.

"Please don't call out to him," Sir Eugene murmured. "I don't want him to die in a panic and without warning."

Both Quincy's mouth and mine were open, competing to make the first protest, when Paul and Alec Dryden emerged from our tent, having put up the inner lining. They moved toward Quincy's sled to find and erect Sir Eugene's and Quincy's tent. Dryden moved like a man at his ease, like a reliable country doctor, all his secrets being homely, West Country secrets.

"A little slow with that cooker, Tony," Paul called to me, and he smiled absent-mindedly. The expeditionary zest of the boy. He should have been able to see our pallor, even under that blotted moon.

"Dryden knows?" I whispered.

"Of course."

The weight of Stewart and Dryden was more frightening still—the weight of their stability, of their harmony. I thought for the first time that the concept of execution was not an aberration of Sir Eugene's. It was high policy. The king and the chancellor had put it together.

"He wore a false face?" Quincy asked. "All day?" He sounded hollow, as oratorical as I did. Sir Eugene answered only by telling Quincy to take the cooker to the door of the main tent and asking me to carry the canvas supply pack indoors.

"You won't do it," I asked, "while we're . . . ?"

I see now that by such questions Quincy and I were giving consent.

I did what I was asked, dragging and wriggling through the canvas entry, wriggling and clawing my way out again. Upright, I went straight to where Paul worked on the frozen lashings of Quincy's sled.

"Paul," I said quietly, "Sir Eugene has some idea about executing you."

He raised his face to me. There was a slight frown on it. Then he turned back to work on the knot.

"He said I could go to Cape Crozier."

Paul sighed when the frozen lashing came undone. One of the pleasures of polar sledding, he seemed to be saying.

"Quincy and I won't let him do it."

"Oh?" he said, loudly, raising his eyebrows slightly. "Does that mean I have nothing to fear?"

I saw Alec Dryden pause in his work and dump the sleeping bags he had just unloaded. He knew what we were talking about.

"I'm telling you so that you'll be able to . . ."

"To run away?" he suggested.

He brushed past me as if I were irrelevant, and walked to the point where Sir Eugene stood alone by the front sled, making no pretense of unloading. Alec and I trailed behind him.

"Sir Eugene," he said. "You want to punish me. Is that right?"

"Not punish you, Paul," Sir Eugene told him primly.

Quincy had also joined the audience. I had the dismal sense that that was all we were—an audience, the witnessing citizens prescribed by law.

Taking his time, Sir Eugene inhaled and raised his chin so that it pointed at Paul in what was somehow a gesture of immeasurable authority. I don't know what it is that suddenly endows the average features of a man with that kind of authority. I saw it later when officers with everyday faces, someone's uncle, someone's perhaps not too loving husband, would all at once take on a mysterious authority adequate to make a thousand humans stop running and face front—sometimes misguidedly but sometimes to their benefit.

Quincy said loudly, "It doesn't have to be, Paul. Tony and I . . . we'll get in his way."

The promises rattled like gravel against the two in the middle, the assiduous two who seemed to be working together toward the execution, defining it, declaring it inevitable.

They were the two who spoke to each other.

"You said I could go to Cape Crozier."

"That isn't possible, Paul. You killed a man. Very savagely, Paul. Very savagely."

"If I'd done it less savagely—would you still want to execute me?"

"Yes, but the savagery gives me certain indications. I'm very sorry, but I couldn't give a man who performed such savagery the option of taking his own life. I couldn't put a weapon in such hands."

Paul began crying softly. "Do you trust me so little?"

Sir Eugene comforted him by the elbow. "Come, Paul. Come."

"I suppose it's to be straightaway?"

Sir Eugene nodded. "We aren't jailors," he said. "Since you know that it's to be, it has to be now. We can't contain you, Paul."

Quincy denied and threatened. "Let him live out here," he called. Admitting his belief that some sort of casting off might be necessary.

I may not have Quincy's words exactly, but I know there was a point where he gave in, having yelled and argued his way around to Sir Eugene's view.

When that stage came, I had already moved to the sled and taken hold of Quincy's ice pick. "I'll attack you, Sir Eugene," I promised. My trembling left hand, I remember, could not get an adequate grip on the handle. "You'll have a second act of bloody savagery," I insisted. My voice reminded me of an escaped bird. It fluttered and was not subject to me.

Sir Eugene didn't answer. Paul answered. "For sweet Jesus's sake, Tony!"

"What?" I said, for I found it hard to distinguish words. I was locked up in a dazed intention to use the pick on Sir Eugene if he produced the gun.

"Let it all happen with a little decency," Paul said.

I lowered the sharp end of the pick to the ice. "You're going to die graciously?" I asked.

"The news we'll take home," Sir Eugene promised him, "is that you fell into a crevasse on this journey, this estimable journey. Your mother . . ."

"My mother won't really understand whatever you tell her. Her address, you'll notice on the envelope, is a nursing home in Hampstead."

That statement unstrung me further. The point of the ice pick wavered. I had always thought of Thea Gabriel as enjoying eccentric and spirited retirement, dancing among jonquils somewhere in the country. I thought, if they can put Thea Gabriel in a nursing home, perhaps they can execute her son.

Sir Eugene said, "Do you want to speak to Brian?"

Quincy's mouth was wide open. He didn't know what was expected of him.

Paul smiled. "The Reverend Quincy and I . . . we've always been friends."

It was clear Quincy would not rush forward, anxious to confer an instant, institutional salvation.

Sir Eugene himself wanted to see things more formal. "Perhaps a prayer," he said.

"No," Quincy said, "no prayer, no blessing. No."

"Come now," Sir Eugene argued.

"You'll have to do it without a blessing," Quincy reiterated.

Yet I could see that that was the extent of his protest. I raised the pick again, and again said that I wouldn't permit it, but this time no one answered me. I was excluded from the tableau. My gesturing with the pick, they implied, was painful to everybody, and futile. In the end, I dropped it and went directly to Paul.

"You haven't made any protest," I accused him. I tried to shake him by the shoulders.

"What happens in *The Sea Wolf*, Tony?"

"For God's sake!"

Yet I could see it was not gibbet gallantry. Like a child, he wanted to know, and not to leave a half-resolved plot.

I found myself saying, "Wolf Larsen gets harpooned and Peter van Weyden takes command of the whaler and turns it home toward Holland." It was so improbable a gallows duty that I turned mean. "Would you like the plot of *Trilby* while I'm at it?"

Paul smiled and began eating snow. We all knew: He did not want to die thirsty. Although we were all thirsty too we did not stoop to eat snow with him.

He stood up after a second mouthful and said, "You're all my friends, all four of you."

Sir Eugene coughed. "Would you like a restraint, Paul?"

Paul said, "No," and instantly turned his back, at the same time pulling down his hood to expose the back of his neck. This movement seemed rehearsed.

I suppose I have always been grateful that Alec Dryden threw his arms around me then, implying that I was a danger to the event. Yet what can anyone do for a victim who performs his execution so professionally?

Grappled, I saw Sir Eugene put his hand on Paul's shoulder,

pressing him gently to a kneeling position. He took out his revolver and placed it to the back of Paul's head. At this second Quincy's mouth and mine both opened in wails of pain of which Paul would have heard only the beginning.

Sir Eugene asked us for no help. Quincy and I mourned, raved, threatened, got in the way while he and Alec covered the stains on the snow, wrapped and tied Paul in sailcloth, carried him a little way off to an unlidded crevasse, lowered him with a rope, threw the rope in after him.

Necessities then sealed the event. We had to get inside the tent; we had to take the offered food into our bodies.

When he had eaten, a virulent Quincy said, "It occurs to me, Sir Eugene, that Paul may have been the sort of man to take crimes on himself, whether or not he had committed them. It seems to me that that would be his nature."

I saw with useless joy the second's fear as Sir Eugene looked up from his mug of hoosh. "We don't know," I said, turning the knife, "who Victor's friend was. We won't know ever."

But Sir Eugene shook his head. "Gentlemen," he told us, "you know I would not proceed with an action like this unless I had made sure . . ."

"I want to go to Crozier," said Quincy, helplessly trying to give Paul some continuance.

"Don't forget," Sir Eugene said gently, "your responsibility, the responsibility of survival."

He left the next morning, hauling the half sled behind him. He had not asked for our future silence.

In the next two weeks we lacked time knowingly to grieve. One night our tent blew away and we sheltered in the lee of our sleds, under a sheet of canvas, debating with shouts whether this was death by exposure. In the morning we recovered the tent, fortuitously blown a mere two hundred yards instead of a similar number of miles, and with its double canvas we retrieved our lives. We collected a half-dozen emperor eggs; grotesquely, Alec fell into a crevasse with one in each hand. He was hauled out unhurt but the emperor's eggshell is one of the most fragile.

Returning toward Frye on an afternoon of −80°, Quincy—the man with an eye for surfaces—fell with his sled into the worst of pits. By lantern light we saw the shattered load on an ice ledge thirty feet down, and Quincy lying in the midst of it with a broken wrist. Only Quincy was recoverable. The following day a week-long blizzard began, and we sat inside the tent and Alec fed Quincy tiny amounts of morphine, mindful of the perils of the drug and also that our supply was small.

And during that time of darkness and bemusing cold and Quincy's fever, I came to accept Sir Eugene's act the way you accept the acts of statesmen and generals, aware of the neat and detached mechanisms of their decisions. It was an acceptance necessary to my survival in that place where loading the sled teased your burning fingers for an hour morning and night, and the cold frosted the brain and froze the lubricant of your eyeballs, where thirst was a delirium as pronounced as Quincy's delirium as he rode crooked and mumbling on top of the sled.

The world knows how Stewart and the others died on the return from the Pole—Stewart and Dryden, Troy and Mead and Percy Mulroy. I have always wondered what influence the business of Paul's crime and execution had on Sir Eugene and Alec in the part of the brain that says *go on* or *no, stop and sleep*.

I wonder what influence it had on Quincy, to make him leave the church in 1914 and become an eternal ranker in one of those industrial-city regiments that were used for battle mulch on the Somme.

As for me, I have already indicated: It was the act that rendered the condition of the century terminal. Nothing ever since has surprised me.